BOOK TWO IN A SERIES

MAGIC & MELODY

A NOVEL

RAIN NOX

CASTLE BRIDGE MEDIA
DENVER, COLORADO, USA

CASTLE BRIDGE MEDIA
Denver, Colorado

ISBN: 979-8-9917855-0-1

Chapter 1

LUCY GULPED FROM HER ALUMINUM water bottle in an effort to settle the fire burning in her stomach. She knew her nerves would try to get the better of her, but she wouldn't let them take control, not today. She clutched her sheet music and forced her legs to walk from the car to the front door of the Northbrook Fellowship Hall.

Inside the lobby, a paper taped to the wall read, "Quiet Please, Auditions in Progress," and beneath, in smaller letters, "Please sign in and wait for us to call you." She looked down the hallway and saw a clipboard on the table to the right of a pair of double wooden doors with small, glass windows. She knew she should walk that way to add her name to the list. Instead, her legs carried her to the left, towards the restrooms.

There was an outer area with mirrors and a couch, and a little table with fragrant potpourri that smelled of spiced apples. Lucy looked in the mirror. "You can do this," she whispered to her reflection. The face looking back at her seemed uncertain.

"You've taken voice lessons for five months," she told herself. "You even sang in a recital—you are ready." The woman in the mirror seemed to consider this; facts could sway Lucy away from the lies her anxious brain told her.

"It's just a community choir, there's no reason to be nervous," she added. But that was a lie. The truth was, this meant a lot to her, and that made the stakes higher, the chance of failure devastating. She had such fond memories of singing in choirs from when she was a little girl, but by high school she had been too shy to sing in front of other people. It had taken her all these years to summon up the courage to get here.

Lucy took a deep breath in and released it slowly, the way her voice teacher had taught her. Then she imagined herself entering the audition room and singing her piece with confidence and expression. She even envisioned the auditioners clapping profusely at the end, though she knew they usually just said, "Thank you."

Feeling slightly more determined, Lucy strode back to the hallway just in time to see a woman entering the audition room. She picked up the pen and was about to write when her eyes widened. She recognized the last name on the list.

Noor Khanna.

She dropped the pen and crept up to the audition room window, longing to know if the rumors were true. She tried as inconspicuously as possible to peek inside the room. Luckily the two auditioners were to the left, so the window was not in direct view of them or the person auditioning.

Lucy's eyes were drawn to Noor. She was quite tall and wore a mid-length, blue paisley dress and tan sandals. Her long brown hair was pulled half back so it was away from her face and fell like a curtain around her shoulders. She wore long teardrop beaded earrings that shimmered when she moved her head.

The piano accompaniment began, and Lucy could see Noor grounding herself, readying to sing. Then, as smooth as glass, Noor's first notes drifted outward towards the auditioners and Lucy. The words felt like warm, gentle ocean breezes, the graceful soprano melody reverberating through the hall.

When the soundwaves enveloped Lucy, her world morphed. Mist began to rise from the floor of the lobby, the overhead fixtures replaced with the light of a silvery moon. Lucy was in a forest, the ground covered in blooming lilies and violets, illuminated by the moonlight. Horned creatures pranced about her, dancing, surrendering to the enchantment of the music and the night. She turned her head, trying to catch the motion she saw in the corner of her eye, sure that fairies lingered on the edges, just out of sight. Lucy reveled in the song and her body joined in a lilting sway, swept away by the magic.

But soon it began to fade away and Lucy reached out her hand to the forest creatures, longing to stay in this fairy world. But alas, a voice speaking snapped Lucy back to the hallway. She froze her swaying body and blinked her eyes, trying to remember where she was.

So, it was true, she realized in an instant. Noor knew song magic.

Lucy peered in through the window again. The auditioners were talking with Noor, and although Lucy couldn't hear what they were saying, their enthusiastic smiles must mean they were complimenting her performance. Lucy hoped her audition would go as well.

She realized she had momentarily forgotten to be nervous. Noor's singing had made her forget her anxieties and brought her to a place of joy and wonder. Her heart rate was measured, and her shoulders were loose. Lucy smiled to herself. Singing that could calm someone as anxious as she felt must be a special kind of magic. Lucy wrote her name on the sign-up sheet and waited.

After a minute, Noor opened the door, so lost in happy thoughts that she didn't see Lucy standing there. Noor turned the other way towards the exit and was soon out of sight.

One of the auditioners came out and checked the list. "Welcome Lucy—come on in," she said warmly as she held the door open.

Lucy smiled at her and stepped into the room. She greeted the other auditioner and gave her music to the accompanist.

"Whenever you're ready," the second auditioner said.

Lucy took a deep breath in, sang through the first line in her head, and nodded to the accompanist. The music started. Lucy was still feeling centered and calm after Noor's performance, and her opening phrase poured out of her effortlessly. All the hours that she had practiced technique with her teacher faded to the background, and she allowed the meaning behind the words to guide her voice.

Before she knew it, the song was over. She thanked the accompanist, then waited for a response from the auditioners. The woman was pointing to a spot on the clipboard and the man was nodding his head.

The woman turned back to Lucy, "Thank you for auditioning. We always need good altos in the choir, so we are happy to invite you to join our twentieth season. We'll see you at our first rehearsal, next Wednesday."

Lucy's whole face lit up, her eyes bright with the sweet elation of success. "Thank you so much!"

She was thrilled. She had achieved a goal that she had been working towards for several months, but secretly dreamed of for over two decades. But more importantly, now she also had an opportunity to sing with Noor Khanna. Lucy was determined to find a way to learn the secret behind the woman's enchanting voice.

Lucy stopped by the grocery store on the way home to get a special treat to celebrate her victory. She had a serious sweet tooth and a celebration for her was not just some ice cream. No, this called for ice cream, hot fudge, caramel, whipped cream, and sprinkles.

She opened the front door, holding the grocery bag in one arm and fumbling to take the key out of the lock. She took a step and felt something under her foot, nearly causing her to trip and spill her groceries.

You stepped on my tail! Cloud wailed woefully. She heard the voice clearly in her mind.

Lucy put the grocery bag down and stooped to pet the luxurious gray cat's head. "I'm so sorry, Cloud. I couldn't see you with the bag in the way." She scratched the sides of his cheeks in apology.

Cloud started to purr and rubbed against Lucy, then the grocery bag. *That's okay. Did you get me anything?*

"Of course! Let me put this away first."

"Meow!" he said aloud.

Lucy laughed, because Cloud only talked to her with human words when he was hurt or especially hungry. Now that he was getting his food, he sounded like a regular cat again.

Although technically she and Cloud could communicate using Lucy's animal magic anytime, Cloud seemed happy just being a normal cat and letting Lucy know what he needed and how he felt the old-fashioned feline way, through meows, head butts, and paw taps. Lucy was happy with that too.

She took out a package of liver and chicken cat paté and emptied it onto a small plate. Cloud started wolfing it down immediately and Lucy scrunched up her nose, trying to block out the smell. It was hard to imagine something that was so stinky to her could be so delicious to him, but it obviously was.

She fixed herself an extravagant sundae and settled in on her little purple velvet loveseat. Lucy loved to watch old movies. Nowadays it was even better because she had Cloud to snuggle next to on her blanket and watch with her. Sure, sometimes he fell asleep in the middle, but that was okay.

She most enjoyed black and white movies from the 1930s and 40s. She also loved to watch films that followed along with the current themes in her life. She scrolled through her classic movie streaming channels and spied the perfect option—*Maytime*, a 1937 picture starring Jeanette MacDonald as an opera singer looking back on her career and tragic romantic past.

As soon as the opening credits rolled, Cloud jumped up on the loveseat beside her and started taking a proper post-meal bath. Lucy took a bite of her sundae and sighed in happiness. Life doesn't get better than a good dessert, a good movie, and a good cat.

Chapter 2

MONDAY STRIKES AGAIN, LUCY THOUGHT as she settled into her cubicle, her white pear tea in hand. She took the scrunchie off her wrist and pulled her strawberry blonde hair back into a neat ponytail at the nape of her neck, then fired up her laptop, ready to start her latest assignment, designing a series of maps for a water quality report.

She actually liked working at TerraPlaya much more these days. For fourteen years she had spent all her days making maps, until six months ago, when wildlife biologist Maya Morales had joined her team. Before Lucy knew it, she was helping with fieldwork surveying birds in the breathtaking Sienna Falls Forest. Making maps continued to be Lucy's primary job, but now she could also look forward to the occasional outing that was sure to take her somewhere she had never been and expose her to flora and fauna she had only seen in books.

Lucy wrapped her long black sweater around her and headed to the conference room for the Monday mid-morning staff meeting to discuss work allocation for the week. She took the seat next to Maya and greeted her friend and other groggy looking coworkers. Guess Mondays are rough for most people, she chuckled inwardly.

Anuk, the office manager, who always gave Lucy the impression that Mondays were the highlight of his life, started out the meeting. "Good morning, team! I have some exciting news. Late Friday, we received a signed contract for new bird surveys in Brighton Island Nature Preserve."

Bethany, the self-appointed office team spirit captain, ever enthusiastic, whooped, "That's like, amazing!"

Maya and Lucy cheered as well, knowing that their previous work had helped make this happen. Even Tyler seemed somewhat interested in the news, and Tyler looking up from his phone for something was a rare event.

Anuk beamed, taking in the excited energy of the office. "Since Bethany is pretty booked up on the Crystal Beach sampling project, we need to think about hiring another person who knows birds well to work with Maya. We are just on the cusp of having enough work to need another person."

Tyler immediately blurted, "I'd like to get out to do more fieldwork. I can learn more about birds."

Lucy's pulse skyrocketed. Tyler was always so pushy and confident, and he always got what he wanted because of it. Lucy was just learning to stand up for herself, and she knew in her heart that she was already better at fieldwork than Tyler. She knew more about birds than Tyler too.

She had literally flown with birds after she learned to see through their eyes. She had soared with a falcon through a forest, glided with a pelican across the ocean, and circled the beach with a laughing gull. She knew more than Tyler not just because of her animal magic—she had also practiced identifying bird calls with Maya and spent many a lunch hour with guidebooks and binoculars.

But Lucy would never even have thought to volunteer herself instead of Anuk hiring a true expert—it seemed egotistical to her. She read Anuk's face and could see he was actually considering Tyler's suggestion. Maya kicked Lucy's foot under the table and gave her a pressing look. Lucy knew exactly what her friend was trying to tell her.

She clenched her fist in her lap for courage. "I'd also like to do more surveys, and I have been making a lot of progress on bird identification from working with Maya." Lucy couldn't believe it was her voice saying the words. She was advocating for herself, just like Tyler. She still didn't think either of them were replacements for a true bird specialist, but she wanted Anuk to know she could do anything Tyler could. She was beginning to learn that there is no harm in asking, just the risk of mild discomfort if the answer is negative.

Anuk nodded his head, showing no sign that he thought her request unreasonable. "Thanks, Tyler and Lucy. I will certainly consider it. However, because of the intensified focus on office overhead and profits, TerraPlaya won't be able to pay for additional training right now. You both would have to learn on your own time."

Tyler looked unsure and hesitated, but Lucy agreed enthusiastically. "No problem! I will start studying right away."

Tyler eyed her with suspicion, not used to such a forward Lucy. "Yeah, me too," he echoed. Bethany gave him a nod of encouragement.

Anuk continued to cover the rest of his agenda, assigning both Lucy and Tyler some new mapping projects for the week.

As they exited the conference room, Maya whispered, "We are going to kick Tyler's butt. You are already awesome at bird identification for someone so new to it. And I have tons of stuff from class I can give you and there are lots of great apps available now that will help too."

"Thanks. I didn't even know I was a competitive person until I thought about Tyler getting all the new fieldwork!"

"I know. I'm so proud of you for sticking your neck out. You got this." Maya waved and headed to her cubicle in the other wing.

As Lucy headed back to her corner desk near the window, she overheard Tyler and Bethany talking.

"You just, like, need more practice, that's all," Bethany was saying. "I can help you."

"Yeah, I probably need to try harder now that Lucy is getting all uppity," Tyler replied.

Lucy continued walking and their conversation was soon out of earshot. Her teeth were clenched, and her face was aflame. Uppity? She was uppity just because she asked for the same opportunity and consideration that Tyler had? That's it. She would practice as much as it takes—Tyler is going down.

Chapter 3

WEDNESDAY FINALLY ARRIVED AND IT was time for Lucy's first choir rehearsal since elementary school. She kept telling herself that she had worked hard with her voice teacher to prepare, not to mention that she wouldn't have passed the audition if they didn't think she was good enough. Even so, from the moment she woke up that morning she was a bundle of nerves. If she drank any more calming tea she might burst.

Before Lucy left the house, she did a deep breathing exercise and spent some time petting Cloud, which always soothed her anxieties. Despite the preparation, her misgivings grew as she drove back to the Northbrook Fellowship Hall, and escalated further when she saw that the parking lot was over half full and cars were pulling in one after another. She grabbed her water bottle and tried not to panic as she followed the herd.

She knew there were around two hundred singers in the Northbrook Community Choir, but she still wasn't prepared for the assault on her senses when she entered the door to the foyer. There were dozens of people milling about the hallway in groups of twos and threes, greeting their old friends from last season. It was Lucy's worst nightmare—these people all knew each other, and she was there alone, feeling like the unpopular new girl in a junior high cafeteria.

She glanced at her watch and frowned when she realized she was twenty minutes early. Out of desperation, she once again found herself in the restroom, giving herself a silent peptalk in the mirror. *Lucy, you are here to sing—there's no need to worry about making friends or being popular. Just focus on the singing,* she told herself. That made her feel better, to concentrate on one thing that she could control.

By the time she was back in the hallway, people were starting to filter into the rehearsal room. It was a large space with a wooden floor and four tiered levels that each held a row of chairs. Lucy started to panic about not knowing where to sit, but a friendly woman with a clipboard approached her, recognizing her deer in headlights look. She asked her which voice part she was and then showed her where the altos would be sitting. She handed Lucy a music book from a tall stack on the table and told her to write her name on it.

Lucy sat down towards the back of the alto section. Before long, the seats filled in all around her. The women to her right and left both welcomed her and she was already starting to feel more at ease. Then the conductor entered and stood in the middle of the floor to address them. She was wearing a casual gray suit jacket and gray pants with a cream-colored top. The suit matched her silvery hair, which was short and spiky. Lucy thought she looked very hip and modern and instantly liked her.

"Good evening singers! I'm so glad you all joined us as part of our twentieth season!"

The long timers in the choir applauded and a few even whooped or whistled.

"I'm your conductor, Darlene Braxton. This is my seventh season with this group. Show of hands—how many newbies do we have today?"

Lucy reluctantly raised her hand halfway. She hated when people made her single herself out. But as the other choir members turned around to see behind them, their smiles seemed so friendly and welcoming that Lucy didn't even mind the attention.

"Welcome! I'm sure our long-time members will make you feel at home. Let's get started—shall we? Everyone stand up!"

Darlene led them through a series of exercises to warm up their voices. At first, Lucy sang nervously at half volume, but the exercises were simple and easy to follow, and soon she was focused on the conductor and being part of the group, and not so much on herself. Then Darlene had each voice part hold one note in a chord, and she gestured with her hand to raise or lower the volume of certain sections to achieve the perfect balance.

Lucy could feel the power of two hundred voices singing in harmony. When the chords were balanced just right, she could hear the overtones ring out above them, like a great beam of light extending from the choir up into the sky. Her heart felt full.

After the warmups, they started singing through the featured piece for the season, Mozart's *Requiem*. Lucy stumbled through it rather painfully. She didn't have much experience sight reading. She wasn't the only one who was struggling, but luckily there were some loud and confident altos in her section, so she just kept her voice low and followed their guiding voices.

Halfway through the piece, Darlene announced it was time for mid-rehearsal break and they had fifteen minutes. Lucy sighed. She hated this part because she would have to stand awkwardly alone in the lobby once again. She could pretend to check her phone at least. She had only just gotten it out of her purse when she realized someone was standing next to her.

"It's Lucy, right?" said Noor. The two women studied with the same voice teacher and had met briefly a few weeks ago at the student recital.

"Hi Noor! Nice to see you."

"How do you like it so far?" Noor gestured towards the rehearsal room.

Lucy considered it for a moment. "I like it a lot. It's so different from just singing by myself. It's like there is a totally different energy."

Noor's eyes twinkled. "Absolutely. That's a great way to put it. The energy *is* different—the power of hundreds of singers is immense."

Lucy nodded, but then frowned. "I am a little worried about learning such a long piece in such a short amount of time. And I'm not used to staying on my part while other people are singing different notes."

"I can help you with that. If you ever want to practice together, let me know. You can come to my studio."

"I'd love that—thank you!"

The two women exchanged phone numbers, then Noor excused herself to get a drink from the water fountain before rehearsal resumed.

Lucy was about to head back in and find her spot when she heard a shrill scream.

"Bat! Bat!"

People in the lobby started to panic and some exited the doors to the parking lot. Others flocked towards the scream to see what the fuss was about. Lucy wove her way through the crowd to the source of the commotion. She peered into the rehearsal room and strained her neck to see what the woman was pointing at. Yep, there was indeed a bat flying around high up in the rafters.

Lucy had seen bats in the wild before and she knew they were an important part of the ecosystem and performed critical functions, like eating insects. But she also knew bats in urban areas were sometimes infected with rabies, but that seemed more often when someone found one floundering on the ground.

"Open the windows—maybe it will fly out!" someone suggested. A brave older man gingerly walked into the room and turned the hand crank that opened the upper windows.

Good, that would make her job easier, Lucy thought. First, she needed to figure out if the bat was sick, because if it was, then calling animal control would be an unfortunate necessity. Lucy backed up against the wall and held her music up to her face, pretending she was rehearsing her part in her head.

Instead, she closed her eyes and allowed herself to fall into a state of mindfulness. It was a little harder with so many people around, but she focused on the smell of a strong perfume wafting from someone near her, the feeling of her back pressed against the wall, and the sound of the fan circulating air. Soon, the noise of the crowd became a background hum, and she reached out with her mind up to the ceiling. She quickly found the bat and sent him feelings of calm reassurance.

Then she spoke to him in her mind. *Are you okay? I'm here to help you.*

I can't get out! I can't get out!

Lucy could tell this bat was frantic due to its situation; it didn't feel like sickness. Lucy had communicated with injured animals before, and there was a certain darkness there that she wasn't feeling now. This was pure panic. She knew she could guide him out safely.

I can lead you out if you let me.

There was no response, so Lucy breathed deeply in and out and focused on finding her way into the bat's mind. After a few seconds she saw it, a deep mahogany door, and she pushed against it and tumbled inside. She felt the bat panicking and she sent out more calming energy.

Let me take control—I promise you will be okay.

She felt the bat acquiesce and then she was looking out from the bat's point of view, seeing through his eyes. She saw some slightly blurry people pointing up at them from the doorway. She spied the open window.

Ready?

Lucy took a leap of faith and forcibly pushed the bat off the rafter in a swoop towards the window. She heard a woman scream again. Lucy had flown with many birds before, but a bat was a new experience; it felt like she was rowing through the air. The window was coming at them fast, and she worried she wouldn't be able to navigate through the rectangle without clipping its wings. Thankfully at the last moment, she felt comprehension click in the bat's brain and Lucy allowed the bat to take over and glide through gracefully.

Thank you, the bat said as he flew off into the night sky.

My pleasure, said Lucy and then jumped out of the bat's mind. She was back in the hallway again, her music book still pressed against her face. The older gentleman had run to crank the window closed again and everyone was sighing and chattering with relief that the bat was gone.

She smiled with a renewed sense of purpose. Animal magic had become a part of her; maybe in time, music would someday become a part of her, too.

She lowered the music book and jumped when she saw Noor staring at her thoughtfully.

Lucy's heart raced. There was no way Noor knew what she had done, right?

Chapter 4

LUCY LOOKED OUT THE CAR window. Was she in the right place? She wasn't in this part of Northbrook often and she didn't know the neighborhood. But the confident lady in her phone said she had arrived, so she parked her car on the side of the road. She was looking for number 10600.

A small sign on the door at the end of a small strip of stores read, "Northbrook Harmony." She wiped her sweaty palms on her pants and headed for the door. There was nothing to be nervous about, she knew, but she was uncomfortable in new places, and with new people. At least she had found parking easily.

The inside front window of the business held draped tie dye scarves in purples, blues, and greens, blocking most of the view from the street. As Lucy pushed the door open, the tinkling of wind chimes filled the air. The studio was lined with white pine flooring, broken up into sections with large woven rugs. Two of the walls were pale marble green, and the other two were a creamy peach, giving the room a calming, but cheerful atmosphere. The space smelled faintly of vanilla.

In those few seconds after she opened the door, Lucy could sense that this was a place of peace and healing. She smiled as Noor sprang out of the back office to greet her.

"Lucy! Welcome to Northbrook Harmony. Let me give you the

grand tour."

The studio appeared to be only one large room plus a small back office, but she could feel the pride emanating from Noor. "That would be great. Thanks for inviting me."

Noor led her to the right back corner, which had an old upright piano with a brass lamp and was stacked high with music books. Next to the wall there was an acoustic guitar on a stand, and above it was a bracket that held a ukulele. "This is where I give my music therapy lessons. A lot of kids respond well to the sounds of the piano, but some do better with guitar."

"Wow—so you play all those instruments?"

"I do. I'm not virtuosic on any of them, but part of my music therapy program required competency on keyboard and guitar, as well as voice. The ukulele is a fun extra."

Lucy was impressed. She was working hard just to become decent at singing; she couldn't imagine learning several instruments at once.

Noor moved to the back left side of the room. "Over here is where I hold small group sessions." She waved her hand over a large square rug with fringes. There was a large wooden chest that looked like it could hold pirate treasure, but Noor opened the lid and revealed a variety of small percussion instruments—red and yellow painted maracas, a blue tambourine, a wooden block, plastic green and white finger castanets, and a purple egg shaker.

Lucy grinned as she imagined a group of children raiding the box—it probably did feel like treasure to them. "That looks fun!"

"It *is* fun with the right group of kids. Group music sessions can work wonders for some children who struggle with social interactions. Some parents tell me this is the only time their children participate in activities with other kids."

"Huh. I don't know much about music therapy, but it sounds like it has incredible potential. How did you get in this line of work?"

"Well, my father, my grandfather, and my older sister are all doctors. It was always assumed I would be a doctor too. But ever since I was a little girl, I was drawn to music. My parents were practical, so when I said I wanted to be a musician, they said absolutely not!"

"That's understandable. It's such a difficult field to make a living in."

"Exactly, and I don't blame them—they were probably right. I wanted to help people, but the idea of being a medical doctor felt wrong for me. Then I found music therapy by accident, and it seemed like a good balance of music and medicine."

"Did you have to study both for your degree, then?" Lucy asked.

"I had to study psychology as well as neuroscience. The research in this field is growing rapidly and there is more and more evidence that music can affect the brain in ways we never imagined a few decades ago."

Lucy wondered what the implications of that were for song magic. Could dark song magicians directly influence people's brains? She shuddered at the thought.

Luckily Noor didn't notice her reaction as she beckoned Lucy over to the last area in the main room. "This is my latest pride and joy, a Celtic lap harp." Noor sat down on a wooden stool and picked up the walnut harp, intricately carved with Celtic knots along the base.

As Noor's fingers began to pluck the strings, Lucy imagined geometric patterns radiating from the harp towards the edge of the room, like a stone thrown in the water, creating expanding circles. The song she played was sweet and melancholic, and filled Lucy with nostalgia for something she couldn't put her finger on, a distant memory, foggy and faded. One thing was evident; Noor's song magic wasn't limited to singing. It made Lucy itch to find out more, but she didn't want to scare Noor off by pushing too soon.

Before Lucy had a chance to figure out how she could naturally broach the subject of magic with Noor, the front door flung open. A young boy barged in and went right up to Noor, ignoring Lucy entirely. Lucy assumed Noor knew the child, since she continued playing the remainder of the tune, unalarmed by the intrusion.

"Blue and violet," the boy declared when Noor put down the harp.

Lucy looked at Noor quizzically.

"Lucy, this is Evan. His mom Debbie rents the studio from me part time when I'm not using it. I said I could watch him for a few minutes while she runs an errand."

Lucy waved at the boy and smiled. "Hi Evan, I'm Lucy."

The boy looked down at the floor.

Lucy wasn't great with kids, never having been around them since she was one. She was the only person she knew who had never babysat as a teenager in high school, and none of her adult friends had young children.

"It's okay Evan, Lucy's my new friend," said Noor.

"Can I play piano until my mom gets here?" Evan asked, ignoring Noor's introduction.

"Sure, you can. Wash your hands first, please."

Evan took off for the sink and then stood at the piano and pressed various keys one by one, listening to the overtones of each note ring out in the room.

Lucy looked at Noor. "What did he mean by blue and violet?"

"It's called synesthesia. Evan sees music as colors."

Somehow that made sense to Lucy. She didn't exactly see colors when Noor played, but she did see and sort of *feel* patterns, as opposed to just hearing the sounds. It wasn't something she could explain, it just was what it was.

Maybe this was her chance to get Noor to admit she had song magic. "Synesthesia. That's fascinating—I've never heard of that. It seems like different people have very different relationships with music," Lucy said, trying to give Noor a knowing look.

If Noor took the hint, she pretended otherwise. "I suppose that's true."

Lucy wasn't giving up so easily. "Like you. Your singing is enchanting, and the audience really responds to you."

For a split-second Lucy thought Noor looked uncomfortable, but she recovered instantly and smiled. "Thank you for saying that. Singing and performing has certainly become a great joy of mine. Evan's mom should be back in a minute—let me make us some tea before we start practicing. I mean, if you like tea? I have a vanilla infused green tea that is divine."

Lucy soon forgot to be disappointed that Noor had changed the subject. She was a huge fan of tea and loved to find other tea drinkers in a world of coffee fanatics. "That sounds lovely, thank you."

As Noor stepped out to the back office, Lucy racked her brain for ways to get Noor to reveal her secret but came up empty. She would have to wait until another day to find out about Noor's song magic. But Lucy was even more certain that she possessed it and was purposely hiding it. She couldn't blame Noor at all—didn't Lucy herself hide her animal magic from almost everyone she knew? It simply wasn't safe to admit such things in this world, and who would risk attracting unwanted attention?

Noor returned with two mugs of tea, and Lucy thanked her. The steaming liquid smelled wonderful and as she breathed in the calming vanilla scent, she felt there was no reason to rush. For now, Lucy would just enjoy practicing the choir music with a new acquaintance.

Chapter 5

ANOTHER MONDAY, ANOTHER MONDAY MORNING staff meeting. Once again, all the groggy faces joined Lucy in the conference room, Maya with her lifeline cup of coffee, Tyler with his phone glued to his hand, and only Bethany and Anuk chipper as birds at dawn.

"Good morning, team!" Anuk began. "Today I have something different to share with you. Our new parent company wants to help us streamline our productivity."

The conference room filled with groans and a few gasps.

"No! Not talking layoffs, people. Not this time," Anuk clarified.

It had only been a few months prior that headquarters had sent an efficiency specialist to evaluate each employee. Luckily, in no small part due to Lucy and Maya bringing in new clients, it was determined that the office could stay whole. But it served as a reminder to Lucy and Maya that working for a corporation meant they could be downsized at any time the company didn't meet its financial goals.

"Well, what then? I feel, like, pretty productive already," said Bethany, which garnered some nods and murmurs of agreement.

Anuk sighed. He was used to leading an outspoken team of environmental professionals, who tended towards the less corporate side of the workforce. "Calm down, folks. If you'll let me finish…we are all taking part in a special survey that is designed to give us more awareness of our communication and workflow styles."

"So, basically a personality test? I took one of those in college," said Bethany.

"It's not a personality test, it's just a series of questions that help us identify our strengths and weaknesses," said Anuk.

Maya scrunched up her face and said, "That sounds like a personality test," causing another round of nodding and agreement among her teammates.

Poor Anuk was growing flustered, and Lucy began to take pity on him; she knew he was constantly caught between corporate and the team, and she suspected he sheltered them from more than he let on. Ignoring the protests, he continued, "You'll each get a link in your e-mail to the survey later today and you'll need to complete it by end of business Friday. Once the surveys are analyzed, a representative from the testing company will talk through the results and advise us on how we can apply the information to better our team. Corporate will schedule that workshop sometime within the next few weeks."

Lucy's stomach tightened. The last time corporate made her take a questionnaire, she had almost been fired. She probably would have been if not for a random coincidence providing her the opportunity to help the corporate efficiency expert's precious papillon dog with her animal magic. But still, a personality test was different, right? Not like this one is a screening tool to classify employees by value like the efficiency test was. Lucy hoped so, anyway. Her stomach churned for the remainder of the meeting and she only half-listened to the rest of what Anuk was saying.

As they always did when the weather was nice, Lucy and Maya took their lunch break in the gated courtyard between the two buildings. It was no ordinary office park garden; this one had paths of limestone, a trellis with purple wisteria cascading over the edges, two large oak trees, and a deck with iron patio furniture, an oasis made private by vine-covered wrought iron fencing around the perimeter.

"What's that?" said Maya, pointing to a bird on a wire behind the office complex. It was quite far away, which Lucy knew meant that Maya thought it had an obvious feature that would allow her to ID it from a distance. As she squinted her eyes, she noticed the extra-long, forked tail and she smiled.

"Scissor-tailed Flycatcher."

Maya grinned. "Nice. That was an easy one, though."

Lucy rolled her eyes.

"I'm just saying, it takes a long time and a lot of effort to become really good at bird identification. I know you can do it, though. And I doubt Tyler has the discipline," said Maya.

"We'll see. I can only control my side, anyway."

"True and wise. Not many birds around today," Maya said, scanning the trees. "How did it go with Noor yesterday—did you find out anything else about song magic?"

"Unfortunately, no. We just practiced our choir music. It's frustrating, because ever since your grandmother told me about song magic, I've been dying to learn more."

"Maybe you can teach yourself like you did with animal magic."

Lucy considered this. Before Maya came to work at TerraPlaya, Lucy had no idea animal magic, or any magic at all, existed. But once Maya taught her some basic animal communication techniques, Lucy quickly surpassed her teacher, learning not only to talk with animals, but to see through their eyes, and even control them like she had with the terrified bat at the choir hall.

It was like becoming aware of magic suddenly made it accessible. She likened it to if you never knew what a piano was, then one suddenly appeared, you would instinctively press the keys and delight in the sound. Even without a teacher, you could experiment and eventually learn to make music. Animal magic had been like that for her.

But song magic felt different. Lucy was insecure. She had only taken voice lessons for a few months before singing in a recital, then auditioning for the choir. Before that she hadn't been in choir since elementary school. Animal magic felt more organic, like it was about intent and focus, but when she heard Noor sing at her audition, Lucy worried that there was a technical side to song magic that could take years of practice to learn.

"I don't know—maybe I can. I haven't tried, really. I don't even know what song magic can do yet. I'm still hoping Noor will open up and I can learn from her."

Out of the corner of her eye, Lucy spied a squirrel scurrying down the oak tree, eying the women.

"Hi squirrel," Lucy and Maya said at almost the same time, breaking them into giggles. The courtyard squirrels were the spoiled beneficiaries of Lucy's animal magic training, which had involved ample volumes of nuts.

"He wants to know if we have any snacks for him today," said Lucy.

Maya thought for a moment. "I don't think I have any more nuts in my desk, do you?"

"Afraid not. I'll tell him."

Lucy focused on the squirrel, letting him know they didn't have anything to share, and he darted back up the tree in disappointment, showing no interest in having a conversation if there was nothing edible involved.

"I'll bring him something tomorrow," said Lucy.

Maya closed her lunch cooler. "Back to the song magic question, what's your plan?"

Her friend knew that Lucy always felt better when she had a plan. It calmed her to formulate small, sequential steps towards her goal, then to focus on one part at a time, refusing to take in the big picture so she wouldn't become overwhelmed. And it worked. After all, Lucy and Maya were able to defeat dark animal magicians last time using this method.

"I've only gotten as far as making sure to talk with her at choir rehearsal on Wednesday and asking her if we can practice at her studio again next weekend. If she says yes to that, then I'll come up with some ways to get her to admit she does magic."

"Sounds like a sensible, *Lucy* sort of plan."

"I'll take that as a compliment," Lucy said with a grin.

Maya chuckled. "And so you should."

Chapter 6

LUCY FELT MORE AT HOME with the Northbrook Community Choir by her second rehearsal. She knew where to sit, and she greeted her fellow altos with brief exchanges on their well-being. She felt more prepared with her singing as well since Darlene had distributed a schedule detailing which movements the choir would focus on at each rehearsal.

That, combined with her session with Noor and additional practice on her own, made her feel more confident than she was the week before. For Lucy, preparation was always the key to managing her anxieties. She would practice as much as necessary to learn her parts and become a valuable contributor to the choir.

The evening had started out promising because she ran into Noor as soon as she arrived at the Northbrook Fellowship Hall. She didn't have to spend those excruciating minutes alone in the lobby or be the first one to sit by herself in the rehearsal room, pretending to study her music. Instead, she and Noor chatted about work and made plans to practice together again on the weekend. Lucy was elated that she would have a second chance to learn about Noor's song magic.

Darlene entered the rehearsal room and the chatter faded.

"Good evening, singers! I hope you all practiced—we have a lot to get through today. Everyone stand up!"

Lucy admired that Darlene was so commanding. Her job as director was to lead the choir towards her vision of the works they were performing. Lucy imagined it was no easy feat to earn and keep the respect of this many singers, not to mention please the board of trustees. Plus, Darlene had to find a balance between being inspiring and strict, making rehearsals enjoyable enough to keep people from quitting but serious enough to produce high quality performances.

Lucy was pleased with herself as they worked through the "Kyrie" section of the *Requiem*. She was able to stay on her part reasonably well. She was still following some of the section leaders, rather than focusing on balancing with the choir, but her voice teacher said that would come with experience.

Another challenge for Lucy was singing in Latin, which she had never done before. She had prepared a song in Italian for her audition, but Latin was new. Darlene spent time separating the lyrics from the music, the choir repeating the words after her for pronunciation, then speaking the words in rhythm with the music. Then they sang the music without words, and finally married both together.

This was perfect for Lucy, who preferred methodical, multi-step approaches to reaching goals. It made her feel like anyone could reach the finish line if they just put in the energy and moved one foot in front of the other.

Ever since Lucy had joined the choir, she had this extra underlying current of joy in her life. Not just because she loved singing, but that she had made a plan to audition, had started voice lessons, prepared meticulously, was accepted into the choir, and now she was becoming part of a community. She had never had that before, and it felt different.

Given that in the past six months she had met Maya and learned animal magic, it was odd that joining the choir was in some ways just as empowering as actually having the power of magic, but nevertheless, it was.

The first half of the rehearsal flew by as Lucy was lost in concentration. Before she knew it, Darlene was addressing the choir.

"Before we take our break, I have an announcement. I'd like everyone to welcome one late addition to our choir this season, Kayla Quinn." Darlene motioned for a woman sitting in the row in front of Lucy, several seats to the right, to stand.

Kayla stood up and tossed her light blonde hair away from her eyes. She had an edgy but professional look, with faded black jeans, a crisp white v-neck, and a fitted black blazer with oversized silver buttons. She didn't appear self-conscious at all, as Lucy would have been at being singled out. Instead, she made a sweeping smile to her right and left and behind her as people welcomed her.

Lucy froze when she saw Kayla's face. It couldn't be.

Could it?

She had only seen the face of the dark magician who sang in Sienna Falls Forest for a brief minute, and that had been a good four-hour drive away from Northbrook. It seemed unlikely that the same Kayla had just joined her choir. But it was her, Lucy knew it.

Lucy's eyes bored into the back of Kayla's head as she tried to make sense of this new development and she accidently caught Noor's eyes across the room in the soprano section. Noor had also been staring at Kayla and looked visibly upset. For a second, Lucy and Noor shared a moment of recognition. They both knew Kayla. Noor turned away quickly and glued her eyes to the conductor.

Darlene continued, "Kayla brings with us a generous new sponsor, her employer, Scordatura Solutions."

The choir applauded and whistled in appreciation.

"Alright. Back in fifteen, everyone!" Darlene released the choir for break.

Lucy tried to push through the crowd towards Noor, but by the time she made it to the lobby she was nowhere to be seen. Instead, Lucy went outside away from the others and tried to regain her composure. She hadn't realized how fast her heart was racing until she stood still again. Her hands were trembling, and her palms were clammy.

Why was Kayla there? Could she just be there to sing? It was possible, Lucy reasoned. She had learned that dark magicians lived regular lives just like everyone else, with families, hobbies, and PTA meetings. On the other hand, it was just as likely that Kayla was there on business. Dark magician business.

Lucy was crestfallen. Her happy feelings about joining the choir were dampened now. She had hoped that her battle with the dark magicians was a one-time thing. But what if now that she knew about magic, it would always be a filter that tainted how she saw the world?

Lucy took some deep breaths in and out, trying to re-center herself. Her years of therapy had taught her many useful coping mechanisms for when her anxiety started to spiral out of control. One of them was to narrow her focus to the present reality of the moment and not allow herself to get swallowed by a tidal wave of what-ifs.

Right now, she was going to go back into the rehearsal and concentrate on singing what she had practiced, and that was it. Her pulse slowed and her breathing returned to normal. She walked calmly and purposefully back to her seat in the rehearsal room and buried herself in reviewing the next movement of the piece.

Since the music was still challenging for Lucy, she was thankfully forced to concentrate on the task at hand. She tried to avoid stealing glances at the back of Kayla's head, but it was hard. She was distracted a few times by picking out Kayla's voice among the altos. Once she did, Lucy knew for sure this was the same person whose song nearly helped devastate a forest.

When rehearsal was over, she tried again to race over to Noor. She wasn't sure how Noor knew Kayla, or if she knew about dark magicians, but Lucy needed to find out as soon as possible.

She caught up with Noor in the parking lot, pretending that nothing had happened. "Hey, thanks again for helping me practice. It made a huge difference."

Noor eyed Lucy with suspicion, then responded somewhat coolly, "Sure, anything to make sure the choir performs well."

Then Noor sped off to her car, leaving Lucy standing alone.

Chapter 7

LUCY WAS TAPPING HER FOOT impatiently at Maya's cubicle. "Finally—you're here!"

"Good morning to you too, Lucy." Maya ran her fingers through her long, wavy dark hair, still damp. "I was running a little late today."

"Sorry—didn't mean to jump on you first thing. I need to ask you something. The paper with the list of Sepharine Holdings Inc subsidiaries— do you still have it?"

Maya sat down in her office chair and opened her filing cabinet. She dug out a folded piece of paper from behind the last divider. "I'm scared to ask why you want this. I thought you were done with fighting dark magicians."

"I was. But I don't think they're done with me. Guess who showed up at choir practice last night? Kayla."

"From Sienna Falls? No way." Maya whistled between her teeth. "That is some coincidence."

"Tell me about it. I don't think she recognized me though."

"Well, she was only there for a few minutes and was focused on her singing. She left before the real battle began. Plus seeing people out of context makes it harder to place them. I'm almost surprised you recognized her."

"Her voice is forever imbedded in my brain." Lucy shuddered as the scene replayed in her memory. "How could I forget the song of a dark magician who could make forest animals flee from their home in terror?"

Maya held out the piece of paper to Lucy. "I hope you know what opening this paper means. When I tried to give this to you last time, you practically smacked my hand away. Maybe ignorance is bliss?"

Lucy sighed deeply. "Yes. Potentially opening a can of worms here. But I have to know. Kayla joined the choir along with a large corporate sponsorship. I need to know if it is associated with the same people." Lucy made a silent plea to the universe that just this once, things could be simple. She slowly unfolded the paper. Her face immediately paled two shades.

"Well, crap," said Maya as she saw her friend's face fall.

"Yep. Kayla's corporate sponsor is owned by Sepharine Holdings." Lucy pointed to a name on the paper.

"Scordatura Solutions? What does that mean?" said Maya.

"I had to look it up. Scordatura is an old term for tuning a string instrument like a cello different from the standard tuning to get a certain effect. It was popular in the sixteen and seventeen hundreds."

Maya's eyes widened. "Are you thinking what I'm thinking?"

"If you're thinking that Scordatura Solutions is a front company for dark magicians using song magic for nefarious purposes, then yes." Lucy refolded the paper and handed it back to Maya.

"It makes sense. We knew they were using ZRC Laboratories, posing as a cosmetics testing company, to train people to use dark animal magic, so why not do the same for song magic? It's probably not a coincidence that there are five subsidiaries and my lita told us there were five types of magic." Maya hid the paper again in the back of her filing cabinet and shut it, as if keeping the secret hidden would somehow make it not true, would keep the evil contained.

"Nope. We have to assume Sepharine Holdings is training people all around the country in how to use the five types of magic through five separate companies."

Maya rubbed the bottom of her chin. "Why keep them separate? Why not train people in all types of magic at once?"

Lucy shrugged. "I don't know. We barely understand anything about the world of magic yet. Maybe there is a reason. Maybe most people can only be good at one type. That's what I need to find out."

"How's it going with Noor? Have you thought of a way to bring it up? Get her to admit she knows song magic?" Maya turned on her computer.

Lucy's face soured. "That's the other thing—I got the impression that Noor recognized Kayla last night."

"Uh oh," said Maya, shaking her head, "That's not good."

"But she seemed more surprised and upset. And then she acted weird after the rehearsal."

"If she was upset to see Kayla then they probably aren't working together, right?"

Lucy paused to consider this. "I suppose that could be true. It's not like they ran over to each other and said hi."

"Maybe the song magic community is small, and they all know each other?"

"Maybe. At any rate, I'm working on it. I'm just getting to know Noor, and I don't want to scare her off. We were supposed to practice again this weekend, but I wrote her last night and look how she replied." Lucy held up her phone.

Noor: I'm pretty busy this weekend, in fact I'm getting so busy with my studio lately—might not have time to practice with you much after all.

"Yikes, that's not very subtle. She's definitely blowing you off," said Maya.

"Ugh, I know. It has to be because of Kayla." Lucy looked defeated. Noor was the only lead she had on song magic, and now she couldn't even follow it. It seemed that everything in her life was always one step forward, two steps back.

"You didn't reply yet?"

"No, I wasn't sure how to—I wanted to talk it through with you first," said Lucy.

"You have to try harder to make this happen. Maybe if you let her know about your animal magic she would open up," Maya suggested.

"Maybe. That feels like a big risk though, and I'm not saying all that in a text. And there's always the off chance that your grandmother was wrong, and Noor doesn't even have song magic." Even though Lucy knew what she experienced during Noor's audition couldn't have been her imagination, she couldn't be one hundred percent sure of anything until Noor admitted it.

Maya shook her head firmly. "Unlikely. She wouldn't have said it if she weren't sure." Maya typed into the web browser. "So, Scordatura Solutions sells instructional products—music books and such. This website isn't like the animal magic one, though. It looks functional—you can make online orders. I'm going to order something, just for kicks, see if it actually arrives."

"Interesting. I was wondering why a shell company would sponsor a community choir—seems like they wouldn't want their name out there too much," said Lucy.

"It does seem weird."

"I need to find out more about the sponsorship—what they get out of it. I mean, maybe it's just a tax write-off."

"Oh Lucy, forever trying to overlook the bad side of people. You don't really think that, do you? After everything we went through. Getting attacked by wolves and ravens, and battling for the lives of a forest full of creatures?"

Lucy sighed again, even more deeply this time. "Of course not, I'll never forget everything that's happened. I'm sure Scordatura is up to no good. I just don't know what it has to do with a community choir."

"I wish I could help you more, but I can't sing a note in tune to save my life. You're going to have to run point on this one."

"Yeah, I know. I guess I need to make connecting with Noor a priority so we can freely discuss magic and get to the bottom of this."

"I really hope Noor is on the good side," Maya said quietly.

Lucy grimaced, then she remembered to trust her instincts. "Noor is definitely not a dark magician, I'm sure of it. Dark magicians don't have day jobs helping children through music therapy."

"Perhaps not. I hope you're right about her."

Lucy looked worried. "Me too." She left Maya's cubicle and returned to her desk; no matter where Noor's allegiance lay, Lucy had a lot of maps to make today.

Chapter 8

IT WAS FRIDAY NIGHT AND Lucy was still crestfallen about Noor's reply message. She didn't have much experience making friends and this felt like a stinging rejection, even though she knew it was about something much bigger than the two women. She had to somehow let Noor know she was on the good side, but without divulging too much. She was sure that Noor was a nice person, that she wasn't a dark magician like Kayla, and she bet Noor didn't feel any better about ditching Lucy than Lucy felt getting ditched. She held her breath as she finally typed a reply.

Lucy: That's disappointing. I really enjoyed practicing with you. Did I do something wrong?

The three dots appeared, then disappeared, then appeared again. Curious, thought Lucy. After a few minutes, words appeared.

Noor: How do you know Kayla?

Whoa. Lucy was not expecting that, but at least Noor was direct, more like Maya, than Lucy, who had to summon up a lot of courage to ask a simple question. But how should she answer? She wasn't going to explain in a text that she had witnessed Kayla using dark song magic to clear a forest of its animal inhabitants, that she knew Kayla was working for some truly evil people.

Lucy: I just saw her sing somewhere once.

That was technically the truth, but without any of the important details. When she didn't get an immediate reply, she sucked in her breath and forced herself to type what she was dying to know.

Lucy: How do you know Kayla?

Noor: I went to school with her.

Interesting. That didn't tell Lucy anything definitive and it brought up a whole other host of questions, like did Noor learn song magic in school, from the same person who taught Kayla? At any rate, Noor's mistrust of anyone who knew Kayla could only mean Kayla was no friend of Noor's.

Noor: Let's meet at 11 tomorrow.

Lucy heaved a sigh of relief. Not only did she want to get to know Noor better and hopefully learn about song magic and Kayla, she also still needed help with her choir music. She loved singing in the choir, but she liked it more the better prepared she felt. She didn't want to just be a follower singing softly and listening to a more confident person sing in her ear. She wanted to hold her own parts and be able to focus on blending and emoting and she was willing to work hard to achieve her goals.

Lucy and Noor were practicing the following day when Evan stormed in the front door. "There's something wrong with Evan."

The two women rushed over, wondering if they needed to call an ambulance.

"What is it—are you hurt?" Noor asked.

"There's something wrong with Evan," the boy repeated, setting a small cage with a gerbil down on the floor.

Noor's eyes widened in understanding, and she stooped down to ask, "Is your gerbil named Evan, too?"

Evan nodded.

Noor smiled gently. "It's a good name. Now what makes you think there is something wrong with him?"

Evan shook his head. "There's something wrong with Evan," he said louder, waving his hands frantically.

Noor pulled Lucy aside, "When he gets upset, he has a harder time communicating."

"Is there a vet nearby?" Lucy asked.

"Not that I know of," Noor said.

Evan pulled on the end of Lucy's sleeve. "There's something wrong with Evan," he said, his eyes imploring.

Lucy's pulse began to race. She had planned to tell Noor about her animal magic soon, maybe even today, but what if she was wrong? What if Noor didn't know song magic or anything about magic and thought she was nuts? But what if there really was something wrong with gerbil Evan and she did nothing about it? Could she live with breaking that boy's heart?

As she looked at Evan's agitated face, Lucy made a decision. She was going to take a huge risk and assume that she was right, both that Noor practiced song magic, and that Lucy could trust her with her secret.

Lucy looked Noor directly in the eyes and said, "I'm going to do something now, and I ask you to trust me, and we can discuss it later."

Noor looked confused but nodded her head.

Lucy kneeled next to the gerbil and went to her place of mindfulness, breathing in the vanilla fragrance, feeling the floor beneath her shins. Then she reached out to the gerbil with her mind. His response was less words and more a wailing of discomfort, reminding her of when she stepped on Cloud's tail. There was definitely something wrong with gerbil Evan. Sometimes Lucy could communicate with an animal in a conversational way, but the gerbil was too distraught. She tried one more time.

Where does it hurt, my friend? I want to help. Lucy spoke telepathically into the gerbil's mind.

The gerbil squirmed with confusion, not understanding where the voice was coming from. Lucy had no choice but to take it a step further and jump into the gerbil's mind. She visualized the door, this one a light pine, and easily forced her way in.

She immediately became aware of a pain beneath the animal's stomach. It was more uncomfortable than sharp, but human Evan was correct that this animal was not in good shape. Lucy tried to send calming vibes to the gerbil before she jumped out of its mind.

When Lucy opened her eyes, she found Noor staring at her with a curious gaze.

"I don't think it is an emergency, but there is something on the gerbil's stomach that is hurting it."

Lucy was surprised that Noor accepted her words with no explanation, just a nod. "Poor thing. Let's search the web for gerbil problems."

Evan was pacing back and forth impatiently, pulling the sleeves of his jacket over his hands.

Noor took out her phone and started typing. After just a few seconds she had a list of common gerbil ailments. "Look at this." Noor pointed at the screen.

Lucy looked at the entry on gerbil scent gland tumors, complete with an illustration of the gerbil's anatomy. "That could be the problem—it's in the right spot. He probably needs to go to the vet."

Noor lowered her voice and turned her back to Evan. "Evan's mom does not have the money to spend on surgery for a geriatric gerbil."

"We can't let him suffer," protested Lucy.

"No, we can't," said Noor.

"So…"

Noor turned to Lucy and looked her straight in the eyes with intensity, "I know you practice animal magic, and you know I use song magic. You're not going to deny it?"

Lucy shook her head, speechless at Noor's forward confession.

"I may be able to use my song magic to heal the gerbil," Noor said.

Lucy gasped. She hadn't learned much about the application of song magic, but if Noor could use it for healing, it was very powerful magic indeed. Lucy could tell if an animal was injured, but she couldn't do anything about it other than take it to the animal hospital or wildlife rehabilitation center.

"What about Evan, human Evan?" Lucy asked, glancing over at the distraught child.

"Don't worry about him. He has a unique outlook; he can see colors in music, after all. Even if he tells his mom exactly what happens here today, she will probably just accept it as part of his inspired imagination."

"Okay, what do we do now?" asked Lucy.

"I'm wondering if we can work together on this," Noor said.

"It's worth a try."

Noor turned to Evan, who was still pacing, and said firmly, "Evan, Lucy and I are going to try to help gerbil Evan. You will hear some loud sounds, okay?"

Evan nodded and pivoted to walk to the other side of the room.

Lucy opened the cage and cradled gerbil Evan on her legs with his belly upwards and his back propped up.

Noor's eyes glazed over as she let out a low tone. Lucy shivered as she felt the soundwaves penetrate her body. She could feel gerbil Evan shudder, then relax. Noor cupped her hands on either side of her face, focusing her sound downward. Lucy could feel the resonance through gerbil Evan's body resting on top of her.

The pitch of Noor's voice slowly ascended, trying to find just the right frequency. "Lucy, can you tell if it's working?"

Lucy closed her eyes and jumped back into gerbil Evan's mind. She was shocked to find the gerbil calm, seeming to enjoy the vibrations. As Noor moved her voice higher, Lucy felt a slight release in the gerbil's stomach, but then it was lost again. "Wait—go back down a bit, I think that was it," Lucy said.

Noor descended the scale until Lucy signaled her to stop. Noor held the single pitch for as long as she could, then took a breath. "It will be more powerful if you harmonize with it," Noor instructed.

Lucy stared, hesitant to proceed. "I don't know anything about song magic."

"But you know how to harmonize, just like in choir. Just hold this note, with as much resonance as possible," Noor said, demonstrating the pitch.

No time like the present to learn something new, this was not the time to be self-conscious. Noor began to sing once more, and Lucy joined in, nervously at first, but growing more confident as she found her footing. Lucy was surprised at the power she felt when she matched Noor's resonance, causing a high overtone to ring out in the studio.

"I think it's working," Lucy exclaimed, as she felt the pain and pressure on the gerbil's stomach recede. "Let's do one more round for good measure."

The two women focused once more on the gerbil, directing all their healing energy on the beloved pet. "I think that's it," Lucy said, finally. "I don't know if he is cured, but he definitely feels better."

Noor grinned. "That was amazing! I haven't done song magic with anyone in ages."

Lucy's eyes widened with curiosity. She had so many questions for Noor. Who taught her song magic, who had she practiced it with before, how does she use it? But there would be time for that later. Right now, they needed to focus on human Evan, who was still pacing back and forth across the room, as distressed as his gerbil was a few minutes prior.

Lucy put gerbil Evan back in his cage, and he immediately started gnawing on his chew toy happily.

"Hey Evan, come here," Noor called.

Evan trotted over and sat down in front of the cage. After staring at gerbil Evan for a while as if listening to him, he looked up with bright eyes and said, "You fixed him."

Lucy wondered if Evan had picked up some animal magic himself; he seemed more attuned to his pet than the average child.

"We did our best," Noor said and looked at Lucy with a wide grin.

Lucy watched Evan as he whispered to his gerbil, both human and gerbil Evan calm now, no sign of the agitation either had before. She stood back in awe, realizing she had just performed song magic for the first time.

Chapter 9

A KNOCK ON THE DOOR startled both Lucy and Cloud, who had been enjoying a good petting session, purring, and even showing his fluffy belly.

Lucy dashed to the door and swung it open to find Maya. "Come in, I have so much to tell you!"

Maya took off her coat and made herself comfortable on the couch, getting a sleepy raised eyelid from Cloud. "So you said in your text. What happened? Did Noor admit she has song magic?"

"Not only that, but I got to see it in action. And I even helped Noor heal a gerbil," said Lucy.

Maya looked confused. "Um—what's a gerbil got to do with anything?"

Lucy laughed and filled Maya in on the events of the day.

"I can't believe you learned animal magic so fast, and now you are already doing song magic—it's incredible what a quick learner you are," Maya said.

"I know, right? It's a crazy coincidence that I had a chance to use both at once. You know I love animal magic; it's a part of me now, but Noor can *heal* with her magic! Imagine how many animals I could help with that power?"

Maya grinned. "That would be awesome. I have no doubt you'll get there. Did you ask Noor if she could train you?"

"No, we didn't get a chance to talk much after that. But she's already helping me with the choir music; I don't want to ask too much of her."

"I doubt she would mind. She volunteered to help you practice music, didn't she?"

"Yes, but still."

"Maybe she'd enjoy having someone to talk song magic with. Assuming she doesn't belong to some song magic club."

"Actually, she mentioned she hadn't done song magic with someone else in a while."

"Well, there you go, then. I love teaching you about birds, and if she's anything like me, she'll love sharing about song magic. I guess that means you didn't learn anything else about Kayla?"

"Nope, just that Noor knew her from college."

"Hmm. When are you going to talk with her again?"

"I was actually thinking maybe you could come with me to her studio next weekend. I need you by my side if we're thinking of taking down any more dark magicians."

"And here I was worrying that Noor was going to replace me," laughed Maya.

Lucy threw a pillow at her. "Don't be absurd."

"Then yes, I'd love to meet Noor and find out what she knows about Kayla."

"I'll set it up," Lucy said.

Maya opened her bag and set a pile of books on the table. "Alright. Let's talk birds."

"Yes. No way Tyler is beating me at this."

"I like this competitive side of you. Too bad birds don't know what humans call them, then you could just ask them, magic-style."

Lucy chuckled. "Now I'm imagining a blue jay telling me 'Why yes, good lady, Cyanocitta cristata at your service.'"

"Why is he British?" Maya said through laughter.

Lucy shrugged and picked up the top book, causing a plastic sleeve to fall out. "A CD?"

"Yeah, it's old. The new ones have MP3s, but this one is free. That along with some phone apps will get you where you need to be."

Lucy put the CD in her stereo system. A narrator said, "lesser goldfinch," and then a messy call played, full of wheezes, trills, and stutters.

Cloud leapt off the couch, ears back, tail high, eyes darting left and right and up and down, searching for the intruder. Lucy and Maya couldn't help but laugh, and Cloud gave Lucy an icy stare, a betrayed look in his eyes.

"I'm sorry buddy, I should have warned you. These aren't real birds, they're just recordings."

Cloud turned his back to Lucy and started washing his paw, as if he knew it all along, and meant to get up anyway.

"Uh oh. I think you owe someone a treat," said Maya.

"Good idea." Lucy took down Cloud's favorite treats and gave the sweet gray puffball two.

"Maybe I'll work on the listening part with headphones on, or outside," said Lucy, not wanting anything to disturb her little Cloud, who had quickly become a part of her heart, not to mention ruler of the house.

"There are so many aspects to learning to identify birds," said Maya. "Their calls are the most important since they're often hard to see. But of course, you'll need to learn the visual part too, including seasonal variations, male versus female patterns, and juvenile and adult."

"Ugh! It's overwhelming."

"It is a lot, but the other part of studying is learning the right habitat for each bird. The truth is, in practice, when we go out to do surveys, it's not like any bird in the world will be there at any time of year. If we can narrow down which birds would reasonably be present, there are fewer possibilities to choose from."

"Good point. That makes it seem a little more manageable."

Maya pulled a small box out of her bag. "You're going to love this—flashcards!"

Lucy grinned as she looked at the deck of cards showing over a hundred common bird species. "You know me so well. That will be a productive thing to do when I take a break from work. And I love studying, so this should be fun."

"You're alone there—studying would never be on my list of fun activities. And I got the impression it's not high on Tyler's list either."

"Well, I kick butt at studying. I don't know why I got overwhelmed for a minute."

"It's a lot of pressure to compete with a coworker," said Maya, "especially one who is confident. Overconfident, in my opinion."

"I agree, but he has Bethany helping him, so I wouldn't count him out," said Lucy.

"Nah, we got this."

Lucy gathered up the books, CDs, and flashcards and set them on the bookshelf. "I've been cooped up inside all day. Want to take a walk down to the pond?" asked Lucy.

"Sure. There might still be some waterfowl you can identify."

Lucy rolled her eyes. "Not everything has to be about practicing," she moaned.

"Okay, okay. Let's just go for a walk."

At the end of the street there was a narrow dirt path that followed along a stone wall. Once they passed the last of the suburban mini mansions, the area opened into a grassland with straggly sunflowers, bunches of blue-green switchgrass, and mounds of mahogany little bluestem swaying in the breeze. They walked down the slope towards the pond. Late blooming bladderworts floated on the surface, their delicate yellow flowers providing contrast to the greenish water.

"What's that pretty pink flower?" asked Lucy, pointing to a plant on the water's edge with tight clusters of coral blooms.

"That's smartweed. Ducks love to eat the seeds. I don't see any waterfowl right now—we must have scared them off."

"Too bad," joked Lucy, grateful to avoid a pop quiz by her well-meaning, but hard driving friend.

The sun was falling below the tree line and the sky turned from scarlet to blue gray. Lucy looked up to take notice of the first star she could see. Probably a planet, she thought. As her eyes adapted, she started to make out more stars appearing in the evening sky.

The sounds of frogs, toads, and crickets suddenly seemed to grow ten-fold as the creatures of the night welcomed their time. A small splash made Lucy and Maya turn their heads, but they missed whatever had caused the sound.

"We should probably head back soon; it's getting dark fast," said Lucy.

"A few more minutes—I love this time of day," said Maya.

Lucy listened to the chirps, croaks, and trills, forming an amphibian chorus, and imagined herself conducting them, their symphony just as melodic in its own way as any human endeavor.

Another splashing sound jerked her back to the scene.

"What was that?" asked Lucy.

"Who knows? Could be anything—a fish, a frog, squirrels dropping things from the trees. If you're worried, why don't you just check?"

"Duh. Good idea." Lucy had gotten so used to being aware of all the animals in the area around her that she had begun to block it all out. What had at first been novel and exciting eventually became background noise. She surely didn't need to know about every cockroach in a building, or every rat in her back yard while she was trying to sleep. So now she had to focus her senses to inventory the wildlife around her.

"Something's hurt," Lucy said.

"Oh no! Where?"

Lucy pointed to the other side of the pond. Maya tried to use the flashlight on her phone, but it wasn't nearly strong enough to illuminate over the dark water.

A firefly blinked on and off nearby and gave Lucy an idea. She called out to all the fireflies in the area, asking them to gather near to help her. Soon, a twinkling floating mass appeared before her, the glow of dozens of fireflies. Lucy carefully navigated the mass along the farthest edge of the pond. She felt the fireflies growing impatient as she searched for the source of the splash.

"Look—over there!" Lucy cried. A small Red-eared slider turtle was struggling in the weeds, a plastic six pack ring tangled around its head, body, and claws.

"We can't reach him from here, and I don't think we can get around to the other side, either, not in the dark and without boots—it's a marshy mess," said Maya.

Lucy nodded. "I'll have to bring him to us." She slowed her breath, inhaled the mild swampy scent, listened to the sounds of the night creatures, and tried to find her way into the turtle's mind. The panic was unmistakable, so Lucy battered down the mossy stone door and took control.

She knew from experience that it was a waste of time to try and get permission from an animal in pain, so she sent out waves of calming reassurance, and asked the turtle to trust her. Lucy wasn't fond of the idea of controlling an injured animal underwater, but she had to try. She immediately sensed the problem—it was nearly impossible to swim forward without extending the flipper caught in the plastic. She struggled to find her way, unable to see through the turtle's eyes in the black water muddled with aquatic vegetation. "Direct me, Maya—am I going the right way?"

Maya strained to see the small dark spot in the murky pond, the fireflies having dissipated, but she managed to navigate Lucy and the turtle across the pond. She waded out into the water and grabbed the distressed turtle.

Lucy shone her phone light and Maya untangled the poor creature.

"I think he's alright," said Maya. "Can you tell?"

Lucy cautiously prodded his mind, but she didn't even need to enter the door to know he was much improved. "I think so. Doesn't look like the plastic was on long enough to dig into his shell or foot, he just couldn't swim. I think he'll be okay now."

"Thank goodness we were here. You stay safe, little guy." Maya set the turtle back down at the water's edge. Without so much as a glance back, he plopped into the water and was soon out of sight.

Chapter 10

LUCY WAS PUTTING THE FINISHING touches on a wetlands map when she heard music floating over the cubicle wall. At first, she ignored it, but then she stiffened. She recognized that voice. Lucy popped her head around the partition.

Bethany was lost in her phone and didn't even notice Lucy approaching. "What are you watching?" Lucy asked.

Bethany whipped her head around. "Sorry, was it like, too loud? My friend is working this health tech expo and there's this flash mob quartet singing that 'Doctor, Doctor' Robert Palmer song. They're really good." Bethany held up her phone for Lucy.

Lucy's stomach twisted when she saw none other than Kayla Quinn singing before her eyes. If Lucy hadn't immediately wondered what evil intent was behind the impromptu performance, she would have been amused at seeing prim and proper Kayla singing something so modern. Lucy had only heard her haunting vocalizations during the forest battle, and of course, classical music with the choir.

"Where is this?" asked Lucy.

"At the Lockwood Conference Center," said Bethany.

"When was this video taken?"

"My friend's live streaming it. What's with the inquisition?"

Lucy stammered, not sure how to answer the question. "Um… no reason. Bye."

She grabbed her purse from her desk and sprinted to Maya's cubicle on the other side of the office.

"Can you get out of here for a bit?" Lucy asked.

Maya looked surprised, but after everything they'd been through, she recognized that tone of voice.

"Yep, let's go. Tell me on the way."

Lucy nodded and the women raced to the parking lot. The conference center was only a few minutes away. Lucy filled Maya in on the video.

"You think she's doing dark song magic at this expo?" Maya asked.

"I have no idea," said Lucy. "I guess it's possible she has regular singing gigs too."

"It's safe to assume if she went to music school, she probably intended to be a singer."

"Yeah, I'm thinking it's Franco all over again. He studied animal science because he loved animals and accidentally fell in with the dark animal magicians. Maybe the same thing happened to Kayla."

"Maybe so. Of course, with Franco, he quit as soon as he knew what they were doing, but obviously Kayla didn't."

"No, it seems not. But still, not all of her singing has to be about song magic, right? She might sing for fun, sometimes. Or extra money."

"Oh Lucy, I love how you still always hope for the best."

Lucy grimaced. "But prepare for the worst?"

Maya laughed.

The parking lot was packed, and Lucy and Maya wove through the sea of cars with urgency, hoping Kayla and her quartet would still be performing when they got inside. The expo center was enormous, with partitions creating a maze-like structure of booths and rooms. The two women fought through the crowds, twisting and turning, listening for any sign of music.

They turned a corner and Lucy spied Kayla on the other side of a large clearing with booths lining the outside.

"Wait!" she barked at Maya, and grabbed her arm, pulling her back. "She's over there."

Maya nodded and they looked around for a safe vantage point. They found a spot behind a square column. Lucy peered cautiously around the edge.

"Looks like they are getting ready to sing again," Lucy said.

"Wait—if she is doing song magic, are we safe?"

Lucy paled. "Oh crap. I didn't think of that." She rummaged through her purse and pulled out some foam earplugs.

"Maybe these will help?" Lucy said, handing her friend a pair.

Maya grinned. "Why do you have these?"

"They help my anxiety. And Bethany can be annoying to work next to."

The women slipped the plugs in their ears just as Kayla stepped out in front of her quartet. With the earplugs, the sounds were slightly muffled, but they could plainly hear Kayla's voice singing a sultry, resonant "Fever," Peggy Lee style, the other three singers providing backup.

Lucy's jaw dropped. "Say what you will about Kayla's life choices, but holy moly she has an amazing voice."

"Agreed. It's a shame, really."

The two women tore themselves away from focusing on Kayla and her quartet and scanned the audience. The swarms of people had stopped moving and talking, all eyes focused on Kayla. Lucy watched as attendees turned the corner from behind them and halted when they heard Kayla's voice. Lucy scanned the faces she could view to the right and left of Kayla and they were all the same, mesmerized.

Maya whispered to Lucy, "Are they hypnotized?"

"I don't know. Maybe."

As Lucy watched on, she nudged Maya. "Look at that woman in the blue top with the curly, black hair. She doesn't seem entranced like the others."

Maya glanced where Lucy pointed.

"No, she doesn't. Maybe's she's hard of hearing?"

"Or maybe she's with Kayla."

The enchantment broke the second Kayla released her final note and she quickly retreated down the hall to another area. Suddenly the room was filled with movement and chattering again.

"Come on," said Lucy, pulling Maya around the corner and out into the clearing. Lucy expected to hear people talk about Kayla and how good a singer she was, but they weren't. No one seemed to be talking about Kayla at all. Instead, they were all converging around a booth that had started showing a video about a new high tech health monitor. People began pressing in, crowding the staff at the booth as they sold unit after unit.

Lucy and Maya pushed their way through to see the video screen. It seemed like a pretty standard health monitor that could measure heart rate and blood oxygen saturation, and transmit the data to an app. Nothing about it seemed that compelling to Lucy, yet this crowd was ravenous, nothing short of purchasing this product would sate them. Lucy started to feel unsafe as people jostled her, angling to get ahead in line, and pressed against her like a pack of sardines.

"Let's get out of here," said Maya, pushing back through the throngs. Lucy followed and both were relieved when they were free from the crowd. Lucy took a couple of deep breaths, realizing her heart was racing.

"I think my blood pressure just spiked," Lucy said.

"Maybe you should buy a health monitor," Maya quipped.

Lucy narrowed her eyes. "Don't even joke about that."

As they made their way to the exit, Lucy's brain flooded with questions, trying to make sense of what she had just witnessed.

The second they reached the car and were safe inside, Maya turned to her. "What the heck was that?"

"I don't know, but I have ideas," said Lucy. "Do you think song magic can control people?"

"Who knows. You can control animals, so maybe. But the singing seemed to hypnotize them or something and it wasn't until after that they became obsessed with getting their hands on that device. It was like a Beatles concert level of fandom madness."

Lucy rubbed her temples in thought. "Maybe song magic can make people more suggestable?"

Maya's eyes widened. "Yes! Like the song opened their minds and then they believed the video telling them they needed the health monitor?"

"Maybe. We can't know for sure, but it's a good theory. But then what does that mean for Kayla?"

"Could she be a freelance dark magician? We only saw her that one time at Sienna Falls Forest, and she just showed up and sang once and left."

Lucy shook her head. "But she works for Scordatura Solutions."

Maya frowned. "Oh yeah, I forgot for a minute."

"We can guess all we want but we won't be able to figure everything out today. We need to find out more about Scordatura," said Lucy.

"Hopefully Noor can tell us what song magic can and can't do, and how we can combat it."

"And everything she really knows about Kayla. There's more to her than what we've seen, I'm sure of it."

Chapter 11

LUCY WAS NERVOUS AS THEY arrived at Northbrook Harmony. What if Maya and Noor didn't get along? She knew that was ridiculous because Maya got along with everyone and had what seemed like hundreds of friends, family, and acquaintances. It was Lucy who had a hard time making new friends. She even amazed herself with how quickly she was starting to become comfortable with Noor; maybe once you make one close friend it is easier to make another.

But there was still the question of if Noor would trust Maya enough to open up about Kayla. Maybe if Lucy and Maya told her everything they had learned about Sepharine Holdings and the dark animal magicians, Noor would want to help fight against the dark song magicians, especially if Kayla planned to cause problems at the choir.

"You must be Maya," Noor said as she held the door open.

"I am, so nice to meet you, Noor," said Maya, "I've heard a lot about you."

A shadow crossed Noor's face, but then returned to its normal friendly glow. Lucy thought perhaps Noor wondered what Maya already knew. She regretted not setting the situation up a little better for Noor, and she wanted to fix that straight away.

"I want to address the elephant in the room," said Lucy. "Noor, Maya knows animal magic and she and I had a bit of a run in with a group of dark animal magicians a few months back. I told her you know song magic."

Noor and Maya held each other's gaze for a moment, then broke into a giggle, easing the tension.

"That's the short version," said Maya.

"I want to hear all the details later," said Noor.

"And we want to tell you," said Lucy, "but first, we need to know about Kayla. We know she is a dark song magician, but that's it. When I saw that you recognized her, I was worried you did dark song magic too."

"Likewise. Of course, I don't, but this is a long story; why don't I make us some tea? Do you drink tea, Maya?"

Maya grimaced. "Oh no, I'm outnumbered! I don't like tea much, but I'm fine, really."

"I do have a pod coffee maker too, if you prefer."

"Aah, that would be great, thank you."

When the women had their drinks in hand, they sat down on cushions resting on the woven rugs.

"This place has such a pleasant vibe," said Maya as she took a sip of coffee.

Noor's face lit up. "Thank you! I tried hard with the wall colors and the rugs, to keep it bright and cheerful but not busy. Some of the kids I work with don't like too much visual stimulation."

"It's a special place, for sure," said Lucy, and Maya nodded in agreement. A gentle silence settled over the room, waiting for someone to take the lead.

Noor cleared her throat. "I met Kayla in grad school. She was a vocal performance major while I was studying music therapy."

"Were you friends?" Lucy asked.

"No, not really. We overlapped by one year, me a year ahead of her. In my second to last semester, the school hired a guest vocal teacher, Pierre Martel. Kayla and I were both assigned to his studio."

"And you learned song magic from him?" asked Maya.

"It's a little more complicated than that. He had about ten students, mostly undergraduate, plus Kayla and me. It was pretty typical that renowned voice teachers didn't want to waste their time on students who weren't vocal performance majors."

"Because you wouldn't become famous and bring prestige to his teaching?" asked Lucy.

"Exactly," said Noor. "But a weird thing happened. Instead of focusing on the performance majors, who frankly, need the attention if they want a successful career, he began to focus on Kayla, an undergrad education major named David, and me. He told us that he saw something special in us, that we had potential only he could develop."

Maya winced. "That sounds kind of creepy," she said, prompting an elbow nudge from Lucy.

"Oh no, Maya's right. I did think it was creepy. But Kayla loved it. She has a fantastic voice, and she really could have had a fine career. She was so pleased someone finally believed in her that she fell under his spell, no pun intended."

"That's understandable. What artist doesn't want encouragement?" said Lucy.

"It's true. I knew I was going to be a music therapist and not a career singer, so I didn't care as much, but I will admit, even I felt good when Pierre said I was exceptional at some of the exercises he gave us. By then I had taken several years of voice lessons, so I knew the things he was asking us to do were a bit left of center, but he said singing was all about resonance, and he had a unique way of helping us to focus our voices."

Lucy looked thoughtful. "Like we did to heal the gerbil. So, he taught you light magic, also?"

Noor shook her head violently. "Oh no, Pierre was a true dark magician. I doubt if he even knows how to use it for good. The healing was something I learned way later."

Maya drummed her fingers on the floor. "What happened next?"

"Pierre subtly started suggesting that soundwaves could be used to influence people. As a student in music therapy, I already knew this was true, but my courses were approaching it in a purely scientific way. Like how music affects the brain and the nervous system. One day, Pierre brought in a mouse and asked me to use my voice to calm it, and I was able to make it fall asleep on the first try. Pierre was ecstatic."

"I bet that made Kayla jealous as anything," said Maya.

"It did. Kayla wasn't successful at first, but she practiced more than anyone I knew, and soon she could focus her voice better than me or David, and she could make the mouse, which now lived in Pierre's studio, fall asleep instantly. But then one day something deeply disturbing happened. Kayla was singing through a song as part of our preparation for the end of semester recital. She started to get annoyed because another student was playing trombone in the hall and the noise bled into the studio. She kept singing as we are taught to do, ignoring any outside distractions, but I could tell she was getting angrier by the second, and her hands started to clench into fists by her side. She kept going though, and after her final note, one of the undergrads shrieked. The mouse was dead in its cage."

"Holy moly. Kayla killed the mouse with her voice?" asked Maya.

Noor nodded. "Of course, Pierre said it was a coincidence. But Kayla, David, and I knew it wasn't. We knew we were messing with something much more powerful than we ever imagined. And Kayla loved the idea, drunk with the potential for power. But I was terrified."

"What did you do?" asked Lucy.

"Pierre must have realized I wasn't the student he was looking for and he requested that I transfer to a different teacher for my final semester. After that I didn't work with him again."

"And Kayla?" asked Maya.

"Kayla stayed on as his student. I didn't run into her much the next semester, and then I graduated and didn't see her again until choir rehearsal a few weeks ago."

Lucy and Maya relaxed into the cushions, their backs aching from leaning in to listen to Noor's story so intensely.

"That's not the first time we've heard that dark magicians recruit college students," said Maya.

Lucy and Maya filled Noor in on how they learned that ZRC Laboratories set up screening interviews with animal science majors at Winkler Tech, just outside of Northbrook, to find young people with aptitude for dark animal magic and how the same dark magicians targeted a forest with endangered birds.

Noor looked puzzled. "How does Kayla fit into that? Does she do animal magic too?"

"We're not really sure how Kayla was connected to ZRC. She helped them though. She sang a song that made forest creatures flee as fast as their little hooves, paws, or wings could take them," said Maya.

"We do know one thing though, and that is that ZRC was a shell corporation, and their parent company is called Sepharine Holdings. And the place that Kayla works, Scordatura Solutions? They are also a subsidiary of Sepharine Holdings."

Noor whistled. "This is much bigger than I thought."

"Oh, it's bad. Sepharine has five subsidiaries. Our theory is there is one for each type of magic. Five shell companies that employ dark magicians."

"Whoa," Noor said, looking pallid and shaky as she stood. "I need more tea to process this."

Lucy followed Noor into the kitchen to help. "Are you okay? This was a lot to lay on you. And maybe you'd have been better off if you didn't know anything about Kayla or that there is a corporate syndicate of dark magicians. I didn't even consider that we could be putting you in danger."

Noor smiled. "Ignorance is never better. If there are dark magicians here, in our choir, in our city, I'd rather know and be prepared than hide my head under a blanket."

"I feel the same way. On one hand, finding out about the dark magicians changed everything, shattered my entire perception of the world. On the other, learning animal magic has opened up a new and joyous door for me and I'd never trade that for anything. Here, look at my best guy, Cloud," Lucy said, and showed Noor a picture of her sweet gray cat on her phone.

"Aww, he's gorgeous," Noor said.

Lucy beamed. "Thanks!"

When they returned to Maya with fresh drinks, Maya gave Lucy a raised eyebrow.

"What?" said Lucy.

"Did you ask her?"

"Ask her what?"

Maya looked at them both with exasperation. "Don't you think it's suspicious that Kayla, a known dark song magician, spontaneously joined your community choir?"

Noor looked thoughtful. "You think she's planning something?"

"Not Kayla. My guess is she just does her employer's bidding. But her company, Scordatura, they are up to no good, for sure. And you two need to be ready."

"I'm not sure where you're going with this," said Noor.

Maya smacked her forehead. "For Pete's sake, making me be the pushy one. Noor, can you train Lucy in song magic?"

Lucy blushed. "I was going to ask her when I found the right time."

"You saw what happened at the health expo. We are already out of time," Maya said.

Noor looked serious. "Of course, I'll train you, Lucy. It would be an honor to have you as my first song magic student."

Chapter 12

LUCY WAS DELIGHTED THAT CHOIR was becoming more enjoyable and less anxiety-producing with each rehearsal. She practiced her parts most evenings after work and sessions with Noor on Saturdays helped build her confidence. The more certain she was of her parts, the more she could focus on blending with the other singers and helping the group achieve the right tone, the intensity of the "Dies irae," the triumph of the "Sanctus."

When all two hundred singers were unified in harmony, Lucy felt a profound sense of belonging. It was that phenomenon of being in the moment that allowed her to enjoy being part of a choir with Kayla Quinn as a member. When they all sang together, there was no Lucy, or Noor, or Kayla, but instead, an enormous cloud of sound. That is, until the director announced the calls for the solos and quartet sections of the *Requiem*.

"Many community choirs hire outside singers to perform the solos, but here at Northbrook I prefer to fill these roles from our regular choir membership when possible. The auditions are open to anyone. Please sign up during the break," said Darlene, waving a paper before placing it down on a table at the front of the room, signaling that their fifteen minutes had begun.

One of the other reasons that Lucy felt better about rehearsals is that she had Noor to talk to during breaks; she didn't have to feel awkward standing alone anymore. Sure, she had started making small talk with some of the other members, especially the ones who sat next to her, but Noor was the closest thing she had to a friend here.

As Lucy moved towards the front hallway to find Noor, she noticed Kayla had made a beeline for the sign-up sheet. Of course, Kayla would audition for the alto solo. She did have a gorgeous voice, and just because she was a dark magician didn't mean she wouldn't be an awesome soloist. But then a worrying thought crossed Lucy's mind.

She pushed through the crowds and found Noor filling her water bottle at the fountain. "Hey. Are you auditioning for the soprano solo?" she asked.

Noor shrugged. "I hadn't thought much about it, really. There is a lot of competition in the soprano section."

Lucy pulled Noor away to a more private corner. "Look, Kayla signed up for the alto auditions. What if she's planning something?"

"Maybe she just wants to sing the solo, we don't know."

"Now you sound like how Maya says I always sound; trying to see the best in people."

Noor frowned. "Even if she is planning something, what can I do about it?"

Lucy realized in that moment that Noor was Lucy six months ago. Even though Noor knew of the existence of dark magic, it didn't seem like she had ever faced dark magicians trying to use song magic for their own gain. Now that Lucy had seen the faces of the mesmerized people at the health expo, she was sure that song magic had darker uses that could cause serious consequences. And six months ago, Lucy had also asked Maya the same question, what could Lucy possibly do about it? And Maya had convinced her to fight, that it was her obligation to do so now that she had found the power of animal magic.

But was it fair to force the same obligation upon Noor? Noor had said she was glad to know the truth, but that was different than getting involved in something that was potentially dangerous.

"For one, it can't hurt to be there with Kayla at the quartet rehearsals. You might learn something or figure out what she is trying to do," said Lucy. "And second, you tell me—if you sing in the quartet with Kayla, could you prevent her song magic from working?"

Noor's faced crinkled with worry. "I don't know. It's not like I've tried before. I guess it's theoretically possible that I could counteract her magic if I was singing with her. But I don't actually know how to stop her."

Lucy put her arm on Noor's shoulder and looked her in the eyes. "I understand what you are feeling, but you aren't alone. I will figure this all out with you. But if you don't get the soprano part of the quartet, we won't be able to monitor Kayla. Will you audition?"

Noor scrunched her eyes shut, blocking Lucy's imploring gaze. When she opened them again, she said, "I can't sit by and let Kayla use this choir for who knows what. Yes, I will audition. But that's all I can promise for now."

"Good enough for me. One step at a time is all it takes."

As they walked back towards the rehearsal room, Lucy turned the corner and noticed a folded-up paper fall from a woman's purse. Lucy bent down to pick it up and ran to catch up with her.

"Excuse me—I think you dropped this."

The woman spun around. It was Kayla.

Without any hint of recognition, Kayla grabbed the paper. "Thanks," she said as she stuffed it in her purse.

Lucy was kicking herself for not taking a closer look at it, but she hadn't realized it belonged to Kayla.

By then, Noor had caught up to Lucy. Kayla looked at Noor, then Lucy, then back to Noor.

"It's been a long time," said Kayla.

"It has," replied Noor. "How have you been?"

"Never better. Now, remind me what you were studying at school? I remember it wasn't performance," Kayla said, with a faint overtone of superiority.

"Music therapy. I have my own practice now."

"How wonderful for you," said Kayla.

"It is. And you, how's your performing career going?" said Noor.

Lucy had to contain her surprise; she didn't think Noor was one to bait someone like that, but Kayla had started it.

"Not bad, I've had several featured roles with the Northbrook Opera."

Noor smiled. "That's fantastic, congratulations," she said, and it sounded sincere to Lucy's ears. Maybe Lucy had misinterpreted Noor's intentions.

One thing Lucy had learned from Maya during their previous adventure was to never let an opportunity go by without trying to get a new lead. "Didn't Darlene say you work for Scordatura Solutions when she introduced you?" asked Lucy.

Kayla's eyes narrowed slightly. "That's right."

"I'm not familiar with them, what do they do?" Lucy asked innocently.

"We sell music instruction books, for elementary, junior high, and high school choirs, bands, and orchestras."

"Ah, so you're in sales, then," said Noor.

Kayla's faced turned crimson, "No, I assure you, I am not. My role there is of a much more creative and impactful nature."

"Oh, I see, my apologies," said Noor sweetly.

"Looks like rehearsal is starting again, we'd better get in there," said Lucy, grateful for a reason to break the tension. The three women returned to the room without another word, and the rehearsal resumed.

Sitting two rows behind, Lucy swore she could feel Kayla's anger in her singing, a sharp bitterness that pricked at Lucy's skin like needles. Perhaps Lucy was just imagining it, but she thought of Pierre's poor dead mouse, and a chill ran down her spine.

Chapter 13

SEEING TYLER READING A BIRD book in the break room on Thursday served as a stark reminder that Lucy had better get serious about her studying. In truth, she had barely cracked the books that Maya had lent her; she was thoroughly distracted by the demands of Northbrook Community Choir, continuing to hone her animal magic, and now exploring the world of song magic. All that, combined with her regular job duties and spending time with her favorite feline, had caused the days to slip away.

As Maya munched on her sandwich, Lucy just moved her salad around with her fork. "I think knowing Tyler is really studying made me lose my appetite," Lucy said.

Maya looked up. "He is? I'm surprised. But he does seem ambitious when he wants to be."

"I know I need to try harder," said Lucy, "but I feel pulled in a lot of different directions at once."

"Hmmm. Maybe you need something to recharge your interest in birding. Something fun that reminds you why you want to keep doing fieldwork."

Lucy watched a cardinal splash around in the bird bath that Lucy and Maya had installed during the summer. "Maybe so. It's been a while since I've gotten out in the woods."

Maya's face lit up. "I know! Why don't we go visit my cousin Jeremy this weekend?"

Lucy grinned. "Do you think he'd mind?"

"Nah. I'll text him. Are you practicing with Noor on Saturday?"

"No, she has the quartet auditions then, so we're meeting Sunday."

Maya nodded and dashed off a text.

Lucy closed her eyes and remembered the first time she had been out to Red Bluff Ranch and a warmth filled her core. Yes, a trip to the country was exactly what she needed.

Two days later, Lucy got out to open the gate at Red Bluff Ranch, then closed it behind her after Maya drove the car through. The familiar feeling of serenity began to wash over her as they drove down the winding dirt road, grasses swaying in the breeze and wildflowers showing the last of their summer colors.

A few minutes later they arrived at a clearing in front of a split-level farmhouse, painted a grayish green with stark white trim.

A huge smile crossed Lucy's face as she saw her friends. Not just Jeremy, but his falcon Silver. Maya had taken Lucy here to meet the majestic bird and try to see through an animal's eyes for the first time. With Silver, Lucy had soared high above the trees, and even witnessed the harsh circle of life up close, as Silver hunted for prey. Jeremy and Silver had been a key part of the battle to defeat the dark magicians, and now she considered them both family, bonded in war.

As Jeremy approached, with Silver seated on his thick leather glove, Lucy could tell the falcon was just as pleased to see her.

Hello, my friend, Lucy said telepathically, and lowered her head with respect to the bird.

Silver gave a slight nod in return, never taking her yellow-ringed eyes off of Lucy. Lucy had been surprised to find that Jeremy didn't use animal magic like she did, so Silver wasn't accustomed to being spoken to in human language. It was here that she learned the hubris of expecting another species to bow to human ways; instead, Lucy became more sensitive to the subtle body language unique to each animal.

"Hi cousin," Maya said to Jeremy, careful not to approach too near the falcon.

"I'm glad you came out. It's nice to see you both. And I can tell Silver's happy to see you too, Lucy," said Jeremy.

Lucy smiled. Worries did have a way of falling to the wayside whenever she was nearer to nature. And seeing the relationship Jeremy had with Silver reminded her of the closeness she had with Cloud, built on mutual understanding and respect.

"What have you been up to?" asked Maya.

"This is great timing because I have something awesome to show you. But I'll need to put Silver in her mew for this."

"Aww, I was hoping I could fly with her again," said Lucy.

"That's up to Silver, of course. Ask her."

Lucy asked her avian friend if she could accompany her once again and she answered in the affirmative

"I can tell how delighted she is—she might like you more than me," joked Jeremy.

"Don't be ridiculous," said Lucy, knowing that she and Silver shared a special bond, but it was nothing compared with that of falcon and falconer. She centered herself, focusing on the sounds of the trees creaking in the wind and the earthy smell of fallen leaves decaying. When she searched for Silver's mind, the door was waiting wide open, and she walked right through.

Jeremy held up his arm and Silver took flight. Lucy watched through Silver's keen eyes as the farmhouse grew smaller and smaller as her wings pumped harder. The speed was intense, and the rush of the wind against her face was exhilarating. But most of all, what she cherished about sharing the experience of flight with a bird was the sense of freedom.

The view of the forest from above the trees was so different from the view from the ground. It was easier to see the forest as a system, an ecological community, to observe the transitional changes from dense woods to riparian to grassland. Silver took her down by the stream, following the course as it meandered through the ranch, and dove down to land on a branch in an oak tree. Lucy knew Silver had stopped there just for her, as the merlin could read her mind just as easily and knew she longed for beauty and peace on this day.

The view was from a fairytale, a small waterfall trickling over a rocky ledge into a pool of water. Lush green mosses and maidenhair ferns lined the grotto. Lucy half-expected to find out that fairies and elves existed as well, but this was enough magic for her.

After Lucy absorbed the serenity of the scene, Silver returned them to the clearing and Lucy thanked her for the gift of flight.

"How was it?" said Jeremy.

"Perfect, as always. She showed me a waterfall."

"Did she? She must really like you, then. That is a pretty remote spot—I don't even make it over there that often."

"This is a special place you have here," said Lucy.

"I know it. Alright, let me put Silver in her mew now and I'll show you my latest endeavor."

The three of them walked around the back of the house to a large wood framed enclosure with screens along three sides, and a sheltered inner room with perches and ledges. Jeremy moved inside, and with a slight flick of the wrist as encouragement, Silver flew to the highest perch. Jeremy secured the door and led the women along a gravel path.

Soon they arrived at another clearing, this one with a series of enclosures similar to Silver's.

Maya and Lucy looked puzzled. "What's all this?" asked Lucy.

Jeremy beamed with pride. "I've been training for the past couple of years and finally got a wildlife rehabilitation permit, for raptors."

"Wow, that's awesome!" said Lucy.

"Really cool, congrats," Maya echoed.

"It is exciting. I've loved working with Silver for the past eight years, and I wanted to do more. Right now, I'm taking in overflow from the local rehab center, some of the easier cases where the birds just need some time to recover before they can be released."

Lucy walked closer to the outer enclosure and admired a bird hiding towards the back. "He's beautiful. Is it a Swainson's hawk?"

Jeremy grinned. "Yes, it is, good call."

Maya poked Lucy. "See? You can totally do this."

"That's pretty good," said Jeremy. "Some people confuse these with the Red-tailed hawk."

"I remember reading that the Swainson's has brown on its upper breast but the Red-tailed doesn't."

"Exactly. Want to try another one?" asked Jeremy.

Lucy felt self-conscious, like she was a contestant on a gameshow, but who knows how Anuk would decide if she or Tyler was more knowledgeable; it could turn out to be a high-pressure situation. "Sure," she said, moving to the next room.

Lucy smiled. "This one is easy. One of the smallest raptors, with those sophisticated slate-blue wings and rusty back. American kestrel."

"That's right," said Jeremy. "And they often bob their tail when perched."

Lucy was starting to enjoy herself, much easier to do when she was successful. She moved to the next one, but as soon as she started examining the bird, sorting through the possible species in her head, and the associated identifying markings, she deflated.

"This one's a little trickier," said Jeremy. "In fact, many expert birders wouldn't be able to correctly ID this bird without seeing it in flight."

"I'm not totally sure either," said Maya.

Lucy wasn't sure if her friends were just being supportive, but she was certainly stumped. "I'm sure it's a falcon, just not sure if it's a prairie, merlin, or peregrine," Lucy said with a sigh.

Jeremy waved his hand. "That's close enough. He's a prairie falcon, and if you saw him from underneath, you'd see the dark underwing and armpits that the peregrines and merlins don't have."

Maya nudged her friend with her shoulder. "Don't be so hard on yourself, Lucy—you're still learning. You'll always be learning. I know I am. Bird identification is part science, part art. It takes time to develop your own style."

Lucy didn't look convinced, so Jeremy said with a little too much enthusiasm, "Aunt Elisa sent me home with some conchas last night; I'll make some coffee back at the house and we can catch up some more," said Jeremy.

"Sounds delicious," said Lucy, grateful for the shift away from her studies.

A few minutes later, Lucy and Maya sat in the kitchen and Jeremy brought out a plate of round breads resembling seashells, decorated with pink and yellow crunchy toppings. Lucy realized she was famished. She sunk her teeth into the soft bread and melted. This is exactly the break she had needed.

"Did your aunt make these?" said Lucy.

Jeremy and Maya laughed.

"What's so funny?" demanded Lucy, always worrying that she might say something wrong, and accidentally insult her host.

"No, we're not laughing at you—it's just a running joke. Aunt Elisa pretends that she makes these, but we all know she really buys them at the bakery near her house."

"Oh, I see. Well, they are delicious, no matter who made them," said Lucy.

"They should be, that's the best bakery in the whole city," Jeremy said, laughing.

Lucy laughed now too. She felt at home with Maya and her family, even Aunt Elisa, who wasn't there but now Lucy knew she faked her own baking. The choir and trouble brewing with Kayla seemed a thousand miles away. Today was about friends and birds.

A buzzing sound from her pocket broke the moment. She took out her phone to read the text.

"Noor and Kayla got the solo parts for the *Requiem*," said Lucy.

"I guess that's good? Now you'll really have to learn song magic," said Maya.

Jeremy looked confused. "Am I missing something?"

Maya and Lucy sighed in unison, and Maya began, "Remember in Sienna Falls Forest how that woman came out and started singing and drove the animals away? That woman is Kayla Quinn, and she's in Lucy's choir."

Jeremy shook his head. "Please don't tell me you're getting into more trouble."

Lucy frowned. "Me? All I did was join a community choir—a perfectly normal thing to do. I didn't know there would be a dark magician in it."

"Trouble just seems to find our Lucy," said Maya.

"That's unfortunate. Well, I am not musically inclined in the least, but if you need my help, or Silver's, we are here for you."

"Thanks, Jeremy," said Lucy, hoping it wouldn't come to that.

"Yeah, thanks cousin," said Maya.

Lucy took the last bite of her concha and as the sweetness faded away, she thought, so much for putting the world of dark magic out of her mind. Oh well, sometimes it seemed the only way out is through.

Chapter 14

LUCY SAT IN HER CAR down the street from Noor's studio, taking a moment to reflect before heading inside to start her first day of song magic training. For the first forty years of her life, she had generally been seen and not heard. Then Maya had joined the company and before Lucy knew it, not only had she learned animal magic, but she had become the de facto leader of her ragtag group fighting against the dark magicians. It wasn't that she had been brave, it was just that for the first time in her life, the need to try and fight for the innocent outweighed her fears and anxieties. And here she was yet again.

It was with this resigned sense of purpose that Lucy tried to focus herself on the task at hand and resolved to train her hardest. She didn't know what Kayla and Scordatura had planned, but Lucy knew there was no way she could turn a blind eye now. And a resentful streak in Lucy was furious that dark magicians were ruining the one thing she had been looking forward to for years, singing with the Northbrook Community Choir. The sooner she could take them out, the sooner the choir would once again become a sanctuary.

Lucy pushed open the door to Northbrook Harmony, causing the now familiar jingle of chimes that brought to mind fairies dancing. Noor had captured a special ambience in her studio, particularly given it was part of a suburban strip mall. Further proof that magic can be created anywhere.

Noor waved Lucy over. She was standing next to a large metal plate covered in fine sand.

"What's that?" asked Lucy.

"Your first lesson. This is a Chladni plate. Watch," said Noor as she picked up a cello bow and ran the hairs along the side of the plate, creating a low tone.

Lucy looked on in disbelief as the sands on the plate began to bounce around in a choreographed dance resulting in an unmistakably geometric pattern. "Whoa. That's amazing. Is that song magic?" asked Lucy.

Noor grinned. "Nope, it's physics. And that's a great foundation for song magic. Ernst Chladni developed this method for visualizing the patterns of vibrations in the late 1700s."

"Different frequencies make different patterns?"

"That's right. It's easier to show with amplification." Noor turned on another device that emitted a steady tone, and turned the frequency nob, this time playing a higher pitched note that rumbled the speaker beneath the plate.

This time the sand danced into an x-pattern with half circles on the perimeter of each side.

"This is so cool—can I try?"

"Sure," said Noor, moving away from the device.

Lucy turned the frequency modulator dial higher and watched as a new pattern formed. She was mesmerized by the movements, awed by the power of nature. "This seems pretty magical to me."

Noor laughed. "That's what I thought when I first learned about music therapy, how music can affect the brain. I realized that some of what we call science is as incredible as what we think of as magic."

"I know what you mean. I remember when I met Maya's grandmother for the first time. I told her that I could communicate with animals, but it didn't seem like magic. But she said magic is just a word for something that people can't explain. And I can't explain how my animal communication works. But this—these patterns, they probably would be considered magic by some, if they didn't have Chladni to explain them."

"Perhaps," Noor said with a shrug. "I've never been too hung up on defining science versus magic. What's important is to learn as much as we can and then use it to help people."

Lucy smiled. "I love that idea."

"What these plates are demonstrating is that sound is energy. And that energy has two basic parameters, frequency, which is what we perceive as pitch, and amplitude, which we perceive as volume. Part of song magic is learning how to focus our soundwaves to achieve a particular outcome."

"Like we did when we healed gerbil Evan," said Lucy.

"Exactly. Another good example is the singer breaking a wine glass. Not that many people can actually do that without amplification, but a few select can. It's easiest if the glass is very thin, and if there are already flaws in the structure. Then the singer has to find just the right frequency, and smash, the glass shatters."

"Wow. I always wondered if that was really possible."

"Here's the important part though, with amplification, anyone can shatter the glass. And with strong enough amplification, any frequency can break glass."

"That sound dangerous."

"You don't even want to know. The military already uses ultrasonic weapons. And there are even some minor commercial applications, like devices that emit ultra-high frequency soundwaves that only teenagers hear to deter loitering."

Lucy grimaced. "That's pretty creepy."

"I know. But then there are good applications too, right?" said Noor. "Like ultrasound used for sonograms, that's just soundwaves too. And they can use soundwaves to break up kidney stones without having to cut anyone open."

"I never thought of that. So, when does it become song magic?"

Noor frowned. "That's where I have to admit I'm stumped. I can teach you what I know, but Kayla, she was training with a dark magician, and it's likely she continued her training after I knew her in college. Who knows what she's learned by now."

"But you said you learned healing magic later, right?"

"I did," Noor said, "I knew that if I could make Pierre's mouse calm and put him to sleep, but Kayla could kill that mouse with just the anger in her singing, that meant there was much more to it, more than just the notes and the volume; there was intent, projection. And I'm still trying to figure it all out to this day."

Lucy was disappointed. It was animal magic all over again, wishing there were some master teacher to impart magical wisdom upon her, but instead, finding she had to figure it out on her own, or at least in combination with Noor. "You taught yourself to heal, then?"

"Yes, through trial and error. I practiced calming animals at first, and that became easy unless they were violently raging, like a rabid dog."

"Did you try it on people?"

Noor blushed. "I'm embarrassed to admit what I've done. I don't want you to judge me. I have tried song magic on people, but I swear it's never been for personal gain or to hurt anyone. I've used it to prevent heated arguments from becoming physical. I've used it to soothe parents grieving for their sick child."

"Oh Noor, that's wonderful. I'm not going to judge you. I've done the same with my animal magic. As long as we aren't using our magic to manipulate people, I think we're okay. But where it crosses a line is something I've been pondering since the beginning."

Noor looked sheepish. "And if I'm totally honest, sometimes, when I perform, I use my song magic to relay the images I see when I read the lyrics, just so they can share the experience with me."

Lucy's eyes widened. She remembered listening to Noor's audition from the hallway, and the feeling of being in a moonlit forest, surrounded by woodland creatures. Noor had been using song magic then, as Lucy suspected. "You used it at your audition. I was there. It was like I could see the mist rising and the twinkle of fairy lights."

"Yes," Noor admitted. "But I didn't use it to influence the outcome of the audition or anything. I didn't even mean to use it, but sometimes when I'm focused on emoting the intent of the song, it just happens."

Lucy laughed. "I know you didn't—why would you have to? You have a beautiful voice. I mean, you just won the soprano solo against fifty other women."

"Thanks. I have worked really hard with voice teachers, including Pierre, on my vocal technique. Even though I didn't focus on performing in college, I still love to sing for people."

"I'm starting to like it, too," said Lucy. "Taking voice lessons has been a great experience. Like another way to get to know my own body and mind."

Noor nodded. "Even though we're going to have to figure a lot of this out together, I have some ideas for how to get started." Noor led Lucy over to the back of her studio, where she had rested two tables on their sides perpendicular to the wall, creating a barricade of sorts. Then she took two sets of safety glasses from a cabinet. "Just in case."

Noor took a green ceramic vase from a box and placed it in front of the wall between the two tables. "Lesson one. Find the crack with your voice."

Lucy noticed there was a light crack running from the rim halfway down the side of the vase. She put on the plastic glasses. Lucy felt self-conscious singing in front of Noor, her voice undeveloped next to Noor's flawless tone. But this wasn't about sounding pretty, it was about training, and Lucy was nothing, if not an excellent student. She opened her mouth and let a random note sing out.

But how could she possibly find the right frequency? She wondered if it was like finding the door to each animal's mind like she did with her animal magic. But the vase was an inanimate object, surely, she couldn't see inside it. Lucy closed her eyes and reached out to the vase, imagining it in her mind. She explored the tiny crevice as she continued to resonate her voice.

Nothing happened.

She continued to explore the full range of her voice, but nothing felt quite right. She didn't think she could find the right frequency by accident. She opened her eyes again.

With gerbil Evan, she had been inside the animal and could feel the vibrations she was making as if from the inside, and that had allowed her to find the correct pitch.

She closed her eyes again, this time pretending the vase was a rabbit. And then it happened. It was as if she was zooming into a maze made of atoms, and she could see the crack in a different way, like it was a ray of light filling an empty space within the otherwise solid vase. Lucy slowly raised the pitch of her voice, trying to expand the light downward, and when she hit just the right note, it gave way and her tone pierced through the darkness, slicing like a sword until it hit something solid.

Lucy opened her eyes to see the vase completely broken in half and turned to see Noor with her mouth hanging wide open. "Whoa! That was impressive!" said Noor.

Lucy grinned. Song magic gave her that same glowing feeling as animal magic, and Lucy knew without a doubt that she was on a journey to become adept in not one, but two branches of magic.

Chapter 15

LUCY HAD BEEN DREADING THE personality test seminar since the day she had taken the survey. It wasn't that she didn't believe there were insights to be had that could potentially help a team work together, she just doubted that it didn't do more harm than good. As far as she could tell, there were dozens of consultants offering various tests to corporations, claiming to improve profits. The whole thing reeked of greed and money.

First the consultant, Bernard, went through the possible personality types the company had devised. Lucy and Maya had to keep from snorting when they heard they were based on animals.

"Each animal type has strengths and weaknesses," Bernard said. "And each one will get along better with some and less well with others. This program will help identify which type you are and how you can work more effectively with the other types."

Lucy had to stop herself from rolling her eyes at Bernard as he described the featured attributes of each animal type. "People in the Tiger category make forceful decisions and stand by them at all costs but can be impulsive and don't think things through. Rabbits are highly efficient, but nuance and detail may be lost in the process. Hawks analyze data carefully but may procrastinate before taking action. Dolphins are intuitive and friendly but may not always see the negative consequences."

Lucy and Maya shared more than a few glances and frowns listening to Bernard's list. Lucy knew it was just a construct to classify workers according to personality traits, but the attributes associated with each animal type were so grossly far from reality that it was laughable. Except for some reason, instead of laughing, Lucy was annoyed to the point of indignance.

"Now I will pass out the survey results. At the top you'll see that each of you has been assigned a primary animal type. But that doesn't tell the whole story. You'll also see a secondary type, and your percentage for each of the four classes. No one is all one type; we are all a mix." Bernard called out names one by one and passed out the results to each employee.

Lucy frowned when she saw hers. Hawk. She hated that it was probably accurate, and she resented that a stupid test could reveal anything about her true self. She couldn't deny that she overanalyzed everything, afraid to make a move. Heck, it took her years just to pluck up the courage to take voice lessons and try out for the community choir.

She glanced over at Maya's paper. Tiger, of course. Lucy wasn't sure why the company paid for this test when the results were so obvious. She bet she could guess every single person in the office.

Bernard interrupted the light chatter that had erupted. "The important thing is not which type you are, but recognizing your strengths and weaknesses and how they interact with the others around you. Let's take a look at an example. When a Tiger is working with a Hawk, they may need to take a step back and offer some reasoning behind their decision."

Lucy winced as she realized that part of the reason that she and Maya got along so well might be that Maya never minded walking through possible actions with her, that she was patient with Lucy's uncertainties and took the time to help her weigh the pros and cons, even though Maya already knew the right decision in her gut.

"When a Rabbit engages with a Dolphin," said Bernard, "they may need to remember to take the time for pleasantries before jumping into a discussion of the task at hand."

That made Lucy think of Bethany and how her coworker would interrupt Anuk's requests by asking how his weekend was or some other social convention. Lucy wasn't naturally talkative, other than with Maya, but she made a note to inquire about Bethany's well-being before she asked for something next time. Then she cursed inwardly as she realized that even she was taking this whole personality test thing as fact. The power of suggestion from someone who claims to be an expert is difficult to resist.

Bernard passed out small cardboard cutouts of the four animal types and the staff stood them on the table in preparation for the team building exercises. "For this first exercise I'm going to pick two employees at random. You," he said, pointing to Tyler, who had a Tiger figure in front of him, "and…" he said, scanning the room while Lucy willed with all her might not to be selected, his finger eventually resting on her, "you."

Lucy cringed. She hated being put on the spot and having everyone watching her do something she was ill prepared for.

Bernard glanced at the name tag stickers they were wearing and said, "Looks like we have Tyler, a Tiger, and Lucy, a Hawk, for this first exercise. Here is the scenario: You get a last-minute request from a client to produce a report that normally takes at least two days, but they need it by the end of business today. Tyler, you are the client manager, and Lucy, you are the one preparing the report. Tyler, how would you approach Lucy with the news?"

Tyler looked at Lucy and immediately blurted, "The client needs the report a day early, so you'll need to prioritize this."

Even though it was just an exercise, Lucy seethed, because she knew that is exactly what Tyler would say, with no concern about how she could get it done or if she had other pressing assignments, or even asking if there was a way he could help. Real teamwork there, she thought. She hoped Tyler was never her boss. She cringed at the thought.

Bernard raised his eyebrow a little but only said, "And Lucy, how would you respond to this request?"

She was so annoyed by Tyler's attitude that she momentarily forgot she was practically on stage, surrounded by a conference room full of coworkers. "Why do they need it early? Did you check if we could have until morning? What am I supposed to do about my other deadlines?"

Tyler frowned, appearing affronted by Lucy's reaction.

With a grin like a stage magician who had just performed a trick, Bernard waved his arms about. "Thank you, Tyler and Lucy. What do you think, folks? Could this interaction have gone better?"

A chorus of affirmatives and nods filled the room.

Maya jumped in first, "Tyler could have explained why the client needed it earlier, maybe that would have made Lucy more empathetic to the situation."

That caused Bethany to jump to Tyler's defense. "Lucy could have, like, been more of a team player, instead of questioning Tyler, she should have said she'd do her best to get it done on time."

"Well, Tyler should have offered to help her shift her workload around to others, and asked her if it was possible, instead of just telling her," Maya retorted.

The rest of the staff sat in silence, not wanting to jump into the fray that was obviously about more than just the exercise at hand.

Bernard interjected, "Great points everyone. This was a great example of a Tiger, who made a decision without consulting other staff, and a Hawk, who needed more information and a moment to digest the situation but also may need to learn to be more flexible working in the often fast-paced consulting world."

Lucy sat with her teeth clenched throughout the rest of the workshop and was relieved when they were finally released for lunch, and she was able to seek refuge in the courtyard again.

"You really hate this whole personality test thing, huh? I know it's dumb and pointless, but who cares?" asked Maya.

Lucy threw her hands up defensively. "I don't know. I guess after everything I've been through over the past six months, how much I feel like I've grown, to be put in a little narrow box that distills me down in such a simplistic way is both depressing and infuriating. You and Anuk are the only ones who even noticed I've changed."

"Aww, I get that sentiment, I really do. But actually, other people *have* noticed. Didn't you say Tyler called you 'uppity' when he was talking to Bethany about you two competing for the bird surveys? In a way that means they see you as a threat now, and they probably didn't before. But even so, this personality test doesn't mean anything, it's just a stupid made-up classification."

"I know, I know. I shouldn't even be upset about it, but I just am. Now everyone is going to be acting all weird, trying to second guess how they should handle each person based on their type."

"Maybe, for like a week, two tops, then people will go back to the way they were before, and it will all be forgotten."

"You think?"

"Definitely."

"You're way too thoughtful to be a Tiger."

Maya chuckled. "Well, actually I'm barely a Tiger—I was almost evenly spread out among the four."

"Ah, that explains it, you're my well-balanced friend. Actually, my second highest percentage was Tiger."

"I'm not surprised. I've seen the Tiger in you, that's for sure. Tyler had better watch his back," said Maya, and then held her hand up like a claw.

Chapter 16

LUCY WASN'T REALLY SURE HOW to practice song magic without Noor around. It had been different with animal magic. When Lucy first tried to speak with animals, there wasn't a risk of something exploding or that she would accidentally break all of her glassware. So instead, Lucy focused on practicing her choir music and strengthening her vocal technique in hopes that she would be able to control her voice when the time came.

The one thing she did practice was trying to find the cracks in objects. The more she tried, the easier it became, and in some ways, it was actually concerning how fractured the seemingly solid things around her really were. Her dinner plate, her front window, even her television set were rife with structural flaws that could be exploited with the right frequencies. But she stopped there, since she certainly didn't want to destroy her own things, nor did she want to damage anyone else's possessions. She would have to discuss a practice plan with Noor.

The first time she stared at her water glass, concentrating on finding its weak spot, Cloud put his paw out and tapped her leg, troubled that she seemed to be lost somewhere else.

Are you okay?

Lucy snapped back to the room and pet his soft, furry chin. "Yes, I'm fine. I'm just practicing my song magic. Or at least part of it."

Cloud seemed appeased and curled up on the couch next to her, but she saw that he kept one lazy eye half open as she continued to practice. Even her feline companion seemed to recognize how dangerous song magic could be, and she hadn't even scratched the surface yet.

With work, choir, and song magic, she was still struggling to find time to practice her birding identification. She set aside everything else and took out her flashcards. At least she could run through the set a couple of times this evening and that would be better than nothing.

No sooner had she retrieved the deck from the bookshelf than her phone rang. Usually, Maya was the only one who called her, so she was surprised to see it was Noor.

"Are you free, Lucy? There's something I want you to see."

"You mean right now?"

"Yes, can you meet me at Emery Square? Near the fountain."

Lucy tensed. She hated last-minute expeditions that she wasn't mentally prepared for, but she had to admit that the more she pushed through her hesitation, the easier it became each time. Plus, not like she was doing anything important, except hanging with Cloud, which was of course one of her favorite things. She promised herself she would give Cloud a proper snuggle and petting when she returned.

"Yes, I can be there in twenty."

"Great!" said Noor.

Once a week, Emery Square was transformed into a bustling community market with vendors selling handmade jewelry or small batch jams, school groups fundraising with funnel cakes, and even a few buskers entertaining the crowds. As Lucy walked towards the fountain to find Noor, she saw a mime dressed in the traditional French-style costume, black and white-striped shirt, red necktie, and black beret.

The man moved in smooth, styled gestures, his facial expressions telling a story of something frightening approaching, realistic enough to send shivers up her spine. She walked away quickly, not wanting to linger any longer on a show that would remind her that her world had changed from safe and predictable to something else entirely.

As she approached the fountain, she spotted Noor sitting on the concrete rim.

"Glad you could make it!" said Noor, standing up.

"Me too, I guess, although I don't know why I'm here."

Noor laughed. "True. You must really trust me."

"I guess I must. One thing I learned from Maya is that we have to find people we can trust and then stick with them no matter what."

Noor turned serious and nodded in agreement. "Now that I know about Kayla and her employer, knowing who to trust seems all the more important. With that in mind, follow me."

The women wound their way through the market, weaving past children holding newly created balloon poodles and giraffes, shoppers eyeing wood turned bowls and vibrant woven shawls. As they moved through the crowds, Lucy started to hear a strange sound, ghostly and violin-like, but not quite something her mind yet recognized.

"What is that?" Lucy asked, her head cocked to the side, trying to hear better.

"*That* is why we are here," Noor answered with an evasive smile, beckoning Lucy to follow.

They turned a corner at the end of the row of stalls and came upon a clearing with a woman standing behind a small rectangular instrument, with a silver antenna poking out from the top and a looped metal piece attached to the side. The woman moved the fingers of her right hand as if playing an invisible cello, causing the haunting sound to rise and fall in pitch, while with the flick of her left hand, she caused the volume to shrink or swell.

Lucy recognized the sound from old sci-fi movies she had seen, usually accompanying little green men, the soundtrack creating an alien atmosphere unlike any other instrument. A theremin, she thought it was called. As she watched the woman and listened to the lilting melody she played, Lucy started to feel dreamy and light. The movements of the woman's hands were hypnotic, and she couldn't look away.

After a minute, she felt a sharp pinch on her arm.

"Ouch! What did you do that for?" she asked Noor.

Noor gestured for Lucy to step away from the group that was gathered around the woman. When they were further into the market, out of earshot, she said. "I had to. You were drawn in. Didn't you feel it?"

Lucy's eyes widened and she realized she had felt something, but it hadn't alarmed her, which was in itself highly alarming. She had felt peaceful, out of time and place. "What just happened?"

"Song magic, of course. In a minute we're going to go back there. But this time I want you to watch the woman's face, her eyes, and watch the audience's reaction, too. And don't fall back under her spell."

"How do I do that?"

"Focus on anything other than the music. And don't make direct eye contact with her. When she looks at you, look away."

Lucy nodded but didn't love the idea of going back. But she trusted Noor and apparently this was all part of her training.

This time, Lucy and Noor stood on the side, mostly out of the performer's line of sight. It allowed Lucy to take in the scene more objectively. The woman, perhaps in her early twenties, was beautiful, black waves of hair falling down her back, a dark green Renaissance Faire style dress with a lace up bodice giving her a mystical appearance. Her eyes were adorned with smokey eyeshadow and thick eyeliner, and her lips coated in a deep shade of garnet.

Lucy turned her gaze now to the group gathered around the woman. Just like she had seen at the health expo, the audience was mesmerized. She watched as a young man emptied his wallet, depositing the cash in the tip jar on the ground below the woman. Lucy gasped as she saw the jar overflowing, not just with cash, but with jewelry and other trinkets. Another man took off his Rolex and placed it in the jar, causing the woman he was there with, a wife or a girlfriend, to smack him on the arm, snapping him out of his trance, and then she dragged him off, her face shooting daggers back at the performing woman. But the woman's face never changed from her serene and slightly seductive smile.

"She's swindling them," Lucy whispered.

"Perhaps," said Noor as she pulled Lucy back into the market. "It depends on how you look at it."

"She made that guy give up his watch!"

"He didn't really have to. That's the complicated part."

"Shouldn't we stop it? It doesn't seem right, what she's doing," Lucy said, shaking her head.

"How? Tell people they are being mesmerized? They wouldn't believe us. And is it really different from the mime? Giving a captivating show and asking for donations?"

That made Lucy pause. How was it different? "I don't know. Does this mean all musicians are really using song magic?"

"Ahhh, that's a complicated question. I can't say I have a definitive answer, but this is my two cents. All good musicians have natural song magic. That's what we call 'stage presence' or 'charisma' or 'the X factor.' Talented musicians do mesmerize their audience, and they love it, right? What's better than going to see your favorite band perform?"

"Yes, but this is different."

"Is it? People buy tickets to see bands play."

"But they choose to do so when they aren't mesmerized."

"That's true. And I would argue also that the main difference is the intent. Most musicians inadvertently use their song magic without any malicious intent, or with their intent just to show the audience a good time. It's symbiotic, right? Like the fans agreed to be mesmerized by buying the ticket, but there are no other negative consequences. Remind me what our choir does—we sell tickets to our concerts, right?"

Lucy started to nod slowly, working through the logic. "But the theremin lady, her intent was to sort of seduce people with her music, persuade them to give her their money or trinkets just for a few moments with her."

"Yes—intent. That's how I see the difference. There's no handbook for this stuff, Lucy. We will have to figure out the ethics for ourselves. Yes, the theremin player is on the edge, but would you call that dark song magic?"

"I don't know. It's not light magic, that's for sure, and it's not innocent. But it's not dark magic either, not compared with what Kayla does. It's like the difference between a pickpocket and a bank robber."

"Exactly. Now that you've seen this, I want you to start noticing the song magic around you. It's more common than you think."

Lucy shuddered. She wasn't sure she wanted to pull back the curtain on this. What if she saw song magic everywhere and there was no escape?

Chapter 17

"GUESS WHAT CAME IN THE mail today?" said Maya when Lucy opened the door.

"I'm afraid to even ask if it's what I think it is."

"Bingo. The CDs we ordered from Scordatura Solutions. I didn't want to listen on my own, in case, well, I don't even know what could happen. This whole song magic thing is really throwing me for a loop."

Lucy sighed. "You and me both. Ever since Noor pointed out the prevalence of song magic, intentional or otherwise, it's all I can think about."

"Sorry, that sounds rough. I know how much the choir means to you—I hope you can still hold on to the good parts."

"I have to, or that would be letting the Kaylas of the world drag me down. But it isn't easy. And I feel bad that I got Noor involved in all of this too."

"I know," said Maya. "But she already knew dark song magic existed. She's known since grad school, so really she has had longer to come to terms with it than you. I'm sure she'll be fine as long as the three of us stick together."

"I hope so. Alright, so shall we check this out? Remind me what we ordered."

"It's supposed to be accompaniment tracks for some choir music."

Lucy looked at the plastic case. "Funny that they still sell CDs. I've used this CD player more in the past few weeks than in the previous five years."

"Yeah, it's odd. Maybe they had a lot left over? Or maybe there are some older people in community choirs who might not be as comfortable with streaming?"

"Maybe. Hey, this is actually pretty cool—it has just the alto part alone, then with the backing music, then also the alto part and all the other voices and accompaniment. I could sure use this for the Mozart piece, although I've learned it pretty well by now. Maybe next time."

"Whoa, I'd think twice about using any products from Scordatura, don't you think?"

"Good point. But it's still possible that their stuff is legit and separate from whatever it is they do with song magic."

"I will never understand your unlimited willingness to believe in the good until proven otherwise. But…it's one thing that makes you special."

"I can't help it. Call it naivety, but I'd rather that than assume everyone's evil."

Lucy popped the CD in the player and the sound of a single piano line plinking out the alto part of Vivaldi's *Gloria* filled the room. She closed her eyes and focused on the sound, not certain what she was listening for. After several measures she opened her eyes again.

"I didn't notice anything strange, did you?" said Lucy.

"Nope. But I'm not sure if I would be able to tell the difference anyway."

"Let me switch to a different track." Lucy pressed the skip button on the remote.

This time, four-part harmony and accompaniment poured into the space. Lucy had just begun to close her eyes again when a wailing screech erupted. She turned to see Cloud with his fur fluffed out like a Halloween cutout.

Turn it off! Cloud screeched into her mind.

Lucy reached for the power button and the music stopped.

"What was that about?" said Maya.

"I don't know. Let me find out." Lucy turned to Cloud, his bristly fur starting to stand back down to form his normally luxurious gray coat. He rubbed his cheek against her leg, and she knelt down on the floor beside him. "Can you tell me what happened, my sweet boy?"

It felt…bad. Wrong. That is all I can say.

"I'm so sorry, Cloud. It's okay now. I'll never let anything hurt you."

I know. Can I have a treat?

Lucy laughed. Food was always one second away in Cloud's mind. "Of course, buddy." Lucy went to the kitchen and took his favorite crunchy treats out.

"That is one spoiled cat," said Maya, which caused Cloud to cast her a glare. "But that's as it should be," she quickly followed up.

Lucy put the treats away and sat on the couch. "Alright. So, all we know is there is something else on that CD that we can't perceive with our human ears. We don't know what or why. I don't suppose you have a friend that can help with this?"

Lucy had a long-standing joke with her friend that Maya knew so many people that there was always an expert available in whatever they needed help with. It had been quite convenient when she had discovered a hive of bees in her elderly friend's wall.

"Hmmm," said Maya. Her face lit up. "Yes! My cousin Eduardo's wife's brother is an audio engineer. He has a studio here in Northbrook. I'll see if he can help us."

Maya took out her phone and started texting. Five minutes later, her phone chimed. "He has a session ending at 2 and a break until 3. We can stop by then."

Lucy had never been in a recording studio before. The dimly lit room held a large mixer and a computer connected to an extra-large monitor. There was a rack with rows of electronic gear that Lucy didn't recognize, with cords patching in and out in a complex web. Microphones and stands, guitar effects pedals, and picks lined the floor, and absorptive black panels covered the walls.

"Ricky!" said Maya. "Thanks so much for agreeing to help us."

"Of course, my favorite cousin-in-law. Anything for you."

Maya introduced Lucy and then they got down to business. Lucy handed Ricky the CD and he stuck it in an external hard drive. "It will just take a few minutes to rip the tracks and then we can see what we're dealing with."

Lucy tapped her thumb and middle finger together nervously. She wished she had some tea right now.

The CD popped out of the tray. "Second track," said Maya.

"Okay. Let's take a look." Ricky opened his audio editing software and added the file to the program. A waveform appeared. "Looks normal," he said. Ricky zoomed in, studied it for a moment, then zoomed in even closer.

"Wait—there is something in there that shouldn't be. It's mixed in with all the other sound so it's difficult to make out."

Maya looked at Lucy and they both shook their heads. "I can't believe this. Who knows how many people buy these CDs?"

Ricky snorted. "No one actually buys CDs anymore, you know? If that helps…"

Maya punched him in the arm. "Yes, we know. But the target clientele for this still might. And there are streaming versions available too."

"Wasn't there a whole thing back in the eighties about hidden messages in music?" asked Lucy.

"Yep," said Ricky, "but it goes all the way back to the sixties when they started using tape to record. The Beatles took a section of the song "Rain," reversed it, and then put it back into the recording. It's called backmasking."

"You mean there really were subliminal messages?" Maya asked.

"I didn't say that. There have been plenty of bands who use backmasking to get a certain special effect, or for publicity, but that doesn't mean there is some secret message seeping into your subconscious without your knowledge. And a lot of what people imagine they hear is just that—imagination—the brain trying to make sense out of noise, looking for meaning and patterns where none exist."

Lucy vaguely remembered reading that a DJ in the eighties had spread the rumor that "Stairway to Heaven" contained Satanic messages. She knew that wasn't true, but after working with Noor, and seeing what happened at the health expo, she also knew there were deeper, more ominous possibilities that Ricky apparently knew nothing about.

Ricky glanced at his watch. "Can you leave this with me? I can run some analysis on it, dig a little deeper, if it's that important, but I have a client coming soon."

"Yes, of course," said Maya. "That would be great. We'll get out of your hair. Thanks so much."

"Thanks Ricky," echoed Lucy.

There was silence as Maya drove back. As they neared Lucy's house, Maya said, "Are you alright? You're more quiet than usual."

"I don't know. It was one thing to learn about dark song magicians performing at expos, at community markets, in a choir, but now to find out that they don't even have to be in person to do their damage? That just a recording could have the same effects? It's too much. How can we ever feel safe? There's music everywhere. Restaurants, malls, elevators, even bathrooms!"

Maya looked thoughtful as she parked in front of the curb. She turned to look at her friend. "I know this is small consolation, but neither of us were in any danger before we knew about all of this."

"You mean we didn't *know* we were in danger."

"I mean nothing bad seemed to happen before, in all those restaurants and bathrooms. And there isn't any reason that should change now."

"I guess you're right," said Lucy. "But I need to work with Noor to find out how to protect against song magic as soon as possible, or I'll never feel safe."

Chapter 18

ANUK WAS HIS CHEERFUL SELF at the weekly staff meeting, perhaps even more so than usual. "Good morning, team! In the consulting world, the best problem we can hope for is to have too much work," he said with a laugh and a glint in his eye.

Bethany chuckled. "Lucky us..."

"Right now, we are fortunate enough to have that problem," Anuk continued, "so we need to shift some assignments around. Bethany and Tyler will finish the wetland delineations and Lucy, we're going to send you out with Maya to do the first round of shorebird surveys at Brighton Island Nature Preserve."

Lucy broke out in a wide grin but then tried to hold back her smile when she saw the scowl on Tyler's face. She knew he was thinking that this was a great opportunity to practice bird identification and the trip would give Lucy an unfair advantage in the unspoken competition between them. Too bad, she thought. He had plenty of opportunities before that he simply squandered with his laziness.

Lucy had been trying harder to make time to practice her birding skills, with the flashcards, books, and recordings Maya had lent her. Now she would need to focus her efforts on shorebirds, which were at least easier to get a good look at in a spotting scope, unlike forest birds.

"I'd really like to get shorebird practice too," Tyler piped in. "Maybe I could do the second round of surveys at Brighton Island."

If Anuk noticed the undercurrent of competitiveness he had created, he didn't let on. "Yes, we can try and make that happen, pending schedules and workloads next month."

Bethany and Tyler exchanged satisfied glances, and Lucy was surprised to see Bethany give her a little smirk. Lucy wasn't loving the high school atmosphere that had developed ever since she started going after her own goals, but she wasn't about to set them aside because of it, either.

After the meeting, she walked Maya back to her cubicle. "This is going to be great, Lucy! Brighton Island is gorgeous this time of year and wait until you see all the different bird species."

"I *am* partial to the coast, after spending my summers on the beach as a child. Not to mention the awesome experience I had last time we were out there." Lucy had practiced her animal magic on a seagull, a pelican, and a little blue heron, seeing through their eyes and controlling their flight as she navigated the shoreline, with their permission, of course.

"We have a list of previously documented birds on the island, so start studying those first, and I will review some of the less frequent visitors to the area. We can practice using the spotting scope during lunch tomorrow and head down to do the survey on Thursday."

"Sounds like a plan—I can't wait!" said Lucy.

Lucy's phone chimed and she read the message. "Noor wants to know if we'd like to go with her to a cave meditation tonight."

Maya raised her eyebrow. "What's a cave meditation?"

Lucy clicked on the link. "It seems to literally be a meditation session held in Welder Cave in east Northbrook. It says '…this special location enhances the body and mind's connection with the natural world.'"

"I know that place—they give tours and even hold concerts there. Sure, let's go."

"Okay, I'll tell her."

That evening, Lucy once again marveled at how much her life had changed in the past six months as she stretched supine on the limestone cave floor, the woven mat the instructor had supplied only partially protecting against the chill and the hardness.

The woman stepped between the participants, placing crystals and herbal sachets all around them. Out of habit, as Lucy took in the fragrant lavender and mint and listened to the breathing of her classmates, she was soon attuned to the animal world. After spending time with Maya, Lucy knew what types of critters dwelled in caves in Northbrook, bats and beetles, scorpions and spiders, but this was more of a tourist attraction and less of a natural site, so all she sensed were a few moths and other harmless insects, to her relief.

The instructor began to guide the meditation, "Breathe in deeply through your nose, allowing the belly to rise, and exhale through the mouth. Very good. Again, big inhale, notice your breath, then exhale. Keep it going, at your own pace, focus on your breathing."

Lucy felt her muscles relax and soon all her worries about Kayla and Scordatura began to fade away, leaving her mind not empty, but freely floating through thoughts without judgement or attachment to any single one.

The low tone of a Tibetan singing bowl filled the cave chamber and Lucy felt a wave of serenity wash over her. Even with her eyes closed, she could see in her mind the wave pattern emanating from the bowl, bouncing off the cavern walls. This time in addition to the form, she pictured colors, indigo blue morphing into seafoam green. When the tone changed to a higher pitch, the patterns quickened, and the colors melted into golden wheat and pale peach.

She imagined the soundwaves purifying her body and dissolving the dark thoughts lodged in her mind, releasing her from the new reality of which she had recently become aware. Through her eyelids she swore she could see the glow of the crystals beside her, but she didn't want to break the spell by opening her eyes to see if it was real.

The feeling of weightlessness, as if she were hovering above the mat, yet somehow still grounded to the earth, made her feel energized, erasing in minutes the effects of weeks of troubled sleep. The soothing tone of the bowl gave her the same sensation of flying with a bird, like that first time she had flown with Silver, soaring through the sky. Lucy had this nagging kernel in the far reaches of her mind that things were interrelated in ways she couldn't explain, but the more she tried to grasp the concept, the further it drifted away.

"Slowly allow your focus to return to the room," the voice said, and Lucy almost didn't want to come back. "Wiggle your toes, give your shoulders a tiny shake, becoming more present moment by moment. When you're ready, slowly open your eyes."

Lucy looked around and was surprised to find the crystals dark, as they had been before. She must have imagined the glow, after all. She looked at Maya, then Noor, and it was clear that all three women had experienced the same centered, transcendent feeling.

They thanked the instructor for sharing her gift with them and walked together to the parking lot.

"What did you think, Lucy?" asked Noor.

Recognition dawned on her face. "That was song magic too, wasn't it?"

Noor smiled. "Yes, in a way. Tibetan singing bowls have been used for healing for a long time. But not just any person can play them and do what she did. That takes a lot of training and practice."

"And the crystals?" Maya asked.

"And the herbal sachets," added Lucy.

"It's all part of the same thing to me, I don't have words and definitions for everything."

"My lita told us there were five types of magic: animal, song, herbal, elemental, and spirit. So perhaps the sachets are herbal magic, and the crystals are elemental?" said Maya.

"Hmmm, maybe," said Noor. "Does your grandmother think the five types are so distinctly separate?"

Lucy nodded slowly. "I see where you are going. The boundaries surely blur, and I bet some types of magic amplify others."

"That makes sense to me," said Maya. "Lita doesn't have all the answers, not being a magic user herself, but she knows stories about magic in our family. Maybe she can give us some insight. You should come meet her, Noor. And she'd love to see you again, Lucy."

"Definitely," said Lucy.

"I'd be delighted," said Noor.

"What are the chances that the meditation instructor would be doing song and herbal magic?" said Lucy.

Maya looked at Noor and they both laughed.

"What?" demanded Lucy.

"I may have mentioned to Noor that you were getting weighed down by what you've learned lately, not just about Kayla and Scordatura, but the woman at the community market, and the hidden messages on the CD," said Maya.

"And I felt bad when she told me," said Noor. "I wanted to show you that there are also people all over doing light magic, generous and kind people, using their power to make people's lives better. You just have to learn to notice them too."

Lucy didn't know what to say. Not only had the meditation class filled her with lightness and hope, but her best friend and her newest friend coming together to help her balance out the darkness she had uncovered filled her with gratitude.

"You two are the best," said Lucy.

"We know," Noor and Maya said together, causing all three to break into laughter.

Chapter 19

"IT'S TIME TO GET SERIOUS," Darlene said after leading the choir through their warmups. "We only have one more regular rehearsal, plus the dress rehearsal, before the concert. I need everyone to focus. Tonight, we will finally hear what our lovely, featured chorus members have been working on as they sing through the quartet sections. From the top, everyone." She readied her baton, her gaze demanding the attention of the singers. Then she glanced over at the accompanist, and the music began.

The solemn and brooding "Introitus" brought an immediate pall over the rehearsal room. Lucy let the heaviness wash over her, allowing the mood of the music to guide her as she waited for her entrance. When the full choir entered, the resonance of the sound enveloped her, and she felt the power of the full group focused on a single goal, to make music that moves people.

Lucy was entranced as she heard Noor sing the soprano solo in the first movement. Even without using any song magic, she was a delight to hear, her voice was smooth like sea glass worn from decades of crashing waves on the sand. The second movement, the "Kyrie," flowed by like a rushing waterfall, leading into the chaotic runs and rising intensity of the "Dies irae." Lucy was immersed in the unity of belonging, her mind as free as it was during the meditation class.

Until Kayla began to sing her first solo.

Lucy was snapped out of the moment and forced back to the truth of the situation that could not be ignored, that sometime in one of the four movements that had alto solos, Kayla was almost definitely planning to use her dark song magic during the performance.

After that realization, Lucy trudged through the rest of the piece, instead of being carried away by the music, she was just singing notes and words, the emotion forced. The magic had been lost. She secretly fumed at Kayla for ruining her choir experience and stayed resentful for the remainder of the rehearsal.

"You sounded amazing," Lucy said to Noor as they walked through the fellowship hall lobby.

"Thank you."

When they reached the parking lot. Lucy glanced around and having ensured no one was within earshot she said, "What are we going to do about Kayla?"

"I don't know yet," said Noor.

"I was thinking if she were to use her song magic in the concert, it would be during that first section where she sings by herself, in the "Tuba mirum.""

"Agreed—it would be much easier when she is not having to fight against the harmonies or counterpoint of the other soloists."

"So now we just need to figure out how to negate her dark magic," said Lucy.

Noor scoffed. "Sure, that's all we have to do...no pressure. Can you come to the studio tomorrow after work?"

"Shoot—I can't. Maya and I have to go out of town for fieldwork, leaving tomorrow afternoon. How about Saturday?"

"Okay. I think Debbie is done with her classes by two and the space will be free after that."

"See you then."

#   #   #

Lucy and Maya reached the long bridge that connected the mainland to

Brighton Island just as the sun was setting. With Maya driving, Lucy was able to take in the painted sky, tangerine near the horizon melting into mauve, then dissolving into the darkening blue of night. Whenever she saw the ocean, a strange expansion occurred in her core, like she was able to breathe more deeply and fully. All the anxious, shallow concerns of Northbrook no longer existed. Here, she was free. If only she could be ocean Lucy all the time.

They checked into a run-down motel, a far cry from the gorgeous lodge they had stayed at in Sienna Falls Forest.

Maya chuckled as she kicked a beer can down the sidewalk outside the row of rooms. "I told you not to get used to that place; this is much more typical of what clients will pay for."

"It's only one night—I'll live." Lucy opened the door to her room while Maya did the same. She looked around at the stained carpet and worn bedspread. "On second thought, let's be here as little as possible."

"Yeah, let's go find somewhere to eat and hang out there awhile. We can bring our field maps and go over the survey details there."

They walked a few blocks down the main road towards a cluster of stores and restaurants and were deciding where to eat when they heard a man declare, "Well I'll be damned—a ghost wolf!"

Lucy and Maya exchanged glances. "Did he just say, 'ghost wolf?'" said Lucy.

"I think so. Let's go find out," said Maya.

"What? No! I've had enough of wolves to last a lifetime. And we can't just go talk to some stranger."

Maya raised her eyebrow, "After all we've been through? Of course we can!" Maya marched over. "What are you looking at?" she asked the man.

"Ghost wolf. See him?" he said, pointing out towards the vegetated sand dunes between the shops and the beach.

There stood an animal, certainly some type of canine, eyes gleaming in the twilight. Maya frowned. "It's pretty dim out but looks more like a coyote to me."

The man waved his hand at her, dismissing her opinion. "You ain't from around here, I can tell. You girls don't know about the ghost wolves of Brighton Island?"

Lucy and Maya shook their heads.

"Back in the day, red wolves roamed this here island. But no one seen 'em in forty years. Then just a few years back, these critters started appearing, half red wolf, half coyote," he said.

Lucy tapped Maya on the arm, nudging her head to the right, hoping she'd take the hint that this guy was nuts and they should leave.

"Hold on, I do recall reading about that. They did genetic testing," said Maya, looking out into the dune with more interest. She squinted her eyes to try and make out the animal's features more clearly. "It *is* a bit large for a coyote, and the ears do seem oversized."

The man rolled his eyes. "Whatever you say, missy," walking away muttering, "these out-of-towners think they know more than Big Teddy…"

The women looked out into the dunes, but the animal was gone. They continued on to the restaurant, but as soon as they were seated, Maya pulled up an article on her phone. "It's fascinating—like our new 'friend' Teddy said, the red wolf was declared extinct in the 1980s, but people kept reporting seeing them along the coast down here. And then it turns out at some point the coyotes and red wolves interbred."

"Wow, that's some story. So, they call them ghost wolves because they are remnants of the past, not quite real, but not imaginary either?"

"I guess so, like they are haunting the island in retribution for the habitat destruction and hunting that destroyed them."

"Maya! Don't say that. I still have nightmares about the wolves in Sienna Falls Forest. Now I'm never going to sleep tonight."

"Sorry. The good news is that it means this area could be a potential place for reintroduction of red wolves, that they could survive here."

"I guess that is good. And most wolves aren't trying to kill us."

"No. Although technically the wolves at Sienna Falls weren't out to harm us, their handlers were."

"True. Let's talk about something else."

Maya nodded and they turned their attention to the pending bird survey they would perform just after sunrise the next morning. They lingered until the restaurant was about to close, then reluctantly returned to the motel.

The next morning, they were checked out of their rooms by 6 a.m. and on their way to Brighton Island Nature Preserve. The flats of Brighton Bay were spotted with migrant birds stopping over to fuel up before their journeys back to Central and South America. Maya set up the spotting scope and Lucy took out her data sheets.

Maya listed out each bird as she identified it, "Three Spotted Sandpipers, two Western Willets. Oh—look at that Long-billed Curlew."

Lucy took a quick look with her binoculars at the speckled brown bird with an extraordinary bill half the length of its body. She never got tired of all the endless variations in nature. Even one little flat of shorebirds in the off-season was brimming with biodiversity.

"It's fantastic!" said Lucy.

Maya listed off more birds and Lucy returned to her documentation.

"All right, that's everyone here. Let's take down the time, wind speed and direction, temperature, a GPS point, and then we can head to the next spot."

They repeated the procedure three more times at different locations within the preserve.

"One more," said Maya.

They began to climb up towards the top of the next dune, Lucy following a few paces behind.

"What the…" said Maya as she stopped and stood at the peak. Lucy quickly scrambled up next to her and gasped when she took in the scene before her.

"Have you ever seen anything like this?" asked Lucy, breathless.

"Never," replied Maya.

Chapter 20

ELEGANT PATTERNS HAD BEEN CARVED into the valley of sand below them, like a linear mandala pathway. Petal-shaped borders brought to mind flowers blooming out of the dune, and Lucy's eyes followed the intricate linework weaving through the sand.

Both women looked around them, hoping to find a clue of its origin, but they were alone as far as they could see, which admittedly was only until the next dune.

"Could this be natural? Maybe an alligator dragged its tail through here?" asked Lucy.

"That would be one artsy gator. There are alligators here, though."

"Aren't there some birds that make elaborate patterns to attract mates?"

"Bowerbirds will collect colorful things, flowers, feathers, coins, and shells, and display them as part of courtship, but they are mostly found in New Guinea. I don't know of any birds who make patterns like this in sand."

As much as Lucy wanted to dig further, she never wanted to take fieldwork assignments for granted, not after how hard she had fought to get her chance six months ago, and especially not with Tyler breathing down her neck. "I don't want to derail our survey. Let's get our count here, and then maybe we can investigate a little more after."

Maya nodded in agreement and set up the spotting scope once more.

Lucy logged more bird species, this time some Black-bellied Plovers, a chunky brown/orange Short-billed Dowitcher, and a cinnamon-colored Marbled Godwit. Once the species were recorded, Maya had Lucy take a turn at the spotting scope, giving her pointers on the identifying features of each species. Birds that at first appeared similar to Lucy soon sorted themselves out by feather pattern and color, bill shape, size, and behavior.

"That's it. Our first shorebird survey here is done," said Maya.

Lucy grinned. She still couldn't believe how much had changed since Maya joined TerraPlaya. She still loved making maps, but now part of her job was fieldwork in some of the most stunning natural landscapes in the state.

Maya finished packing the spotting scope in its case and Lucy put the survey sheets and clipboard in her backpack. "Ready to investigate?" asked Maya.

A nervous flutter in her stomach reminded her that she'd never be as fearless as her friend, but that was okay, she didn't need to be. She just needed to trust her. "Sure, let's go."

The patterned pathway rose over the next dune, and the next, becoming more defined as they followed along. Clearly, they were heading in the right direction because the ocean breeze hadn't had time to wear these designs down yet; they were getting closer.

At the top of the next dune, Maya groaned. Lucy looked down and saw why: the path deadened when it reached the strip of vegetation that transitioned inland.

"Maybe we can still see remnants in there; let's look," said Lucy. She scrambled through the sand. She scanned between the clumps of grasses as she walked along where the path logically should have gone, but soon the sand gave way to soil and leaves. They had lost it.

"Look," Maya whispered.

Lucy lifted her head to see a dog about twenty feet in front of them, standing perfectly still. Her heart started racing. Not a dog, though. A coyote, maybe. Or...

"It's a ghost wolf!" Maya said. "Just like Teddy told us. It really does look like a combination of a red wolf and a coyote."

"Do you think it has something to do with the sand patterns?"

"I have no idea. Can you ask it?"

Lucy considered this. She and Maya had previously discussed the ethics of trying to communicate with animals in the wild. They agreed that it could be disruptive to the natural world and create confusion, especially places that didn't get many human visitors. But Lucy had a feeling that the ghost wolves were different. They certainly didn't fear people, and they had found a way to survive in close proximity to humans.

"Okay, I'm going to try."

Friend, did you do this? Lucy said, pointing behind her to the patterns in the sand.

The ghost wolf looked unsurprised by the interaction, either that, or he didn't understand her or hear her at all. Then he tilted his head slightly, as if assessing the two women.

Three-legged man. Lucy heard the words directly in her brain.

"Three-legged man? Does that mean anything to you, Maya?"

"No, nothing. Can you ask him where this three-legged man is?"

Where?

The ghost wolf gave what almost seemed to Lucy like a sigh of annoyed exasperation, then began trotting back into the scrubby shrubs. He paused to turn around and look at the women.

"I think he wants us to follow him," said Lucy.

The landscape changed as they trailed the ghost wolf, scrubby bushes giving way to gangly, gnarled trees. Lucy could just barely hear the sound of the waves crashing in the distance, the call of the gulls on the seashore. In here it was more private, quiet, with the calls of birds, frogs and toads, a more subdued tone.

After ten minutes of walking, Lucy couldn't hear the ocean anymore, and her fears rose as she considered how far away they were from civilization, and if it were wise to trust some legendary creature to guide them. No point in turning back now, especially when this time they were seeking an explanation for something beautiful; what harm could come from that?

The ghost wolf stopped. Up ahead was what appeared to be a partially falling down bird blind, looking out onto a small pond. Maya cautiously stepped towards the structure, keeping her distance as she moved to where she'd be able to see inside.

A sharp yell shattered the quiet.

An old man, his skin wrinkled and leathered by the sun, was sitting on the floor inside. His clothes were torn and soiled and his long hair was scraggly, his chin sporting a wild gray beard. He looked spooked at the sight of the women.

"I'm so sorry. We didn't mean to frighten you," said Maya.

The man balanced on a walking stick and the wooden plank wall to reach his feet and survey the women. "How did you find me?" he said, his voice deep and raspy.

Before Maya could answer, the ghost wolf moved into the man's view.

The old man shook his head. "I should have known. I trusted you…" he said admonishingly to the animal.

Lucy didn't want to get the ghost wolf in trouble. "Sorry to disturb you. We just wanted to know about the patterns in the sand and when we asked him, he led us here. Did you make them?"

The old man looked her up and down, then looked at Maya, then back at the ghost wolf. Finally, he sighed as if accepting the situation. "I did."

"How?" asked Lucy.

"By singing."

Lucy's eyes widened. Did this random old man in the middle of the Preserve know song magic? That would be a wild coincidence.

"Can you show us?" said Maya.

The man shook his head. "I don't think so. Best if you were on your way."

Lucy took the backpack off her shoulder. "We have snacks. Nuts and granola bars."

His face perked up. "Chocolate?"

"Yes." Lucy gingerly tossed a miniature Hershey's bar towards the man, still keeping a safe distance between them.

He opened the wrapper with knotted fingers, then took a bite. He groaned. "I haven't had chocolate in years." He closed over the bar, leaving it half uneaten, and tucked it into a pouch around his waist. "I'll show you, but then you have to leave me alone and forget you ever saw me."

The old man led them back to the sand, leaning on his walking stick with each step, and as soon as his feet reached the beach, he began to sing, a soft, folksy tune, in a language Lucy didn't recognize. As he shuffled along, the path behind him changed, the sands bouncing around into shapes and patterns. It reminded Lucy of the Chladni plates that Noor had shown her in the studio, but even more elaborate. This wasn't just physics; this was something else, this was art.

"You know song magic!" Lucy declared.

The old man turned around, his eyes narrow. "Never heard of it."

"What do you call what you just did?" asked Maya.

"I don't call it anything, because I don't talk to anyone about it."

"But where did you learn it?" pressed Maya.

"My mati taught me decades ago."

"What did *she* call it?" asked Lucy.

"She didn't call it anything either."

They weren't getting anywhere like this. Lucy wasn't sure if he was being purposely stubborn or if he just didn't have any reason to define or discuss his powers.

"You know most people can't do that, right?" said Lucy.

"Can't they?" he replied.

"No."

He shrugged.

"Could you teach me?" asked Lucy.

The man furrowed his brow, then scrunched up his nose. "I don't know."

"You don't know if you want to or if you can?"

"No one's ever asked me before."

Lucy couldn't let this chance pass her by. "Well, I'm asking you now. Can you try? Please?"

"Do you have more chocolate?"

"Yes, and you can have all of it."

"Fine," said the man. "Imagine instead of pushing the music out in front of you that it's trailing behind you like a fancy wedding dress."

"Can you teach me the song?"

"I don't think it matters, the words or notes."

Lucy thought for a moment, then walked onto the sand and began to hum. She closed her eyes and pretended a strong wind was catching the sounds as they came out of her mouth, and they were falling on the sand behind her. She stopped and turned around.

There was only plain sand, ridged by the wind.

The old man scratched his chin. "You have the right idea, but it's too weak without the words."

Lucy tried again, feeling self-conscious, singing a song that had comforted her through many long nights. This time she focused on the emotion behind the words, and not on the notes.

We are stardust
Born out of time
Forever searching
for a way to combine

We are stardust
Ripped from the sky
Ashes to ashes
Stardust to stardust

This time when she turned around, the sand had formed into swirls and spirals, like the Milky Way. Not as clean and elegant as the etching the old man had created, but still graceful in its own right.

"You did it! That's lovely," said Maya.

"Not bad," said the old man.

Lucy tingled with excitement; using her song magic gave her a buzz of energy like nothing else. She handed the chocolate over to the man. "Here. Thank you for showing me that."

He nodded and accepted the offering. He started shuffling off when Lucy caught up to him and said, "Wait. Is there anything else you can teach me? That your mati taught you? Did she ever tell you how to protect against other people who might be using similar powers to harm you?"

The old man froze, then spun around. "Are you in danger?"

"Not just me, but a lot of people. I'm trying to stop them, but I don't know how," said Lucy.

"Well…There is one thing. I don't know how much it will help since I haven't had to use it in years, living alone like I do."

"Anything you can teach me would be great. Please."

"Fine. Have you ever been in a swordfight?"

Maya laughed at the absurdity of the question, but Lucy remained serious and said, "I used to fence in high school, including saber, but that was a long time ago."

"I didn't know that—you surprise me all the time," said Maya. Lucy shrugged.

"Then you know when you're attacked, you parry," said the man.

"Sure, I know that."

"With sound, the parry is singing something the opposite of what you're hearing."

"Like if you sing low, I sing high?"

He scrunched his face up, like he was struggling to teach something to a small child. "No. Not like that at all. I don't know how to explain it. It's not just the notes, it's the intent, the feeling."

A lightbulb went off in Lucy's mind. Noor had talked about intent as well. It was Kayla's anger that killed the poor mouse, even though her fury was really at the student outside in the hallway, playing the trombone.

"Yes! That makes sense. Thank you so much for your help. We will leave you alone now."

"And don't tell anyone I'm here."

"We won't," Lucy said, and Maya echoed.

They watched as the old man retreated back into the forest, and then they walked along the beach back to the car.

"I can't believe he lives in a bird blind in the middle of a nature preserve," said Maya.

"And that no one knows about it. I wonder how long he's been here."

"Who knows. Years, maybe."

"You know I don't believe in fate, but that was a stroke of luck, the ghost wolf leading us to an old song magic guru who doesn't even know he's special."

"Strange things seem to find you," said Maya. "Especially for someone who considered herself so ordinary."

"Hmmph. None of the strange things happened until I met you!"

"Ha. You got me there."

Chapter 21

"YOU'RE NEVER GOING TO BELIEVE this," Lucy called out to Noor as she walked into Northbrook Harmony.

"Hi Lucy. Hold on, Evan is here—his mom is just getting her stuff together."

The boy ran over to her. "You're the lady who fixed Evan," he said.

Before Lucy could decide how to respond, Debbie came out of the office. She looked puzzled by her son's statement.

Noor quickly explained, "This is Lucy. She made friends with the gerbil when I watched Evan a few weeks ago."

Debbie nodded. "Oh, I see. Nice to meet you. Evan doesn't talk to very many people, so he must really like you."

"He's a sweet kid and takes very good care of his gerbil."

"That he does, he loves that thing," Debbie laughed. "Alright, we're off. Come on, Evan."

The windchimes hanging from the frame released a calm, tinkling sound as the front door closed behind Evan and his mom.

"I think you have a friend for life now, after helping gerbil Evan," said Noor as she turned the key in the lock.

"I just hope he stays well."

"Me too. So, what am I not going to believe?"

She told Noor all about the patterns in the sand, the ghost wolf, and the old man.

"Whoa. That's not what I imagined when you said you were traveling for work."

Lucy chuckled. "It's not always like that. Actually, who am I kidding? The first time I did fieldwork with Maya someone broke into our hotel rooms and stole our laptops. It only got weirder from there. This trip was a dream since there were no dark magicians after us."

"Your life seems wild."

It was an odd feeling knowing that someone else thought Lucy's life was exciting. Really only the past six months had been, but it almost made up for the first uneventful forty years. "I suppose it is, these days."

"We'd better get to work. I was thinking about noise cancelling headphones—in a perfect scenario they generate the exact inverse of the soundwaves they are trying to cancel."

"Oh, I've always wondered how that works."

"That's the theory behind it," Noor continued, "but that doesn't work well in real time, so most of them also generate some constant noise that helps mask other sounds, like the roar of a plane."

"But how can we apply any of this to stopping Kayla?"

"I'm not sure yet. We've been focusing on healing, and using sound to affect objects, but we haven't tried to intercept sound yet. I set up my sine wave generator that I use to demonstrate the Chladni plates. Let's work with that."

Noor turned on the machine and it began to emit a single, steady tone.

"That's going to get annoying fast," said Lucy.

"Let that be our motivation," chuckled Noor.

"What do we do now?"

"Let's try to break it. I'll try first." Noor let out a strong note, focusing on the machine. She tried different pitches, different volumes, with vibrato and without, but it didn't make a difference. She threw her hands in the air in frustration. "Ugh—I don't know. Any ideas?"

"No, but I remember what it was like when I was learning to use animal magic. Sometimes you just have to experiment freely for a while."

"Be my guest," said Noor.

Lucy closed her eyes and focused on the tone. Like Noor, she tried creating her own sounds, but they had no impact on the note emitted by the machine. She thought back to cracking the vase. This time, she visualized the tone as a soundwave, an oscillating "S" pattern moving through space above the generator. She imagined her own sound as a sword slicing through the soundwave. Thwop!

"Wait! What was that?" said Noor.

Lucy opened her eyes. She wasn't sure if she had heard a change in the tone or not. "Did it work?"

"I swore it cut out for a split second. Can you do that again?"

Lucy repeated it several times, and now the tone was more like a "wah wah wah" as she repeatedly sliced it. She explained to Noor what she was envisioning and soon enough, Noor was able to produce the same results.

This was a breakthrough.

Surely interrupting the wave would, at the very least, decrease the effectiveness of whatever song magic was being cast.

"This is great progress. But we have a big problem," said Noor.

"Yeah, I know. We can't ruin the concert."

"Definitely not—two hundred people, plus Darlene, the accompanist, and many others have worked too hard on this performance. We have to interrupt the song magic in a way that will be imperceptible to the audience."

"Let's think. For the parts when you are singing in the quartet or when the chorus is singing, we can use our own voices to disarm her magic. But for her brief solo lines, it will have to be something nearly silent."

Noor turned off the tone generator and flopped down on one of the woven mats. "Let's take a break. I need to clear my mind."

"Why don't I make us some tea?" said Lucy.

"That's a great idea. Thanks."

Lucy went into the back office, filled the electric tea kettle, and plugged it in to boil. She placed tea bags in two mugs on the counter. She saw steam pour out of the spout before she heard the burble of boiling water.

Carrying the two teacups back into the studio, Lucy said, "You know when you boil water for pasta and even after it's obviously hot and starting to bubble, you can barely hear it? Not until it's a really heavy rolling boil does it make a sound."

"I guess so, why?" said Noor.

"When Kayla sings, maybe we could create sounds so quiet that no one could hear them, but we could still learn to direct the waves to intercept hers?"

Noor thought about this as she sipped her tea. "Perhaps. We are still learning what is possible. We could tap our feet silently. It never really occurred to me that just because we can't hear something doesn't mean it isn't making a noise."

"Yes! But if we can't hear it, the soundwaves must not travel far enough to reach our ears or are out of the range of human hearing. We'd have to figure out how to force it in her direction."

"And only cancel out the dark magic in her singing, not her real voice."

"Yes, like the old man at the preserve said, do the opposite."

Lucy and Noor spent the next several hours experimenting. Without knowing exactly what Kayla was planning, it was difficult to come up with a strategy to stop her, but by Saturday evening they had some ideas. Now they just had to keep practicing individually and together over the next week until the concert, and hope that it worked under pressure.

Chapter 22

ALL THE TEA IN THE world couldn't pep Lucy up on Monday morning. Practicing song magic most of the weekend had exhausted her, and she wasn't ready to return to the world of mapmaking. She wished Anuk wasn't always like a robin chirping at the crack of dawn, full of boundless energy and good cheer. It made her feel like a grump.

"Were you able to wrap up the wetland delineation last week?" Anuk asked Bethany and Tyler.

"Yep, all done," said Bethany, "totally no problems."

"Just the typical mosquitos, snakes, and mud," complained Tyler.

"Sounds like fieldwork," said Anuk with a chuckle. "And how was the first survey at Brighton Island Nature Preserve?" he asked Lucy and Maya.

"Great," said Maya, "wind speeds were low, and we catalogued quite a few species. The data we are collecting this season is going to set up a solid baseline for the future."

"Excellent work," said Anuk.

Tyler hid his signature scowl as it crossed his face and said, "Remember that I'd like to be a part of the next survey there."

For once, Anuk seemed annoyed, which was saying a lot since he usually only got frazzled by the constant struggle to meet corporate metrics. "Yes, Tyler, thank you for the reminder. Again, it will depend on what work we have next month."

"But it's not fair if Lucy gets all the birding experience," he whined.

Lucy huffed and shook her head in indignation. Tyler had gotten so much more experience than her over the years, even though he had a similar degree to hers, in mapmaking. He pushed his way into the fieldwork he wanted while Lucy was stuck making the maps he was supposed to be creating.

Anuk sat back in his chair. "I'm sorry that I agreed to consider either of you to take on more bird survey assignments. Perhaps it would be best if I moved forward with hiring an additional staff member."

The blood boiled in Lucy's veins. She couldn't believe Tyler was going to mess up her chance to keep doing fieldwork with Maya. What if she hadn't been the one to go to the Preserve? Then she would never have learned about song magic from the old man.

Maya looked over and Lucy gave her a little helpless shrug in response, not sure what she could do to remedy the situation, but Maya's eyes held an ember of determination.

"I have an idea to resolve this issue," said Maya.

"Oh? I'd love to hear it," said Anuk.

"A bird-off. We used to have them when I was in college. Three rounds—photo identification, bird calls, and listing birds common in a specific habitat. Whoever wins gets first dibs on the Brighton Island Nature Preserve surveys."

Lucy paled. What was Maya thinking? She hated being the center of attention, much less trying to prove her worth in a high-pressure situation with all her coworkers watching.

Tyler also didn't look thrilled about the suggestion. But Bethany's face was lit up like a fireworks extravaganza. "That's a great idea! We could order in lunch one day and make it a fun company event to involve the entire office."

The entire office? Lucy's throat was suddenly dry, and her stomach felt like it was full of pop rocks and soda. She was going to have a word with Maya about this later.

"But who is going to prepare the questions? It has to be someone unbiased," said Tyler, giving a not-so-subtle glance at Maya.

"*I* will," said Anuk, "if it means this can stop being a distraction. I studied enough about birds, albeit a long time ago, to cover all the basics."

"This is going to be, like, so fun," said Bethany.

Lucy just looked down at her shoes. This is not the stress she needed right now, with the concert coming up so soon. And now she would have to study harder than ever to ensure she showed greater expertise than Tyler.

"This doesn't mean that we won't hire another bird expert, though," said Anuk, trying to re-establish control over the meeting. "As much as I try my best to accommodate the career goals of my staff, it's my job to make all hiring and assignment decisions. Now back to my agenda."

Working for Anuk was one of the things that had made her stay at TerraPlaya for almost fifteen years, but sometimes he was too nice for his own good. She knew a little something about not dealing well with conflict, and she hated to put Anuk in this position. Although technically it was Tyler who had pushed the issue. At any rate, she was now committed to going head-to-head with him in a semi-formal competition.

In the courtyard during lunch, Lucy shrieked at Maya, "What were you thinking?"

"What do you mean?"

"I'm not good under pressure, you know that," said Lucy.

"Um, no, you just don't like it. You actually perform great under pressure. Sienna Falls Forest is my case in point."

"I also have a lot on my plate right now. Remember how I'm trying to stop Kayla from doing who knows what at the concert?"

"Yes, and you will stop her, I have faith in you and Noor. Were you able to use the old man's advice?"

It used to bug Lucy how Maya always seemed calm in the face of obstacles that brought Lucy to the brink of an anxiety attack, but now she appreciated her friend's calming influence. And the confidence she had in Lucy helped quiet the negative voices in her head telling her she couldn't possibly compete against the Kaylas, or even the Tylers, of this world.

Her anger at Maya receded. "Sort of. We have some ideas, but since we don't know what Kayla is planning to do, we won't find out until she starts singing if it's going to work. And by then it will be too late if it doesn't."

"It will work, I know it," said Maya.

"I wish I shared your optimism."

Maya grinned. "That's okay, I have enough for the both of us. Let me know if there is any way I can help. I might not know song magic, but maybe there's some other way."

"Thanks. I can't think of anything, but I'll be glad just knowing you are in the audience."

"Of course. Lita and I have tickets already."

Lucy felt better. With Maya by her side, she could beat Tyler in a bird-off, and with Noor part of their lives now, maybe they could beat Kayla too.

Later that evening, Lucy got a call from Maya. When she answered, the sounds of a wailing baby assaulted her ears.

"What is going on over there?" said Lucy.

"I'm watching my cousin's baby and he's been crying nonstop for over an hour. He's teething. I don't suppose you want to come over and try out your song magic?"

"On a baby?!?" Lucy squealed.

"Why not?"

"Because I don't know what I'm doing. What if I hurt him?"

"You're not going to hurt him. Didn't you say it was all about intent?"

"I guess so—I don't know. Let me call Noor."

Thirty minutes later, Lucy arrived at Maya's cousin's house. She could hear the poor boy wailing inside all the way from the front yard.

"Thanks for coming," said Maya, cradling the crying baby.

"Of course. No promises though."

"What did Noor say?"

"She said lullabies are the oldest form of song magic in existence. And if I sing with love and affection there is no risk of harm."

"If Hugo wasn't yelling in my ear right now, I would have time to appreciate how beautiful that idea is. Let me put him in his crib." Maya set the boy down on his back, his arms flailing in protest.

"Now that I think about it, I don't actually know any lullabies," said Lucy.

"From what I've gathered so far, it probably doesn't matter what the song is, just how you sing it."

"You're probably right. Cyndi Lauper it is, then." Lucy leaned over the crib and started crooning "True Colors" over Hugo. He stared up at them with soulful, wet eyes, helpless and hurting. She poured all the soothing that she could into her voice, imagining the sound was a white light enveloping the boy and washing away his pain. She closed her eyes and imagined the throbbing in his gums from tiny teeth trying to push through and tried to use the music as a salve, numbing the area.

When Lucy reached the second verse Hugo's cries lessened, and by the time she sang the last note, he had fallen asleep.

"You are an angel sent from heaven," Maya whispered to Lucy. "If you could patent that you'd make millions."

"Hah—I'm just glad I could help. I don't know how long it will last, though."

"Hopefully until my cousin gets home, that's all I ask," Maya said with a smirk.

Lucy sat back into the couch. "I can't believe that worked."

"I can. I remember my mamá singing to me when I was sick or scared. It's powerful stuff, lullabies."

"It's incredible, right? Noor said the oldest known lullaby is 4,000 years old, from Babylonia."

"No kidding—that's something. I wonder if it's as creepy as the ones I heard growing up."

"Your mom sang you creepy lullabies?" asked Lucy. "I guess the cradle falling one is pretty dark, they use it in all the horror movie trailers."

"Oh yeah, my mom's were mostly about monsters that would eat me if I didn't close my eyes and stay still."

"Whoa—that's wild. And that helped you fall asleep?"

Maya thought for a moment and rubbed her chin. "I guess that is what Noor means about intent. No matter what the words are, people sing lullabies with that same soothing tone that you just did, and it works."

"Hmmm. It does seem intent is the key. That's why Kayla is so terrifying."

"Indeed, she is. Because her intent seems to be pure selfish evil."

Chapter 23

THE NIGHT OF THE CONCERT was finally upon them. Lucy dressed in her new concert black outfit that she had bought specially for choir performances and headed towards the venue. She hadn't slept well, and her throat was sore and dry from nerves and fatigue. She had a travel mug full of soothing tea and honey and sipped it at each traffic light. Her top priority was protecting the audience from Kayla, but belonging to a choir was a lifelong dream of hers so performing to the best of her abilities and helping Darlene achieve her artistic vision was a close second.

Seeing Noor in the green room calmed her nerves. Lucy wasn't in this alone; Noor would be doing her best to assist, and Maya would be supporting her from the audience. Although Lucy had advised her and Carmela to wear earplugs during the solos, just in case.

"How are you feeling?" Noor asked.

"Nervous...about everything. How about you? You have some big solos."

"I always get a little nervous before a performance, but I love singing for people so usually once I begin it melts away."

Lucy knew she didn't need to remind Noor that she had to stay on her toes and wouldn't be able to lose herself in the moment as she usually did while singing.

Darlene gathered everyone around for warmups, followed by a pep talk. "I am so proud of how hard you have all worked this season. It's been my pleasure to lead this amazing group. We know what we need to focus on—watch the dynamics, and the cut offs, listen to your fellow singers. But most of all, enjoy the beautiful music that we are about to make together."

The singers had time for one more bathroom break and last-minute hydration. Lucy finished the rest of her tea. She couldn't help eyeing Kayla, who looked radiant and happy. No one would guess she was a dark song magician.

Lucy couldn't help but wonder if Kayla wouldn't have been happier just having the opportunity to sing the solos in front of hundreds of people. She did originally mean to study vocal performance, after all. Who knows how her career would have turned out if she hadn't been assigned to Pierre Martel in college. Perhaps she would be an entirely different person and in another timeline she and Lucy would be alto section buddies.

Darlene directed everyone to gather their music folders and line up for their entrance onto the stage. They formed their rows and one by one filed out onto the risers. The four soloists stood up front, slightly off to one side.

Once in place, Lucy immediately scanned the audience for Maya. She found her quickly, sitting in front as promised, with Carmela beside her. Maya gave her an encouraging smile and Lucy smiled back. It made her feel stronger to know her friend was there.

When the house lights lowered and the audience began to quiet, Darlene made her entrance and took the conductor's stand. The audience gave her a warm, welcoming applause. Darlene motioned for the singers to raise their music folders, looked over at the accompanist, and with a flick of the baton, the music began.

Lucy never got tired of listening to the opening of Mozart's *Requiem*. It felt so stately and brooding, each beat weighed down with solemnity, as the pall of death descended upon the concert hall. When the voices entered, Lucy was nearly caught off guard by the power and intensity. She could feel the focus of her fellow singers surrounding her, all projecting the plea for eternal rest and perpetual lightness, *"requiem aeternam dona ets, Domine, et lux perpetua luceat ets."*

Noor had the honor of being the first soloist in the piece, and she performed with grace and skill, her clear soprano tone and rich vibrato piercing through the hall.

The next two movements went by as if in a dream, Lucy caught up in the power of two hundred voices united. Then came the quartet section, first the bass, then tenor, taking their turns. Soon Kayla's solo would be upon them.

Before the first note came out of Kayla's mouth, Lucy prepared mentally to thwart her by visualizing the soundwaves coming from the piano accompaniment, like crimson blood swirling in a pool of water, intense, brooding, but without any of the dark malice of song magic.

Lucy tapped her finger invisibly on the underside of her music folder and imagined the pulsating soundwaves, small as they were, infused with protective intent. She willed them to mix in with the overtones of the piano, then directed the drifting mass of sound slowly across the stage toward the soloists.

When Kayla's velvet tone finally escaped, a lioness free from her cage, Lucy immediately felt a shift, like needles pricking her skin. Kayla was definitely using song magic.

Lucy directed the complex swirl of her light magic mixed with the piano music to envelop Kayla like a mist, dampening her enchantment.

Darlene's eyebrows furrowed for a quick second as if she detected something was off about Kayla's singing. The alto solo was short, but Lucy could feel Kayla trying to recalibrate, struggling to cut through the barrier with all her will, but the parts Lucy knew were dark song magic dissipated before they reached the audience, leaving only the pure music for the listeners to enjoy. Lucy could sense Kayla trying to hide her frustration, but her hand was balled into a fist beneath her music folder.

Noor came in on cue, the soprano part taking over the melody, and Kayla's teeth clenched with anger.

They had done it; Lucy and Noor had foiled Kayla's song magic and protected the audience from enchantment.

There were several more solo parts in the work, but they were brief, and for much of it Noor sang along with Kayla or in quick succession and would be able to dilute Kayla's intent without Lucy's help. Still, Lucy remained vigilant for the remainder of the concert.

After the program ended, the audience broke into appreciative applause. This wasn't exactly how Lucy imagined her first performance with the choir would be, but she sang her best and tried to enjoy the parts that she could.

"You were wonderful," said Lucy to Noor back in the green room.

Noor beamed. "Thanks. So were you," she said with a knowing look. "It worked. Did you feel it?" she whispered.

"Felt it, saw it even. I think Kayla's pissed."

"Yeah, I'll bet. I wonder where she is."

The two women left the green room. "I'm going to find my family. Let's talk soon," said Noor.

Lucy went to find Maya and Carmela. Before she reached the turn for the concert hall, she heard voices coming from the loading dock behind the stage. It was Kayla. She was talking with a man, a very angry man from the sound of it.

"I did exactly what we had planned," Kayla said defensively. "I didn't know they were going to interfere."

"You must always be prepared for a fight, you know this. Have you forgotten all your training? We should never have trusted you with this. I'll take it from here."

"But-"

"No. You failed and there will be consequences," he said, and a shiver ran down Lucy's spine.

"Don't give up on me, please," Kayla begged. "I'll prove myself—you'll see."

Just then the sound of a door slamming shut startled Lucy and she ran towards the concert hall before she could be caught eavesdropping.

Chapter 24

MAYA GAVE LUCY A BIG hug in the aisle as soon as she came into view.

"And one from me, too," said Maya's grandmother. "What beautiful singing."

"Thank you, Carmela. I'm so glad you're both here," said Lucy.

The older woman smiled. "I told you that girl had song magic, didn't I?"

"Noor? You were sure right about that."

"I was hoping to meet her."

"Sorry, she already left to get ice cream with her family," said Lucy.

"Oh, that's too bad. The three of you girls will have to come over soon."

"I'd like that."

Carmela's voice dropped to a whisper. "I want to know everything that's going on. That other girl, she does dark magic, yes?"

Lucy nodded. "I'm afraid so."

From the corner of her eye, Lucy saw a woman by the front doors watching them. She looked familiar but Lucy couldn't place her.

"Maya—do you see that woman by the entrance?"

By the time Maya turned to look, the woman was halfway out the door, only the tail of her brown overcoat visible.

"Who was that?" asked Maya.

Sudden recognition dawned on Lucy. "It was the woman from the health expo. Remember—with the blue top and black, curly hair? The only one who wasn't hypnotized."

"Yeah, I remember. If she's here, then she must be with Kayla's circle."

"I guess so. I also have to tell you what I just heard in the hallway. Proof that Kayla is merely doing her assignments as told. She's no mastermind, just a lackey."

"Of course she is—that sounds about right given our luck. Let's talk tomorrow. I need to drop lita off at her house."

"I *am* getting tired," said Carmela. "But I worry about you girls, getting yourselves into more trouble. Promise you'll come by and see me and bring Noor. I need to talk some sense into all three of you before something terrible happens."

"We promise," said Lucy and Maya.

Before she left the concert hall, Lucy checked her phone to see how late the fancy grocery store nearby stayed open. She was going to get herself a treat to celebrate her first concert with the choir. The parking lot had mostly cleared out, the singers and audience members on their way to dinners and desserts or off to bed.

Her car was parked beneath a tree and even with the streetlamps it was dark, with shadows dancing as the wind blew the branches. Lucy didn't see the figure until she was fifteen feet from her car.

It was Kayla. Still dressed in concert black, she looked like a scorned witch, just missing a pointy hat. Her face was like a venomous snake as she hissed, "I don't know who you think you are, but you messed with the wrong woman. Now I have to face the consequences…and so do you."

There was no one nearby to witness the scene, and Lucy's pulse raced with fear. She didn't think Kayla would physically hurt her, at least not seriously, but then she didn't really know what Kayla or her employers were capable of.

"I don't know what you're talking about," Lucy said, but the nervous wobble in her voice didn't sound too convincing.

"Just stay out of my way from now on, or you'll be sorry," said Kayla.

"And give Noor a little message from me—she has no idea how far I've come since college. You haven't seen anything yet."

Before Lucy could force words to enter her blank mind in response, Kayla let out a high shriek, like a cat in heat, and Lucy jerked as she felt something sharp in her hand. She dropped her cell phone and looked down to see blood pooling on her palm. She looked up at Kayla in horror and saw the woman seemed pleased with herself.

"Consider that a warning," said Kayla without a shred of remorse, then turned on her heels and walked back into the shadows.

Lucy was shaking as she bent down to pick up her phone. The screen was not just cracked, it was as if someone smashed it with a hammer, creating a spiderweb of fractures along the glass. Her palm was throbbing, and she was afraid to put pressure on the wound in case there were embedded shards in her skin.

She wrapped her hand in her fieldwork shirt from the trunk, more to protect her car from bloodstains than anything else, gingerly placed the broken phone on the passenger floorboard, and drove herself to the urgent care clinic. Luckily Lucy wasn't squeamish about blood. In fact, she didn't feel that bad at all; she hardly felt anything but a hollow numbness.

She walked into the clinic calmly and checked in at the front desk. The receptionist took one look at the bloody shirt and called the triage nurse over.

"You're lucky, we're slow tonight," said the nurse. "Let's get you taken care of before you make a mess."

Lucy just nodded blankly and followed the woman. She was barely aware as they cleaned the gash, picking out tiny slivers of glass; it was like she was somewhere else, watching her body from above, like an angel in an old holiday movie.

"No stitches needed, just a bandage," said the doctor. "Keep it clean and take some Tylenol if you need it."

Lucy nodded. She handed the woman her credit card for her co-pay and drove herself back home in a stupor. All she could think of was Kayla's icy expression.

As soon as she was inside the door, her sweet gray friend brushed against her leg. When she felt his sidle, she snapped out of her daze, and everything that had happened that night came rushing back to her, almost bowling her over. She touched the bandage on her hand and winced.

Cloud was quite sensitive to her moods and his ears perked up in concern.

What's wrong, Lucy?

"Nothing, I'm fine. Just a crazy evening. I'm glad to be home with you, my sweet boy."

She didn't want Cloud to worry about her. She was meant to take care of him and not the other way around.

Part of Lucy wanted nothing more than to talk to Maya, but of course she couldn't use her phone right now. Tea. She needed her most calming tea and a relaxing black and white movie. And her cat.

As Lucy sat on her couch and pet Cloud's velvety fur, trying to lose herself in the 1938 Katherine Hepburn screwball comedy *Bringing Up Baby*, she couldn't help but ruminate about the evening's events. The conversation she had overheard in the hallway troubled her. It wasn't so much that Kayla sounded scared of the consequences the man was threatening her with. It was that Kayla seemed so eager to please him, like she couldn't stand disappointing the mystery man.

Even as she held her palm above her heart to reduce the throbbing, Lucy found herself feeling sorry for her foe. She knew Kayla could have taken a different path as soon as she found out Pierre Martel's true nature, but she didn't, and although that was her choice, the story that Noor told from their college years was one of a young woman who was seeking approval and found it in Pierre. To be his star student must have boosted her ego. And it was clear to Lucy that whoever Kayla was working for now would never give her what she needed. It was equally clear that there might not be an easy way out for Kayla even if she wanted one. Maybe it was like a dark magician version of the Mob.

In the end, she knew it didn't matter what Kayla's motivations were, Lucy had to keep the troubled woman from hurting anyone else with her song magic. Maybe things would take a turn for the better and Kayla wouldn't continue on with the choir since she failed her mission. Then Lucy could enjoy her time at Northbrook Fellowship Hall without any evil plots tainting her experience.

But if their interaction in the parking lot tonight was any indication, Kayla had no intent on stepping aside from whatever plans Scordatura had with the Northbrook Community Choir.

Lucy believed Kayla when she said tonight was just a warning. Kayla could do much more than damage a cell phone and cut her hand, just ask the poor mouse from Pierre's vocal studio. Lucy snuggled closer to Cloud, trying to shake off the sense that her entanglements with dark magicians were far from over, and somehow she had gotten herself into an even more dangerous situation this time.

Chapter 25

THE PHONE STORE WAS EMPTY of customers when Lucy arrived just after opening. She had wrapped the phone in an old kitchen towel.

"That doesn't look good," joked the man behind the counter. "Okay, triage time."

Lucy carefully unwrapped the phone, taking care not to spill any glass on the counter.

"Wow," he said. "What happened here?"

She hadn't considered that he would ask what caused the damage and she couldn't very well tell him a dark magician threw song magic at it. She was terrible at coming up with lies on the spot and she wished Maya were here. "Um…it was in an accident."

He made a slight frown and raised his eyebrow. "If you say so." He gingerly lifted the phone with pliers and held it up horizontal to the counter. "We don't usually see a screen this smashed without signs of warping to the structure."

"Do you think it might still work?"

"We'll find out soon. Can you leave it with me for an hour or so?"

"Sure. I will be at the coffee shop around the corner. I have my laptop with me. Here's my e-mail address if you need to reach me."

Lucy ordered a cup of hibiscus tea and settled into a corner of the outside patio with her back to the wall, where no one would be able to see her computer screen. She wanted to do some research while she was waiting.

She searched for Kayla Quinn. Thirty-two million search results came up. She added 'singer' and narrowed the results, then narrowed them further by adding the location.

Here was something intriguing. Apparently, Kayla used to provide dining entertainment singing opera arias at an Italian restaurant on Saturday nights. Giorgio's was an upscale joint located in the former warehouse district of downtown Northbrook, an area that was rapidly being revitalized and redeveloped into expensive condos. Lucy had never been there but had heard people from work talk about it, although not recently.

She searched for Giorgio's and found that it was listed as permanently closed. Interesting, but a dead end. Just before Lucy was going to begin a new search, an article caught her eye: "Mass Food Poisoning Sickens Diners."

Twenty-six patrons at the iconic downtown restaurant Giorgio's were treated for food poisoning last night, suffering from nausea, gastric upset, dizziness, and weakness. All were expected to fully recover. An investigation by the health department is underway and the restaurant is closed until further notice.

Lucy searched for related articles and found: "Giorgio's Mishap a Mystery."

Investigators found no obvious cause for the sudden illness of twenty-six patrons who dined at Giorgio's two weeks ago. No health violations were discovered. Samples from food in the refrigerators and freezers found no evidence of any common bacteria that would explain the outbreak. Owner Bobby Giorgio, the son of the original founder of Giorgio's, had the following statement: "We at Giorgio's are devastated by this event and are deeply sorry to our patrons who had a negative experience at our restaurant. Our kitchen and staff have the highest standards, and we consistently hold the highest health score rating. We ask for the support of the community as we move forward."

Poor Bobby, Lucy thought. She wasn't sure how you bounce back from something like that. No wonder they had closed. She certainly wouldn't go to a restaurant that had such a well-publicized outbreak like this.

Sure enough, an article written not too long after the incident announced the restaurant's closing, after fifty years in the same location. It was a heartbreaking report of the demise of a multi-generational dream, all because of one ill-fated night. One section of the article caught Lucy's eye.

Bobby Giorgio has agreed to sell the building to Everett Development Co. "They've been hounding us for three years to sell, so at least someone will be happy now…"

A theory began to take shape in Lucy's mind. She looked for information on Everett Development Co. and found that they had been working to buy out several buildings on that block for years, and since Bobby had finally sold a little over a year ago, the restaurant had already been razed and the area was poised for construction as luxury condominiums with upscale retail on the ground floor.

Lucy searched for the dates for Kayla's performances at Giorgio's and was horrified by what she had found.

Kayla had sung there on the night of the alleged food poisoning.

After everything she had seen in Sienna Falls Forest and then at the health expo, Lucy no longer felt paranoid about making connections between dark magicians and seemingly random events. In fact, she was quite sure it was no coincidence. Kayla used her song magic to sicken twenty-six people. She was a dangerous woman.

The thing that confused Lucy the most was that Kayla seemed to genuinely enjoy singing and performing. Had Kayla relished the chance to entertain the diners the first four times she had sung at the restaurant, before the incident? Had she worn a fancy dress and mesmerized them with her talent before the final night when she used her song magic to destroy a family business? Lucy couldn't imagine how Kayla could sing so beautifully some of the time, then turn around and use her gifts for evil.

An e-mail notification popped up from the phone repair shop. It was ready. Lucy packed up her laptop and returned to the store. Before she even reached the counter, the man said, "This was one of the strangest things I've seen. The damage was purely limited to the screen. I don't know what angle it was hit to crack it that badly but leave the core intact. You said it was in a car accident?"

She hadn't said that. She was pretty sure she just said 'accident,' but his assumption made sense.

"Yeah," she said, but felt her palms starting to sweat like they always did when she lied.

"Well, lucky break, for sure. Try booting it up."

Lucy half-smiled. "Yes, lucky." She entered her passcode on the smooth new screen. Sure enough, it powered up and seemed to be operating fine. "Awesome! How much do I owe you?"

He gave her the invoice and she paid for the repairs.

Now that she had her phone back, part of her wanted to text Maya and see if she was free so Lucy could update her on what had happened with Kayla yesterday and what she had found out about Giorgio's. But the other part of her longed for a normal day without thoughts of dark magicians and evil plots looming overhead. She needed to focus on other parts of her life.

Instead of reaching out to Maya, she went by the grocery store and bought a brownie mix and some wet food for Cloud.

When the brownies were in the oven and beginning to fill the house with that comforting, rich fragrance of butter, sugar, and chocolate, she sat down at the kitchen table with her bird identification cards. She needed to work harder to beat Tyler in the bird-off and now that the concert was over, this was her new top priority.

As she flipped through the cards, she sorted them into two piles, the ones she had identified correctly, and the ones she hadn't. Then she went through the incorrect pile again, sorting it into two more smaller piles of correct and incorrect, until she identified them all correctly. Then she shuffled the incorrect pile and repeated the exercise. Finally, she incorporated her trouble cards back into the full deck for next time.

By then, the brownies were baked, and she took them out of the oven to cool. She scanned through streaming movie options and settled on *Sullivan's Travels*, which starred one of her favorite actors, Veronica Lake, in a story about a young actress who accompanies a wealthy man across the country as he rides the trains, pretending to be a hobo. It made her think of the old man living alone in Brighton Island Nature Preserve, seeming to have the mental capacity to live in regular society, yet choosing an alternative lifestyle for reasons known only to him.

Cloud devoured the treat Lucy had brought him and then he settled in next to her on the couch while she ate brownies and drank orange chocolate tea. This was life, Lucy thought, not that crazy stuff out at Sienna Falls Forest. Not blocking Kayla's magic at a choir concert.

Lucy was frequently tormented by comparing the things she enjoyed with the things she perceived most people enjoyed, that she was *supposed to* like. Drinking at bars, dancing at parties, spa days with giggling girlfriends. Those had never been for Lucy, and she often wondered if that meant something was wrong with her.

As she grew older, she learned to accept herself for who she was, and revel in a quiet night and an old black and white movie. And now that she had Cloud, those hours spent were even more special to her. It had taken her a full forty years to get to the point where she stopped feeling bad about not being like the picture of the perfect, fun-loving woman in her head.

Yet, as soon as she felt like she settled into being herself, her life had suddenly changed. She found a best friend and animal magic in Maya, and now she had another new friend and song magic in Noor. And she enjoyed spending time with each of them, but at heart she knew she would always be an introvert and that was okay.

When the movie was over, Lucy plugged in her headphones, so as to not upset Cloud, and practiced bird call identification. Afterwards, she absentmindedly sang out a trill, imitating a type of sparrow, and the soundwave knocked Cloud's tiny mouse toy off the table. Even though the cat had seemed fast asleep, he sprung up to full attention, trounced across the table and caught the toy as it bounced on the ground.

Lucy had just discovered a new use for song magic, perhaps the best one yet.

The next ten minutes were spent with Lucy guiding cat toys with the invisible hand of sound magic, Cloud jetting across the wooden floors and sliding into the kitchen or leaping and twisting over the couch. It was mad, joyous mayhem. When he was tired, she gave him a treat. Then she watched another movie, ate another brownie, and before she knew it, the day was over, and she snuggled into bed with Cloud draped across her legs. Not a bad day at all.

Chapter 26

AS MUCH AS LUCY HAD needed Sunday to relax and reenergize, she felt a tinge of disappointment when she remembered that Maya was out for a few days at a wildlife conference. She wouldn't get to talk with her friend again until Thursday, which seemed like forever away.

The Monday morning meeting made Lucy remember what work had been like before Maya came to TerraPlaya. Lucy had always crept in early to make her morning tea before the weekly meeting, since social interactions made her anxious, and tea soothed her nerves. Even with that fortification, she sat uncomfortably in the conference room, dreading being called upon by Anuk to report on her work progress. Once Maya had come on board, the meetings barely phased Lucy any longer because she knew she had a friend to sit next to and support her.

Not that her other co-workers weren't nice or friendly enough. They were, it's just that Lucy didn't have much in common with them and it made her long to be left alone in her little cubicle facing the courtyard.

She was trying to concentrate as Anuk enthusiastically reported on the last quarter profits of the office and the bright outlook for their future. Of course, Lucy was happy to hear the office was doing well and that her job was secure. There was a time last year when worries about downsizing after they had been acquired by a larger company had dampened the spirit of the office severely, and she was grateful they had emerged stronger and more resilient, with several new clients and contracts.

Lucy had lost track of what Anuk was saying until she suddenly realized he seemed to be talking to her.

"…and that should be an interesting new opportunity for you, Lucy and Tyler. I will be forwarding you the invitation from the project lead for training this afternoon."

Tyler nodded his head in response, and his expression seemed pleased, instead of his normal look of sheer boredom, so Lucy could only assume it was a good thing and nodded her head in solidarity.

As Anuk turned to other topics, the man sitting next to Lucy gave her a look and she realized she was drumming her fingers on the arm rest of her chair. She gave an awkward shrug and forced her hands to relax in her lap.

Her mind was racing, wondering what Anuk had said. It could be anything. Would she have to work together with Tyler? That would be a first. At most, they reviewed each other's maps for quality control, since Anuk usually assigned a single mapping support specialist per project. She told herself there was no point in worrying, since she would find out more when she saw the meeting appointment, but that did little to settle her worried mind. She brought her morning white pear tea to her nose and focused on the aroma, then took a sip and imagined the liquid soothing her system as it trickled down her throat.

She was the first one to jet out of the conference room after Anuk dismissed them, and a calm enveloped her when she reached her cubicle. She took a moment to stare outside into the courtyard, noting a squirrel at the base of the large oak tree, and a mockingbird perched on the fence post. Aaah…even just looking at nature from inside the office centered her.

Thankfully, when she turned back to work and woke up her computer, the invitation was in her inbox. She scanned the e-mail, then sat back in her chair. This was a different kind of project, nothing like her regular daily tasks. TerraPlaya's parent company had a federal contract to assist with disaster recovery, and Lucy knew that several other offices supported that program. Now there was a company-wide search for staff who knew the mapping program she and Tyler used. But instead of making maps, they would be analyzing the aerial photography that was flown after the recent hurricane on the east coast.

Lucy loved making maps to go along with the technical reports the other staff produced, but it was entirely new for her to use her skills to help communities and people, and that was a different type of fulfillment that she didn't normally get from work. Just when she had thought the only new avenues for her were outside the office, such as fieldwork and bird surveys, she realized there were probably lots of other novel applications of her skills that could be performed within the comfort of her cubicle. That gave her something to think about.

She ate lunch alone in the courtyard, or at least not with any other humans, as she took the opportunity to feed her squirrel buddy some nuts and say hello. Then she went through her bird identification flashcards. Maya would be proud of her dedication.

The afternoon training went well, and Lucy felt confident that she would be able to assist on the project, even though it required different parts of the software than she normally used. So, she was surprised when an hour later, after she was well into the new assignment, a shadow crossed her desk.

It was Tyler. And he was standing over her, looking sheepish.

"Hey Lucy…so, uh, interesting assignment, huh?" he said.

"Yes, it really is," she replied, giving him time to get to the point of his unusual visit to her cubicle.

Tyler looked at her computer screen. "Yeah. Looks like you are digging in already."

"Yep. Did you need something?" Lucy asked as kindly as she could, since she could tell Tyler was struggling with expressing himself.

"Well yeah, I didn't quite catch some of what the trainer was saying. Since you seemed to have it down already, maybe you could show me?"

Lucy was stunned. Tyler was admitting that he needed help from her? No time to gloat though, he was her teammate, and this project was about much more than one upping her colleague, it was about rebuilding lives. "Of course, which part in particular?"

His face reddened to the shade of a pomegranate, and he stumbled through his words, "Um, yeah, maybe you could start from the beginning?"

"Absolutely—pull up a chair."

She spent the next twenty minutes demonstrating the process to Tyler, who took dutiful notes. When they were done, he stood up, looking more optimistic than he did when he first came over.

"Thanks so much, I really appreciate this," he said.

"No problem, anytime," said Lucy.

He started to leave, then turned around. "How's your birding practice going?" he asked.

"Good, good," she said, not wanting to reveal just how much time and energy she planned to invest in order to beat him. "How about you?"

"Not too bad. I even signed up for an online course from Audubon."

It shocked Lucy that he would share that with her, that he wasn't playing it cool. Or was he trying to tell her how serious he was about the opportunity? The paranoid part of Lucy also worried that this was some psychological warfare move and he was trying to freak her out. If that was his plan, it was the wrong move because it only made her determined to study harder.

"That's great, Tyler. Let me know if it's any good," Lucy said, as if she didn't have a care in the world.

"Will do. Thanks again for the help." And with that, he was gone.

Lucy saved her work and packed up her things to go home. It occurred to her that with Maya out and choir not until Wednesday, she had nearly three days in a row free from magic and drama and she was going to enjoy it.

Chapter 27

LUCY'S HEART SANK WHEN SHE saw Kayla walk into the rehearsal room at the Fellowship Hall on Wednesday. She had hoped with all her might that Kayla would drop out of the choir after her failure to complete her assignment at the concert. For a second, Lucy even considered that maybe Kayla was just here to sing now, but she could hear Maya's voice in her head questioning her naivety.

No, if Kayla is here, then it isn't over, she told herself.

Panic began to set in, so Lucy applied her go-to technique, making a list of options and their pros and cons. Using a pencil and paper was ideal, but by now she could easily do the exercise in her head.

One option would be that she could stay in the choir no matter what, no matter how many times she had to try and thwart Scordatura. That would be exhausting and not the enjoyable outlet she had longed for when she joined the group. But maybe they would give up and eventually it would just be a normal, relaxed community choir where her biggest worry would be learning the music.

Another option would be to quit the choir and give up on a decades-long dream. After all, technically she had successfully auditioned, was accepted, and sang in a concert, so she had accomplished her original goal. But she was finally starting to recognize the same faces in her alto section, and even make some small talk with her neighbor singers. She didn't want to give that up. Not to mention she'd be leaving the entire choir vulnerable and abandoning Noor.

Lastly, she could wait and see what happened and reassess the situation later. That seemed like the best option for now because she didn't have all the information yet. She and Maya still needed to find a way to learn more about Scordatura and their endgame. And she wanted to talk it through with Noor. If Noor wanted to quit, then that might change things.

An older man with gray hair, a bushy mustache and boxed beard strode in and stood behind the music stand in the center of the room. He wore an old-fashioned vest over a fitted shirt and was polished right down to his shiny black oxford shoes. He waited for the singers to quiet down and then spoke. "I'm sure you are all wondering where Darlene is. I have the misfortune of telling you that she has fallen ill and is in the hospital recovering."

Shocked whispers and expressions of sympathy for their fallen leader filled the room. The man continued, "I know she loved this choir very much and she wouldn't mind me sharing this information with you. Her prognosis is very good, but unfortunately, she will not be able to rehearse with you for the next concert. The board has hired me to fill in for her until after the new year. My name is Ivan Novak, and I am your new director."

Lucy caught Noor's eyes and both women knew what the other was thinking. That this was no coincidence and whatever happened to Darlene was no accident.

"I know it is a longstanding tradition for this choir to perform Handel's *Messiah* every December with the community orchestra and I hope you will join me in preparing the best concert Northbrook has ever heard, to honor Darlene." He gave a broad smile that showed perfect, white teeth, and even though the words were pleasant enough, he reminded Lucy of a smug crocodile.

Without further discussion, Ivan led the group through warmups, then the choir librarian passed a score out to each singer. The remainder of the first half of the rehearsal was a run-through of the piece, which made Lucy miserable. Most of the choir had sung the piece before, but Lucy had not, so she mostly mouthed the words as she tried to pick out her part, too timid to sing out when she was struggling to follow along. It had taken her weeks to feel comfortable with her part to the *Requiem*, and now she had to start over again. She had never been so glad for the break to be announced.

Noor waited for her in the hallway, and they hurried out to the parking lot where they could talk in private.

"What was that all about? What did they do to Darlene?" said Noor.

"I don't know where to begin—I have so many things to tell you." She filled Noor in on the conversation she overheard after the concert and the warning from Kayla. She held up her bandaged hand.

Noor's eyes widened. "She broke your phone and cut you? That's messed up. I don't like this at all."

"Yeah, and she pretty much implied this was the least of what she could and would do."

"I don't doubt that anymore," said Noor. "I had hoped that there was a limit to how far she would go, but if she has been working with people like Pierre Martel for all these years, she might be a murderer for all I know."

"You're right, it's possible." Lucy told her about the incident at Giorgio's.

Noor shook her head in disbelief. "She's a monster. And apparently, she isn't even very good at song magic, according to her employer. That's terrifying if she's the incompetent one."

"So, do we walk away?" asked Lucy. "I never wanted to be a superhero, I just wanted to sing in a choir."

"I know, Lucy, that sucks. But I can't quit the choir and leave all these blissfully ignorant people in the hands of Scordatura. And even if we did, it's too late, we both see dark magic being used all around us. We'll never be able to shut it out, so may as well face it."

Lucy's stomach churned with the truth of Noor's words. She could run away from the choir, but she could never escape the reality of the magical world unveiled. There was no question that what Maya had accidentally awoken in her was both a blessing and a curse. But somehow it wasn't burdening Maya the same way it weighed on Lucy. Since the forest battle, Maya hadn't had any interactions with dark magicians. Perhaps Lucy had the curse of double magic. Maybe the more she learned, the worse it would be.

Their breaktime was up so they made their way back to the rehearsal room, where they found Kayla laughing and joking with Ivan. Lucy and Noor shared a look, the fact that the two already knew each other confirmed everything they had dreaded.

Ivan readied the choir and jumped right into reading through the remainder of the piece. At the end of the rehearsal, he thanked the group for their hard work.

"I see why Darlene enjoyed working with you all," he said in a charming tone, "and I'm looking forward to the next seven weeks. Oh, and one more thing. Someone asked during the break when solo auditions would be. I'm told that Darlene allowed members of the choir to audition for these parts, but I'm a little old school. The December concert always has the best tickets sales, and we want to lure as many people in as possible to fund the rest of the season. I think you'll be surprised and delighted when I announce the fantastic names we have signed on as our soloists this year. Great rehearsal, everyone!"

On the way out, Kayla turned around and gave Lucy a satisfied little smirk. Lucy pretended she didn't see and went to look for Noor.

"Well, we know who, when, and where now. The concert is set for December 14th. And they are bringing in their own people, all four soloists, plus they'll still have Kayla as back up. We just don't know exactly what they will do or why."

"At least that gives us some time to plan," said Noor. "We need to learn more advanced song magic, maybe call in some reinforcements."

"I'm open to any suggestions. Let's loop Maya in too. Even if she can't do song magic, she can help in other ways." Lucy needed her best friend beside her on this.

"Definitely. We'll figure this out," said Noor.

"Yeah," said Lucy with a sigh. "We have to."

Chapter 28

IT WAS A PERFECT DAY in the office courtyard, the fall breeze rustling the leaves on the giant live oak and the fall wildflowers, a bed of purple aster and blue sage, filling the air with a sweet fragrance. The song of a cardinal brought melody to the space, and Lucy breathed in the sunshine and fresh air. She was learning to savor each beautiful, peaceful moment in her life.

Maya soon joined her, and the women unpacked their lunches while Lucy filled her friend in on everything she missed.

"I can't believe I'm just hearing about all of this. Lita and I should have walked you to the car after the concert. I feel awful."

"Nah, you can't be my bodyguard, you know. And I can't be afraid all the time."

Maya stared at her friend as if seeing her in a new light. "You know, Lucy, you are not the same person you were when I first met you. Aren't you scared?"

Lucy laughed. "Of course. I can barely sleep at night worrying about Kayla and Scordatura and dark animal magicians and dark song magicians, and who knows what else is out there. I feel like I'm trapped in a horror movie. But if I let myself start to drown in it, I can't even get up in the morning. So instead, I've decided that I have no choice but to learn more magic to defend myself."

"Wow," said Maya, her mouth hanging open, "that's inspiring."

"Thanks. In truth, Noor also inspired me. I asked her if we should just drop out of the choir when we learned about Ivan Novak, but she said she couldn't leave all those people unprotected."

"Hmm. Noor does seem like one of the good ones. Just so long as you don't spend all your time singing with Noor and abandon us lowly animal magic users."

Lucy realized that Maya had been feeling left out, with everything that had happened with the choir, not to mention that despite her best efforts, Maya was never able to excel in animal magic like Lucy had. Even though Maya knew her magic was what she needed to follow her life's passion in wildlife conservation, that was little consolation when she needed to help her friend battle dark magicians.

"Never," said Lucy. "In fact, I told Noor the three of us need to get together and come up with a plan. Even though you can't do song magic, that doesn't mean we don't need you."

Maya nodded. "I'm always on team Lucy."

"That means everything."

"Why don't the three of us meet up at lita's on Saturday night? She really wants to meet Noor."

"Sounds good. Let me text and ask her."

Lucy also filled Maya in on her interaction with Tyler, and the new disaster recovery project she was working on.

"That's really cool. I had no idea there were so many different ways to use that software besides maps."

"Oh yeah, it's endless really. I've only ever scratched the surface since I don't know how to program, but even as a basic user there are a lot of ways it could be used to help people."

"You seem excited about this. That's great. Just don't let this new avenue distract you from the bird-off."

"Hah—never! I've been studying like a madwoman, especially since Tyler told me he is taking that class."

#   #   #

Lucy had just finished reviewing bird habitats when her phone chimed. It was a text from Noor telling her to look at a link. It was an article about Pierre Martel, who had apparently returned to France to resume his career as a professor of voice at a prestigious music conservatory. It was comforting to know that he was no longer working in the U.S., but Lucy wasn't quite sure why the article was relevant to their current situation.

She kept reading as the story described his illustrious career as a teacher and performer. And then she saw it: At one time Pierre Martel had taught at the same university as Ivan Novak. Together they formed a new vocal and instrumental performance group specializing in early baroque music, and it became quite the elite ensemble, touring all over Europe to great acclaim.

Surely it was no coincidence that Kayla studied with Pierre and now suddenly Pierre's old colleague was their new conductor. But how did Ivan connect to Scordatura Solutions—was he part of their corporation? Lucy searched the internet for both sets of key words but found nothing. She didn't really expect to find any proof they were connected online, but it was worth a shot.

There was no reason to believe the board of the Northbrook Community Choir had any connections to Scordatura, since prior to Kayla joining, they hadn't sponsored the choir before or been involved with it as far as Lucy knew. So, what led the board to hire Ivan Novak? Had it been Kayla's suggestion?

She had one idea how they might find out. She texted Noor back and made plans for Saturday morning.

Darlene Braxton sat up in her hospital bed as the two women entered. "Ladies, so nice of you to come and visit me. I'm so glad you called."

"We're glad you wanted visitors," said Lucy. "We brought you these."

Lucy put the flowers on the table in Darlene's room as she looked around at the monitors and IV pole. Darlene looked pale and her eyes were sunken, but she looked alert enough.

"Thanks for the flowers."

"You're welcome," said Noor. "We were all shocked to find out you were in the hospital. What happened, if you don't mind me asking?"

said Noor.

Darlene sat up and squinted her eyes as she struggled to recall. "I remember there was a sudden noise, a sort of grating sound, like metal on metal, then so much pressure like my head was going to explode. I remember intense nausea. Then everything went black, and I woke up here."

"Oh my gosh, that's awful," said Lucy.

"Do the doctors have any idea what happened?" asked Noor.

Darlene shook her head. "They aren't sure—all the tests have been inconclusive. They say I have a concussion, but that might have been from when I hit the pavement."

Noor nodded sympathetically. "How are you feeling now?"

Darlene rested her head back on the pillow, as if remembering where she was, lying in a hospital bed. "I'm okay, I guess. I still have a headache, but the worst part is that I just can't think straight. I lose my train of thought, and it's hard to remember things."

"That sounds rough," said Noor. "I hope you get better soon. We all miss you."

A wistful smile crossed Darlene's face. "I miss you all too. The choir is one of my favorite things in life. How is the new director treating you?"

Noor forced herself to keep a neutral face. "He seems okay so far."

"I'm surprised the board was able to find a substitute director so quickly," Lucy said.

"Ah, well we were lucky because our new sponsor heard about our predicament, and they happened to know that Ivan was available for a short-term position. Of course, the board jumped at the opportunity to have someone with his resume fill in."

"Of course," said Noor.

"I hate to miss the holiday concert," said Darlene. "You know it's the biggest event of our season, the 'Sing it Yourself *Messiah*.' Over a thousand people attend each year. The community orchestra plays with us, and the audience is invited to sing along with the chorus parts. It's intense."

Lucy's eyes widened and her stomach began to churn. She had no idea it was that big a deal. Over a thousand people would need protection from Scordatura. They definitely needed backup.

Lucy and Noor were quiet as they navigated the hospital corridors toward the exit. As soon as they reached the open air, Lucy turned and asked, "So, what do you think?"

"There's no way to know, but Darlene's illness could have been caused by a sonic attack of some kind. Concussion and memory problems are known symptoms."

"Could your song magic help with her healing?"

"Maybe. I need to do some more research first, though."

"At any rate, it does seem that Scordatura is responsible for taking her out of the picture, with Ivan waiting in the wings to take over. Darlene's lucky she wasn't hurt even worse."

"Yeah, I'm afraid you're right," said Noor.

Lucy stopped in front of her car and turned to face Noor. "Are we in over our heads?"

"Probably. But what choice do we have? One thousand people…"

Chapter 29

EVERYTHING ABOUT MAYA'S GRANDMOTHER'S HOUSE was imbued with the feeling of home. The bright blue walls of the small living room and the earthy gold of the kitchen were cheerful and cozy. The aromatics of meat stewing in cumin, tomatoes, peppers, garlic, and onion filled the house and made Lucy's mouth water the moment she stepped in the front door.

Maya was already there, and Lucy had carpooled with Noor so her new friend wouldn't have to arrive alone at a complete stranger's house. But knowing how friendly Noor and Carmela both were, Lucy figured they would be comfortable together in no time.

Maya did introductions and ushered her guests inside.

"Thank you for having me, Mrs. Morales," said Noor.

"Please—call me Carmela," said the older woman.

Noor nodded. "They tell me that you recognized my song magic at the recital? Even though you don't practice it yourself?"

Carmela gave a secretive smile. "All true, child. But first we must eat."

Noor gave Maya a puzzled look.

"No serious business until after the meal. Lita says it ruins the taste of the food," Maya explained with a shrug.

"It does!" Carmela said, shaking her head. "You girls set the table while

I finish up the cooking."

Lucy and Noor followed as Maya showed them where the table settings were. With so many hands, the silverware, cloth napkins, and placemats were soon ready and waiting for the feast, and glasses were filled with homebrewed sun tea with sprigs of mint.

The women made small talk as they savored the carne guisada, chunks of lean beef steak that had simmered all day in spices, along with pinto beans and rice. Lucy took one bite and was in paradise. She had forgotten how incredible Carmela's cooking was and realized she hadn't eaten such a delicious meal since the last time she had been here.

This time, Carmela surprised them with a tres leches cake for dessert, and even though Lucy swore she couldn't eat another bite, she somehow managed a small slice. The cake was light and spongy with sweet cream on top, the perfect complement to their meal.

Finally, the food was eaten, the dining room cleared, the leftovers packed away, and Carmela declared it was now time for a serious discussion. She took her place in her big green armchair and the younger women sat on the couch.

Carmela's eyes rested on Noor. "Maya tells me you learned song magic at university."

"Yes, although until recently I didn't use it very often," said Noor.

"And you, Lucy, have found yourself once again entangled with dark magicians," Carmela said.

Lucy protested, "Yes, but it's not my fault! All I did was join a community choir."

Carmela nodded knowingly. "My poor child. When you get to be my age, you begin to see the balance in the world—light attracts dark, I'm afraid."

"Are you saying that since I learned light magic, I'll always find dark magic?" said Lucy, none too pleased with the idea.

"Perhaps. It's just a notion of an old woman," said Carmela. "Think nothing of it."

"A very wise woman," said Maya. "I wouldn't discount anything you say."

"But isn't part of that just not seeing something until you recognize it for what it is?" said Noor.

"Yes!" said Lucy. "Like how I see song magic all around me now… although, it wasn't the same with animal magic."

"Hmmm. I didn't consider that," said Maya. "Lita, do you think fewer people use animal magic?"

Carmela tilted her head as she considered this. "I couldn't say—maybe so. But we do live in an urban environment. We have separated ourselves from animals for the most part. But music, that's different."

"That must be it—we've infused every aspect of our lives with music," said Lucy.

"So maybe there are more opportunities to use song magic," said Noor, "and therefore more chances for us to notice it."

There were nods of agreement all around. Then Carmela leaned forward, her eyes dark and serious. "Even though my mother practiced animal magic and I could recognize magic, it wasn't part of my life. She kept me out of any danger. But you three, I worry about your safety."

"I know, lita. We'll be careful," said Maya.

"Careful? What does that mean, cariño? How will you protect yourself from such powerful people and is it wise to face them?" said Carmela, her brows pinched with worry.

Noor stepped in, "I know we just met, but Lucy and Maya are the strongest women I know. We will take care of each other. I will do my best to make sure nothing happens to your granddaughter."

"We won't be rash; we know when to walk away," said Maya.

Lucy cringed at the statement, because she worried they were past that point. They were in too deep now and there was no way out without leaving a thousand people to suffer the consequences. There could be no walking away, only the chance of a crushing defeat that could leave them hurt or worse, in the hospital like Darlene.

Her silence on the matter didn't escape Carmela's observation. "And you, Lucy? I heard about the cut on your hand. Is your judgement too clouded to see the gravity of the situation?"

"No," said Lucy slowly, "I see it all as clear as crystal. Maya and I battled the dark magicians in Sienna Falls to protect a forest full of innocent creatures. How can we turn our back on the friends, neighbors, and families of our fellow singers, people who are unknowingly putting themselves in danger just to support us?"

"She's right," said Noor.

"We'll be okay. We have each other, and we have Jeremy and Silver as reinforcements," said Maya.

Carmela sat back in her chair and laughed. "It seems I'm outnumbered, but I'm not as worried anymore. Seeing you girls sitting there, I see an aura of strength. Three is a very powerful number in magic. If you stick together, you can do anything, I have no doubt."

Lucy, Maya, and Noor exchanged glances and grinned.

"If we're doing this, then we need to come up with a plan," said Lucy. She always felt better with a plan.

"That's what I like to hear," said Carmela. "Sensible. Plan, prepare, call in backup. That's the way to overcome any obstacle."

"We need more information. What is Scordatura trying to do?" said Noor.

"Well, how can we find out? Last time we used Lucy's animal magic to do a little light spying. Could we do that again?" said Maya.

"Maybe. We'll need to do some research," said Lucy. "Scordatura's facility isn't in the middle of the forest. There's bound to be security."

Maya and Carmela looked at one another. "Daniel!"

"Who's Daniel?" asked Noor.

"Let me guess," said Lucy, "your cousin's neighbor's doctor's son?"

Maya cracked up laughing. "You're not far off. Daniel is my uncle's business partner's son. They contracted him out to do security audits at the new branches. He's brilliant."

"And you think he'd help us?" asked Lucy.

"No harm in asking," said Maya.

"Alright. Step one is consulting with Daniel so we can gather more information," said Noor.

"Yep, I'll contact him tomorrow," said Maya.

"And I'll research their facility," said Lucy, pleased that she now had one simple step to focus on after weeks of feeling like things were swirling out of control.

"And I'll try not to worry too much," said Carmela, causing the four women to laugh again. "Who wants more cake?"

Chapter 30

THE MONDAY MORNING MEETING WAS agonizing as Anuk droned on about changes to corporate policy and reviewing assignments. Not that Lucy didn't care about what he was saying, just that she couldn't wait until lunchtime to find out if Maya had talked with Daniel, and to share what she had learned from her research on Scordatura.

"Lucy, Tyler, they have been very pleased with your efforts on the disaster recovery program. In fact, the project manager confided in me that not everyone was so quick to catch on after the training," said Anuk.

Tyler looked down, avoiding Lucy's eyes. He needn't have, since she was not so petty as to make a coworker feel small for asking for help. The training really was quite insufficient, Lucy had just always excelled at internalizing information. It had made school easier for her and balanced out some of the disadvantages that being quiet and anxious in class brought with it.

The compliment made Lucy blush; she hated being called out, even for positive things, but in truth she felt proud. Something about the project has sparked a new interest in her work, similar to the way that the fieldwork had. It was surprising that projects completed within the confines of her cubicle could be so satisfying, but perhaps that was because her life outside had become so exciting, even occasionally harrowing, that a calm day in the office was a treat.

"In fact, they have asked that I send one of you to the South Carolina office to assist in some related work using a GPS to collect additional information on the ground. It would be a full weeklong assignment."

Before Lucy could even begin to think through the implications of that, Tyler blurted out. "I can do it."

Her initial reaction was to be annoyed that Tyler was once again trying to hoard all available opportunities at this company, but then she realized in this case it was a good thing. She couldn't miss choir practice. She didn't want to leave Cloud alone for too long, even with Maya catsitting. And most importantly, she had to be in Northbrook to progress their preparations for the winter concert.

"Excellent—thank you for volunteering, Tyler. I will put you in touch with the project lead and you can coordinate with the travel department," said Anuk.

Tyler wore a smirk on his face until Anuk added, "Of course, this means that Lucy will need to accompany Maya on the second bird survey at Brighton Island."

Lucy coughed to hold back a laughing snort as she saw Tyler's gloat morph into surprise, then disappointment. Maya stole a glance at Lucy, the corners of her mouth turned up, trying not to broadcast her joy.

Three hours later, the two women sat in the courtyard on another glorious fall day. A blue jay cawed from the oak tree, orange and black fritillary butterflies fluttered around the passion vine climbing the trellis.

"Did you get in touch with Daniel?" Lucy asked, then took a bite of her sandwich.

"Yep. He's in."

"What did you tell him? Does he know about your animal magic and about song magic?"

"Nah. That's on a need-to-know basis. Everyone who knows my family accepts a certain amount of oddness, but they know we are always on the good side."

"So, what does he need from us?"

"If he has the location of the building, he can do a little recon, try to figure out their security situation. Did you have any luck figuring out where the offices are?"

"Maybe," said Lucy. "There's the warehouse, of course, where they ship the CDs and instructional books from. But would they discuss their dark magic business there, keep files there?"

"Why not? What better place to do a shady dealing?"

"I can't imagine the Missy Zimmers of the world sitting in some dank office in an industrial park, meeting clients there."

"Hmmm. I suppose so. Did you find another possibility?"

"Yes, I checked the address on the company's initial filing on the SEC database. It's a suite in an office building downtown."

"Ugh. The question is, even if the CEO of Scordatura has a nice shiny office, would they keep their most incriminating files there? Or in a warehouse on the edge of town?"

Lucy shrugged. "I have no idea."

"Do you remember what year the company filed with the SEC?" asked Maya.

"Not the exact year, but I recall it was the early eighties."

"Then they probably have hardcopy files from back then, and that would be in a warehouse. A decade plus of paper files would be too bulky for a fancy office."

"That brings up another issue, though. Maybe we'd find old files on paper in the warehouse, but what about recent dealings? The stuff we're looking for is probably digital now, and I'm not a hacker..."

Maya frowned. "All good points. Let's see what Daniel can find out for both locations. If we uncover some information about old projects, it could still help us; we're kind of flying blind here about what Scordatura does and how they do it. And even *I* don't know anyone willing to hack into a private business. At least without explaining more than we can risk sharing."

"Okay, I'll send you the two locations and we can revisit this after Daniel has a chance to investigate."

Lucy stopped to get gas on the way home from work and suddenly had a craving for an orange soda. The drink held fond memories for her from her college days when she would stay up late chugging Sunkist and eating Skittles as she studied for finals.

The atmosphere inside the little convenience store was tense the moment she entered. A burly man was yelling at the clerk behind the counter, in such a heated argument that neither turned her way when the door chimed. She considered turning around and leaving, but something made her stay, and she continued to listen as she made her way to the beverage refrigerators along the back wall. She cautiously surveyed the exit options, just to be on the safe side, and clutched her phone in case she needed to dial the police.

"I *did* give you a twenty!" screamed the man. "You're trying to scam me."

The clerk shook his head. "No, you gave me a ten. You're the one trying to pull a fast one. I have to pay for any shortages, you know?"

"Yeah, right, you mean you pocket any money you overcharge."

"Look, sir, you gave me a ten. Please take your purchases and leave."

"I'm not going anywhere," the customer snarled. "I'm standing right here until I get my change. And don't even think of ringing up any other customers." He stood with his body pressed up against the counter, physically blocking the checkout area.

Well, this wasn't what Lucy was expecting when she stopped to get a drink. She certainly didn't want to confront that situation head on. Perhaps she should try and make a graceful exit and pray she could escape unnoticed.

The sound system was blaring "Bitter Sweet Symphony" by The Verve, a popular song she remembered from her high school days. Even though it wasn't her choice of music, she knew every word by heart, it was played on the radio so much. That gave her an idea. Noor had mentioned using song magic to calm angry people. Maybe this was her chance to try it out. She softly started singing along with the music as she pretended to peruse the potato chips.

She imagined her soundwaves traveling over the shelves towards the two men, first attempting to build a protective barrier around the clerk, and then working to calm the belligerent customer. Trying to avoid looking directly at the pair, she monitored them in the security mirrors angled to catch shoplifters. The man was not only red-faced, like a giant pimple about to explode, but his aura was practically fire. Lucy pictured her singing as a steady rainfall, extinguishing his flames of anger. She also took a page from Noor's book and pushed an image of the man relaxing on his couch, watching football, drinking beer, into him along with her song.

Almost immediately, the man's blazing aura gradually began to shrink, and by the end of the song it was a manageable orange glow.

"You know what—this isn't worth my time. I could be home right now, drinking these. But I'm never coming back here and I'm telling all my friends what a scam this place is," the man barked, then grabbed his six pack of beer and stormed out.

"So sad, you will be missed," muttered the clerk under his breath when the man was out of earshot.

Lucy waited a moment to make sure the angry man wouldn't return, but when she saw his car leave the lot, she approached the clerk and put her Sunkist and Skittles on the counter.

"You must be my lucky charm, ma'am," the clerk said.

"Oh? Why do you say that?" Lucy asked innocently.

"That guy was pissed. I thought he was going to pull a gun or something. But then you come in and he suddenly calms down. You're like a lion tamer."

"I didn't do anything," she protested, wondering if he could somehow sense her interference in the matter.

"If you say so. Enjoy your snacks."

She took the items and returned to her car. Once inside, she let out a shudder. That was pretty stupid, she thought. It would have been much safer to leave immediately after she recognized the hostile situation. But there was no point in beating herself up over her questionable choice now.

Instead, she sat back in the driver's seat and allowed herself a moment of pride. After all, she had thought on her feet in a stressful situation and helped the poor clerk who probably suffers constant abuse from customers. At least this one time she was able to help avoid a much worse outcome. Song magic was becoming a part of her, just like animal magic.

Chapter 31

PARKED JUST OUT OF VIEW of the small warehouse, the three women hunched down in Noor's mom's borrowed SUV, which had the trunk space needed for their version of spy gear, a harp and two animal cages. They were dressed in all black with cheap ski masks covering their faces. The last thing they needed was to alert Scordatura that they were poking around in their business if they got caught on camera. Better for them to think they were random thieves hoping to score resalable goods from the warehouse.

"Ready, ladies? Step one, Lucy," said Maya.

Lucy closed her eyes and scanned the area for wildlife, sensing the presence of each individual animal and mentally sorting by species and size. "Got one that might work," she said. She reached out to a black vulture roosting on a light pole, asking for his help. The bird acquiesced, and Lucy watched through his eyes as he swooped down from the pole and flew towards the front of the warehouse. At Lucy's direction, the bird landed atop the security camera, scooched to the back, then spread out his wings, gave a little jump and landed with full force on the back of the camera, forcing it to point upward at the sky. Lucy thanked the bird and released him.

"Camera redirected," said Lucy. Her voice sounded steady, but it was only because she was pretending to be Sidney Bristow from *Alias*. Inside, she was questioning every life decision that led her to this ridiculous situation and couldn't stop the trembling in her hands.

"Let's roll," said Maya, and Noor edged the car forward until she stopped in the shade of a tree in the parking lot.

"Step two—Noor, you're up."

Noor nodded and retrieved her Celtic lap harp from the trunk. Lucy exited the car and followed Noor to the front entrance, which was a recessed alcove with a thick glass door and concrete walls. Noor began to play her harp just around the corner from the alcove, out of sight of the front door. Lucy rapped on the door three times in succession, then sprinted around the corner. The timing was crucial for this part. Lucy focused on directing Noor's song magic towards the front door.

It only took one minute for the security guard to appear to inspect the noise. He cracked the door tentatively, his face confused when he heard the lyrical harp sounds. He let out a mighty yawn, took one labored step, then another. Two more steps and he would round the corner. Lucy concentrated with all her might, humming along with the tune, willing the soothing soundwaves to reach his brain. He yawned again, took one more step, and on the fourth, he crumpled to the ground and began to snore.

This was Lucy's cue and she leapt over the sleeping man, carrying two small cages with her. Daniel had been able to confirm the outside camera and the night security guard, but he could only guess about the inside.

Lucy cracked the front door just enough to allow the tarantula she released from the small cage to go through. She directed him up the wall, onto the ceiling, seeing through his eyes. The hallway going straight dead ended into double metal doors Lucy guessed connected to the warehouse. Lucy didn't see any more cameras on the ceiling, so she had the spider turn down the hallway to the right.

She saw one camera on the ceiling next to an office door, a dome style unit just as Daniel predicted. She navigated the tarantula, while still staying out of view around the corner, and positioned his body so that it covered the camera eye. She implored him to stay put while she explored the adjacent room.

The office door was locked, but Lucy was prepared, practice makes perfect. She let out a low sound, directing her voice like a narrow laser beam towards the keyhole, listening to the sounds that bounced back, like a bat with echolocation, until she found just the right vibration and she heard the click of the lock. She turned the handle gently, then released the mouse she had brought in the second cage through the crack in the door.

Lucy surveyed the room through the mouse. It appeared empty, and there were no signs of a security camera. There were filing cabinets, an entire wall of them, four drawers tall. She would never have time to look through all of these. Noor couldn't keep the man asleep with her magic forever, not with the concentration it took. She recaptured the mouse and set to work, using her phone as a flashlight. She picked a cabinet at random and scanned the folder labels, names and dates, some with just a few sheets and some files several inches thick. Lucy pulled one out.

Dougherty's, 1982. That name sounded familiar to Lucy. As she read on, she remembered hearing about it in a documentary on unexplained phenomena. Since the 1950s, Dougherty department store was the biggest business in Northbrook, four stories tall, until 1982 when strange things started happening. Customers insisted the store was haunted, that they felt an evil presence inside the building, and were consumed with a sense of doom. With no way to combat what Dougherty's said was mass hysteria, the business was forced to shutter. But it wasn't hysteria, it was Scordatura, using song magic.

As much as Lucy wanted to read more about the case, she had only a few minutes to try and find something they could actually use. She rummaged through the folder, her stomach clenching as she discovered the breadth of Scordatura's operations. Many of the cases were minor, with trivial, petty consequences, or small monetary rewards, like winning a beauty pageant over another contestant or sabotaging a car race.

And then Lucy moved to the last cabinet and found a file that took up nearly the entire drawer. *Project Puppet, 1992.* Lucy gasped as she read the document. She took out her phone and snapped photos of random pages, not taking the time to read them, just trying to get as much information recorded as she could. Then a text popped up on her phone.

Maya: Guard awake. Inside.

Shit! Lucy had taken too much time. Now she was trapped. In this situation, the plan was for Noor to run off into the woods and rendezvous with Maya at the gas station around the corner. She was on her own. Her heart started racing and she could barely get a breath in. Don't panic, she told herself. Focus.

She took a deep breath and scanned the area again for animals she could use to help her. She felt the presence of the tarantula and mouse she had brought, a plethora of insects, several birds roosting for the night, a huge raccoon ambling around looking for scraps, rats, and squirrels.

What she needed was a diversion, one that would take the guard to the back of the warehouse. But what would be loud enough to draw his attention? She remembered several large metal dumpsters in the photos.

Lucy reached out to the raccoon and asked him for help. Then she navigated the raccoon out to the dumpsters and used his dexterous paws to open the lid, then let it bang closed with a crash. She did that twice more as she stood behind the office door, cracked just wide enough to see down the hallway.

After the third crash, the guard sprinted down the hallway towards the back. Lucy quickly turned the corner, then settled the tarantula back in its cage, and made a run for the exit. Maya was waiting at the edge of the parking lot with the car running and they sped off to the gas station. They found Noor crouching in the bushes and she jumped in the car, carrying her harp.

"Did you find anything?" asked Maya.

"I sure did," answered Lucy, "and it's bad. Really bad."

Chapter 32

"HOW BAD?" SAID NOOR.

"They have been using song magic for all sorts of weird things for decades. It seems they are mercenaries for hire, without allegiance to anyone but themselves." Lucy told them about Dougherty's. "They used infrasound to make customers feel an uncomfortable dread in the store."

"I've heard of that before," said Noor. "Some researchers think infrasound explains haunted houses. It's a low frequency that people can't consciously identify but it still affects them—they sense it rather than hear it."

Maya frowned. "Someone hired Scordatura to put a department store out of business?"

"It seems so. I didn't have time to find out why," said Lucy.

"That seems such a trivial thing to warrant using dark magic," said Maya.

"Maybe that's because we're thinking about it wrong," said Noor. "To us magic is, well…magical. But to them it's a skill, a product, a service. The same as if you were good at math and contracted out your accounting services. Maybe it's like the gig economy of magic."

"Yeah, exactly," said Lucy. "And there were hundreds of files in there, and that was probably only the cases from before digital files became the norm."

"How could they be operating like this for so long and no one knows about it? It's crazy," said Maya.

Lucy shrugged. "I guess they're careful. They make everything look like an accident or a natural occurrence. Like Giorgio's restaurant—who's going to guess it was the singer who sickened all those customers instead of an obvious cause like food poisoning?"

"I guess that's possible. Did you find anything that links to the choir?" asked Maya.

"Maybe," said Lucy. "I took some photos of documents in a file called 'Project Puppet.' I need to read them, but it seemed like they were using song magic to build an army of people who would be susceptible to suggestion."

Maya's eyes widened. "Like at the health expo!"

"Exactly. But I guess it would be a latent change in their brain that put them sort of on standby. Normal until triggered by a certain stimulus," said Lucy.

"So it's like in movies where someone gets hypnotized in Vegas and they cluck like a chicken when someone says, 'peanut butter' or something," said Maya.

"I've seen studies about how music can increase neuroplasticity," said Noor, "how the brain changes and adapts. Sounds like they are preparing minds to be receptive."

"But receptive to what?" asked Maya.

"I don't know yet," said Lucy. "I'll need to look at the photos and hope that one of them has the answer. There were tons of pages and I only had time to capture a few."

"Let us know what you learn. I hope there's something that will tell us if the choir is part of Project Puppet or something entirely different," said Noor.

"Or both," whispered Maya. "Surely they could grow the numbers in Project Puppet while achieving some other goal."

"Maybe. It depends on how many people they have working on each project. I mean, how many dark song magicians could there be?" asked Noor.

Lucy and Maya exchanged glances, their faces grim.

"What am I missing?" said Noor.

"When we researched animal magic, we found out there were dozens of training centers recruiting college students, in every major city in the country," explained Lucy.

Noor looked horrified. "And since I was nearly recruited into dark song magic in college…"

Maya nodded grimly. "That's right—there may be more practitioners than you imagined, hundreds, even thousands more."

"But if that's true, we really are no match for them," said Noor.

"Oh, but we already were. You and Lucy foiled their plans at the last concert, didn't you?" said Maya.

Noor still looked doubtful but was starting to look a bit less discouraged.

"We're fewer in numbers, but even if they have allocated four people more senior than Kayla to this concert, we can still win. We just need some help," said Lucy.

"Are you thinking what I'm thinking?" asked Maya.

"That we need to talk to the old hermit," said Lucy.

"Yep."

"The man living in the nature preserve?" said Noor, incredulously.

Maya nodded. "I know it sounds crazy, but I think he knows much more than he let on."

"And you think you can get him to leave the park, drive with strangers several hours away to attend a choir concert?" said Noor.

"When you put it like that…" Maya gave a chuckle.

"It's worth a try. We're going there anyway for our second bird survey, we can at least find out if he was downplaying his magic just so we would go away," said Lucy.

"We'll bring treats. Brownies and chocolate," said Maya.

"It works on Cloud," said Lucy with a grin, while Noor looked completely confused. Lucy explained, "He loves chocolate—the old man, not Cloud. Cats can't have chocolate."

"This whole conversation is utterly absurd, you know?" said Noor.

"Yes, and it's two in the morning," said Maya. "Time to go home and get some sleep. We can talk more soon."

Lucy was exhausted from the intense anxiety of their caper, but her mind was spinning, haunted by all the files she had seen. How was she supposed to just go on living her normal life, going to work at TerraPlaya each day, knowing that there were scores of people scheming behind the scenes? How could she sleep a wink? Perhaps from now on she would always sleep catlike, with one eye near open, ready to spring up at the slightest sound. Perhaps she should wear earplugs all the time and run a white noise machine 24-7.

She thought about what Maya had said a few weeks prior, how nothing had changed just from knowing, not really. Scordatura existed long before she became aware of it, and her life had been unaffected by them, at least to her knowledge.

But then a terrifying thought ran through her mind, causing her to jerk and jostle poor Cloud, who was curled up against her knee. He swooshed his tail in protest.

What if she had already been exposed to Project Puppet? How would she know? What if at any moment the trigger would be sounded, and she would become their pawn?

No way she could fall asleep now. She went to the freezer and took out some mint chocolate chip ice cream and a spoon, and turned on one of her favorite old movies, *Singin' in the Rain*. If anything could take her mind off of her current predicament, it was stellar dance numbers and catchy tunes.

With Cloud snuggled beside her, having followed her into the living room, Lucy savored the rich, creamy dessert, and lost herself in the movie. Her lids were heavy and by the time the credits rolled, she was half asleep. She roused herself just enough to put her bowl in the dishwasher and nestle into bed. Cloud followed close behind, jumping up and settling on her chest right away, purring loudly.

As Lucy began to drift off, Cloud's steady purr reverberating through her body, calming her, she realized that a cat's purr was a special kind of song magic.

Chapter 33

BRIGHTON ISLAND NATURE PRESERVE WAS magical in its own right. Although the weather was getting cooler, the area was still alive with activity, a haven for birds stopping over during their migration to Mexico for the winter. Lucy and Maya took the long way to the survey site to visit a flock of sandhill cranes that overwinter on the island, the majestic birds foraging in a field on long, stalky legs, their red crowns moving like rubies hidden among the grass.

The two women took special care with their work, Lucy focusing hard to accurately capture the data Maya was calling out and also further her own skills in shorebird identification. She was starting to be able to discern the subtle differences between the different types of plovers, for instance, the plump little piping plover, puffy like an adorable plush toy. Lucy and Maya were the epitome of professional, but both knew the other couldn't wait to complete the survey so they could talk with the old man again.

After they took their final observations, Lucy packed up their spotting scope and data sheets in her backpack and they headed inland. She hoped they would remember the way without the ghost wolf to guide them. They wandered through the scrub brush, then further in where the trees began to grow taller.

"I think it's this way," said Maya, leading them to the right.

Soon enough, the edge of the bird blind came into view. Lucy's stomach gurgled. They had promised the man they would leave him alone, and here they were just a few weeks later. She didn't feel good about that, but the stakes were high, so she just had to hope he would understand and forgive them.

Not wanting to startle him again, they stayed on the far side of the blind, maintaining his privacy. Lucy wished they had asked his name last time.

"Sir—are you there? It's the two women who brought you chocolate," said Lucy.

There was no response.

"We know you want to be left alone, but this is really important," said Maya.

The only answer was the distant squawk of a seagull near the shore.

"Should we check on him?" said Lucy, her mind filled with horrid visions of the poor old man lying lifeless in the bird blind.

Maya nodded and the two women cautiously circled around to where they could see inside the blind.

Lucy gave a sigh of relief. It was empty. They walked in closer to take a look.

"He's been here recently. Must be out doing whatever he does during the day. Fishing, maybe," said Maya.

"Should we look for him or wait here?" said Lucy.

"I'd rather explore as long as we're here."

"Lead the way, then."

Maya headed back towards the beach, and the two women walked along the tide line, looking down at tangled blobs of sargassum, occasional pieces of driftwood, white, heart-shaped cockle shells, and ridged, spiral welks. The fluctuating rhythm of the waves crashing reminded Lucy that nature had her own soundtrack, songs that told of water or earth, birds or wolves, powerful eruptions or trickling waterfalls. Brighton Island sounded nothing like Sienna Falls, but both were music to Lucy's ears.

They were so absorbed in studying the offerings of the sea as they followed the shore that both women jumped in the air when a voice spoke.

"I knew I hadn't seen the last of you two," said the old man. Thankfully, he didn't sound angry, just resigned.

The two women walked over to him. "We are back to do bird surveys for our company. We'll actually be here several times over the next two years," said Maya.

He looked at her with a raised eyebrow. "Bird surveys, eh? That the *only* reason you're here?"

Lucy looked at Maya, hoping she would know how to answer his question. Maya just shrugged, and Lucy knew her friend was trying to mimic the man's indifferent ways.

"Well, as long as you're here, do you know what this is?" he said, holding up a small brown object that looked like a tiny cookie sandwich, with a tan top and bottom and a black band around the middle.

Maya looked closely. "Is that a sea bean?"

A smile cracked across his face. "Ah, you do know something about nature. Maybe you *are* here for bird research."

"What's a sea bean?" said Lucy, leaning in to get a closer look.

"It's a seed pod that travels the ocean for years, from faraway tropical places, until it finds refuge on a distant shore. This one is called a hamburger bean," he answered.

Lucy grinned. It really did look like a tiny burger in a bun.

The man looked pleased by their interest in his find. He put his hand in the old worn pouch he kept at his waist and pulled out another seed, this one a bit larger, dark brown, and shaped like a heart. "This one's called a sea heart, for obvious reasons."

"That's really neat," said Lucy.

"You take it. Supposed to be good luck—seems like you might need some," he said, holding it out to her, then dropping it in her open palm. When Lucy closed her hand around it, a fleeting impression passed through her, of a tropical paradise and laughter and joy, but it faded before she could truly grasp the image. She tucked the sea heart in her pocket.

"Did you parry?" the man asked.

"What?" said Lucy.

"The folks you were trying to fight—were you able to defend

against them?"

"Um… yes. Sort of. We stopped them once, but now there are more of them, and I'm not prepared for our next encounter. I just learned song magic, and they have been using it for decades."

"Sounds like it's not a fair fight. Best to leave it be if you ask me."

Maya looked at the man, comprehension dawning on her face. "Is that what *you* did?" she said slowly.

"Excuse me?" said the man.

"Is that why you ran away and hid on this island? Because you didn't want to fight?" said Maya.

His face grew tomato-red. "I don't need some young know-it-alls coming to my home and telling me my life. Leave me alone," he barked, and started shuffling away from them.

"Wait!" shouted Lucy. "I really need your help."

"I don't know anything else—I can't help you," he said with his back turned.

Lucy squeezed her eyes shut. She couldn't let him walk away; she had to do something. After all they had been through, after how hard she, Maya, and Noor had worked, this one old man might have the key to beating the dark magicians, and he refused to help. A quiet rage began to boil up inside her, like acid in the pit of her stomach, and without thinking, she let out a shrill note, exploding the sand and seaweed in front of the retreating man, causing him to shield his eyes.

He turned around, astonished by her outburst, then leaned on his walking stick and returned fire with a low growling sound that caused the sand to move like a wave towards the women, knocking them to the ground.

Maya looked at her friend from where she had fallen on the beach. "What are you doing?" she whispered to Lucy, shocked by her rash behavior.

"Trust me," said Lucy.

"Always," said Maya.

Lucy got on her feet and pulled her friend back to standing, brushing sand off their clothes. The man was watching them, waiting for Lucy's next move.

She held her hands up in surrender, then smiled. "I thought you said you didn't know anything else."

He pursed his lips, shaking his head. "You're a sly one," he said with a sigh.

Lucy grinned. "Then you'll help us?" she said.

"I didn't say that. But we can talk...."

That was good enough for her. "Thank you. We brought brownies," she said, and the old man chuckled as he walked back towards them.

Chapter 34

LUCY TOLD THE MAN, WHOSE name they now knew was Leon, about Northbrook Community Choir, about Kayla and her employer, and how Lucy and Noor had foiled their attempt to use dark song magic on the audience at the last concert. He listened carefully and without the slightest display of shock or disbelief.

"And then, we had hoped it was over," explained Lucy, "but Scordatura put our director Darlene out of commission, and appointed a new one, a man named Ivan Novak."

At the sound of the name, Leon's eyes widened, and he stumbled, catching himself with his walking stick.

"You've heard of Ivan Novak?" said Maya.

He recovered quickly and pretended to look at something at his feet. "Name might be familiar."

"Look, there's a big concert coming up and we have to be ready," said Lucy. "If you know something you have to tell us."

His eyes narrowed. "I don't *have* to do anything. You think I live alone out here so I can get sucked back into that world?"

"So, you *were* running away," said Maya.

"So what if I was? I just want to walk along the beach and look for sea beans, watch some birds, collect some shells. Let an old man alone."

Lucy shook her head in frustration. "Fine, I get it. We're not asking you to get involved, just teach me what you know so I can fight."

Leon clenched his free hand as if the decision was physically painful, then released his fingers to fall by his side. "Fine. What do you want to know?"

"Let's start with who really taught you," said Maya.

"It was true what I told you last time, my mati taught me what you call song magic. She didn't call it that though, she called it *pomicanje zvuka*, which roughly translates to 'sound shifting.'"

"Sound shifting, I like that," said Lucy. "Was your mati a musician?"

"Not professionally, but she always sang at home, traditional songs, and lullabies. But you don't need to be a musician to do song magic."

"No?" said Maya.

Leon shook his head. "Not at all, as long as you can make some type of sound."

"You know what this means?" Lucy said to Maya.

"I have some catching up to do," she said sheepishly.

"It couldn't hurt for you to learn enough to provide backup for me and Noor."

"Fair enough," said Maya. "But right now, we need Leon to teach you some new moves."

"What do you say—will you teach me how to fight Ivan and his crew?" asked Lucy.

Leon took a bite of brownie and closed his eyes, savoring the taste. The two women waited in silence while he ruminated. When he had eaten the entire square, he looked at Lucy with a scowl and said, "I guess I'd better, since you couldn't even block a simple tremor roll."

"Tremor roll?" Lucy asked.

Leon grinned. "When I was a little boy, I used to name all the techniques my mati taught me, so I could pretend I was a famous wrestler. The one I threw at you I called a tremor roll because it's like an earthquake."

"All right then," said Lucy. "We'd better get to work. How do I block something like that?"

Leon stood tall and was transformed from shifty vagrant to wise mentor with the simple change in stance. "The first thing I noticed is that you didn't anticipate my move. Your opponent is always going to give you a warning, you just have to pay attention. If someone is using their voice, then they will likely take in a quick breath before they attack. That's your signal to shield yourself or counter."

The next several hours were punishing for Lucy, pushing her physically and mentally to the limit as she practiced blocking techniques, various attacks, and then sparred with Leon. More than once she was thrown into the sand, and Leon would growl, "Get up quick! They won't stop attacking just because you're on the ground. Roll out of the way and counter."

When Lucy tried the attacks he taught her, he yelled, "Is that it? You have to mean it." And when she tried to protest that she didn't want to hurt him he just laughed. "If you land even one hit on me, I will come up there myself and help you fight."

Lucy glanced at Maya and without any need for speech, they knew what to do. Everything they had accomplished had been by working together. Lucy gave a slight nod and Maya said, "I want to try. Like this?" Maya took in a deep breath, preparing to let out what looked to be a huge sound.

Leon turned his focus on Maya, reflexively preparing to block her.

"Pfffh," said Maya softly after her huge breath.

Leon only had a split second to look confused before Lucy hit his shoulder with a move he had named a sound slap, and he staggered back to rebalance. He grabbed his arm.

"You could claim that was cheating, but I'm pretty sure you would tell me there are no rules," said Lucy. The grimace that crossed Leon's face made Lucy's chest tighten. Had she gone too far?

"I would indeed," admitted Leon. "Well done—I guess I must honor my offer."

Something didn't sit well with Lucy. She had won fair and square, but he was right—who were they to drag an old man from his happy life on an island beach back into a dark world? If she ever found a way to escape, she was sure she wouldn't want to be pulled back in, especially by virtual strangers.

"No," said Lucy.

Maya shot her a look. "But we need him."

"No, we don't," said Lucy. "We need to take care of our own problems—it's our turn now." She turned back to Leon. "We appreciate your help—you deserve to live the way you like."

"Thank you," he said with a grateful smile.

Lucy and Maya were quiet on the way back to the car as they thought about the old man living alone on the island. He didn't seem to want their help, so they didn't offer anything other than the brownies. They would be back for the next bird survey soon enough, so there was time to think about how to broach that issue later. They just hoped he would stay safe and healthy until they came up with a plan to help him that he would be willing to accept.

Now Lucy had to teach Noor everything that she learned from Leon, and teach Maya the basics, because Carmela was right: the three of them together were strong and powerful.

Chapter 35

THE THREE WOMEN ARRIVED AT Red Bluff Ranch on Saturday morning. Jeremy and Silver met them at the end of the road near the farmhouse.

"She's magnificent," exclaimed Noor when she saw the majestic merlin perched on Jeremy's glove, while Lucy gave her silent greeting to Silver with a respectful nod.

"You must be Noor," said Jeremy, "welcome to the ranch."

"Sorry, I got distracted," Noor replied, realizing she hadn't even greeted their host. "I've never seen a bird of prey up close before. It's nice to meet you."

"Yeah, thanks cousin. I couldn't think of anywhere else with privacy and open space for us to train," said Maya.

"Not a problem," said Jeremy. "You know you're welcome any time. And I'm fascinated by song magic—and also worry that you three might get yourselves hurt. I want to help if I can."

Maya rolled her eyes. "Have you been talking to lita?"

"She just worries because she loves you," said Lucy.

"I know, I know," said Maya.

"If my parents knew about any of this, they would lock me in the house and never let me leave!" said Noor, and the group laughed at the thought.

"I should put Silver in her mew before you get started," said Jeremy.

"Noor, would you like to see my raptor rehabilitation center?"

Noor's eyes widened with delight. "You have more birds? Yes, I'd love to."

After settling Silver safely in her enclosure, Jeremy led them to the other set of cages designed to house the birds during their recoveries. "I have some new birds since you were last here."

"Wow! How many do you have now?" asked Lucy.

"Five. That might not sound like a lot, but it's a ton of work, feeding them all, especially since they each have their own special diet, not to mention cleaning the cages. And I only take adult birds—there's no way one person could look after young ones too. Since I am a master falconer, the Rehab center said they might eventually send some to me that need help with flight training, making sure they are strong enough before release."

"That does seem like a lot for one person," said Maya.

"I'm hoping to find some extra help in the near future, an intern or something," said Jeremy, leading them down the path. "Come look at this new one, he's a real beauty."

The three women scanned the enclosure. Lucy was the first to see the stocky bird with mottled brown and white feathers tucked up in the highest corner, hidden in the shadows. "Awww, is that a barred owl?"

"Yep, the first owl I've taken in. He's a bit tough to handle, but he's already on the mend. He had a run in with some barbed wire. The Rehab center patched him up and now he just needs to rest and recover before we release him."

"Ooooh, poor baby. I hope you get better soon," crooned Noor.

Lucy and Maya laughed.

"What?" said Noor.

"It's just that you're talking to him like an infant instead of a full-grown raptor," said Maya.

"Well, I haven't been around animals much. My parents didn't believe in pets. But I love them."

"That stinks—sorry we made fun. Look around as much as you like," said Lucy and Maya nodded in agreement.

While Noor took her time oohing and ahhing at each of the enclosures,

Lucy and Maya filled Jeremy in on the latest developments, from Ivan Novak, to their breaking into the Scordatura warehouse, to their visit with Leon. He shook his head in disbelief at every twist and turn of the story, especially the part where Kayla cut Lucy and broke her phone.

"Now I am really scared for you all. These people mean business," he said.

"You're right. The only choice we have is to work harder and beat them at their own game," said Lucy.

"I suppose so. I know better than to think my cousin and her friends would run away," said Jeremy.

"With that settled, we'd better get down to it. Noor, you ready?" asked Maya.

Noor reluctantly dragged herself away from the regal birds and followed her friends out towards the field.

"This should be a good place," said Jeremy.

The next few hours were spent teaching Noor everything that Leon had shown Lucy. She was relentless in her tutelage, and when Noor asked for breaks, Lucy took that time to work with Maya and Jeremy.

Even though Leon had told them that a special aptitude for music and a pretty singing voice weren't required for song magic, Maya was still uncomfortable and self-conscious. Jeremy shared Maya's lack of musical skill, but he was more than willing to give it a try if he could help in the upcoming battle.

By the end of the day, Noor was at least as good as Lucy at both blocking and attacking, and Maya and Jeremy could block or soften attacks roughly half the time, and occasionally throw a clumsy attack that was just as likely to backfire as to hit the target.

Exhausted, Maya begged Lucy to let them retire inside to rest.

"I didn't know Lucy could be so ruthless," Jeremy quipped as they dragged their weary legs towards the farmhouse.

"Oh yeah, she can be real bossy," said Maya with a smirk.

Lucy's face turned red. "Only because I'm trying to protect us!"

"We know, we're only joking," soothed Noor. "Every group needs a fearless leader."

Lucy's face turned from red to pale at the thought of her as the leader. Somehow, she had led the charge at Sienna Falls, and they had won. Even though she felt much more comfortable as a follower, would prefer it really, it seemed the role was naturally falling upon her once again, and all she could do was accept it as both an honor and a curse.

Jeremy made them coffee and tea and they settled around his circular wooden table. An image from an old storybook flashed through Lucy's mind, of the Knights of the Round Table, the men assembled to make plans for war. She chuckled inwardly, wondering if that made her King Arthur.

The room was quiet as the four of them sipped their beverages and snacked on the fruit, cheese, and crackers that Jeremy had set out. Once the food had refueled their energy and the drinks centered their minds, they turned their focus to the second topic of discussion, Project Puppet.

Lucy pulled up the photos she had taken of the warehouse files. With a serious tone, Lucy looked at each member of the group in turn, then began, "What we are dealing with is no less than a small part of a sinister scheme, one that reaches far beyond Northbrook choir."

"You learned something else from your photos?" asked Maya.

"Yes, but only a little more than we already knew. There are still so many holes, I had to make some pretty big assumptions," said Lucy.

Noor leaned in, her arms on the table. "Based on what you read, do you think this concert is part of Project Puppet?"

"Most likely," said Lucy. "But it's just one of many similar events. Project Puppet seeks to create a network of suggestable people so large that in any given location, at any given moment, enough people could be triggered to accomplish a specific task."

"That's pretty vague," said Jeremy.

"Yes, but that's the point, right?" Maya said. "It's not about achieving a single goal. The point is to have this tool ready and waiting, so it could be used for any goal they want to attain."

"Or that the highest bidder is willing to pay to achieve," said Noor in a whisper.

The four of them took in this thought, their faces dour. Lucy gulped her chamomile tea, as if she could drown this new knowledge out of her body.

"But why would the audience for the Northbrook choir be so important that they brought in the big guns this time?" asked Noor.

Lucy shrugged. "I don't know. It could be that someone has hired them for a local job, and they need more susceptible people."

"But if it were so important, why would they trust the operation to only Kayla last time?" Maya said.

Lucy thought back to the conversation she had overheard on the loading dock. "I think it was a test for Kayla, a big one."

"And since she failed, and I'm sure they can't stand to fail, they are taking no chances this time," said Noor.

"Is it possible that they plan to use the trigger at the end of the concert? Like if they were hired for a local job, like you said?" suggested Jeremy.

"Maybe, or somewhere else in the near future." said Lucy. "There's no way to know for sure. All we can do is make sure they aren't successful in enchanting the audience this time."

"And the choir," said Noor.

Lucy grimaced. She hadn't thought about the fact that the two hundred choir members were also potential victims. "Yes," she said, "the choir too."

Chapter 36

THE IDEA THAT ALL OF her fellow singers, and she herself, could soon be soldiers at Scordatura's whim consumed Lucy as she headed to rehearsal. She tried once again to focus on singing, but with not only Kayla there to ruin the experience, but Ivan leading the choir, she questioned her choice to stay.

When Ivan entered the room, she heard a woman in the alto section say, "Isn't he a tall drink of water?" at which several other women giggled like schoolgirls.

Lucy frowned at the thought of Ivan Novak as the object of anyone's lust, as evil as he was, but she knew that he was objectively handsome, so she could hardly blame her fellow choristers who didn't know his true agenda.

Ivan led them through the most challenging sections of the *Messiah*, Lucy begrudgingly acknowledging that he was quite a fine director, guiding the choir to achieve just the right balance among the voice parts, and pulling out the drama of the story, the elation, the betrayal, the renewal. As pointless as it was, she still couldn't help but lament her bad luck, that the very choir she had joined, after decades of building up the courage to audition, was plagued with rats.

The only sliver of light she could fathom was that she was still getting great choir experience, and maybe someday she could find a different choir to join, or, she dared to hope, Darlene would be able to return in the new year, without any further intervention from Scordatura.

Before the break, Ivan made some announcements. He flashed his brilliant smile that made Lucy cringe and other swoon, and said, "I'm so excited to announce to you today the four soloists that we have secured for this performance. You will get to meet them at the dress rehearsal with the orchestra."

Lucy was ready with pencil in hand, to take down the names. The sooner she could start researching, the more she could unearth about the structure of the dark song magic syndicate.

Ivan continued, "We have soprano Ileana Banis, who has sung with the Greek National Choir, alto Fiona Lee, a fine upcoming singer getting her doctorate from our very own University of Northbrook, tenor Sergio Diaz who you might recognize from his role as Don José in the Northbrook opera's production of *Carmen* last year, and finally, bass Russell Penner, a member of the elite Voce Nocturna ensemble."

The choir members applauded, impressed by the caliber of soloists they were going to have the privilege of singing with on December 14th. Lucy would have been excited at the opportunity too, if she didn't suspect that each of these talented singers weren't also practitioners of a darker art. She was crestfallen to know that recruiting was apparently happening at the university in her own town.

Noor had to make a phone call during the break, so Lucy didn't get a chance to ask her if she knew any of the names Ivan listed. It also meant that she was stuck standing alone again, which she hated. Sometimes she chastised herself—anyone else would surely have made friends with other singers by now, but she tried to cut herself some slack by reminding herself that many of them have sung together for years, or even joined the choir with existing friends. She still felt like an outsider.

As she tried to look busy scrolling on her phone, she had the piercing feeling that she was being watched. She looked up to see Kayla and Ivan talking and watching her, but once spotted, they quickly turned away to face the other direction, continuing their conversation, which looked serious to Lucy's eyes.

During the second half of rehearsal, Lucy fretted about the incident, wondering what Kayla had been saying about her and what they were planning. By the end, her anxiety was in full force, having imagined a dozen horrible possibilities. When Ivan released the choir, Lucy jetted over to find Noor.

"Are you okay? You look paler than normal," Noor said with both a chuckle and genuine concern.

Lucy explained what had happened during the break. Noor tried to tell her it was nothing to worry about, that they had to focus on the facts of the situation, without adding on infinite unknowns. "That will just make you go crazy," said Noor.

No sooner had she finished the sentence than the women realized someone was approaching.

Ivan, standing a foot taller than either woman, was an imposing presence, even without knowledge of his true nature. Kayla was standing off to the side behind him. "Lucy, is it?" he said, and his eyes glanced at her bandaged palm as she absentmindedly touched it.

She started to turn from pale to a light shade of green. "Y-y-yes," she stammered. Noor moved closer, protecting her friend in a show of solidarity.

"And you must be Noor," he said, his voice oozing with honey.

"That's right," said Noor.

He nodded. The rest of the choir and the accompanist were filtering out of the rehearsal room, and Lucy became acutely aware that they would soon be alone with Kayla and Ivan. "And how are you enjoying singing with our choir?" he said with his crocodile smile, loud enough for anyone lingering in the hallway to hear.

"It's wonderful, thanks for asking," said Noor with a forced smile.

Lucy could only manage to nod in agreement, her throat clenched tight with panic.

Now Ivan lowered his voice to a whisper. "The thing is, ladies, that I'm not sure this choir is the right place for you."

"You're kicking us out? You can't do that," said Noor.

"No, no, I wouldn't dream of it. I just wonder if our goals aren't in line, and you'd be better off singing somewhere else." His dark eyes flashed a warning, but the plastic smile remained. "Just think about it."

Neither woman replied as Ivan turned on his heels and stepped away from them. When he passed Kayla, he said, "Perhaps you could escort these ladies to their car and help them make the right decision."

Kayla grinned like the Cheshire cat. "It would be my pleasure."

Lucy gave Noor a glance and she shrugged. What could they do? It wasn't any safer staying in the Fellowship Hall with Ivan. They had no choice but to see what further message Kayla had to relay. At least this time it was two against one.

The parking lot was nearly empty when they reached Lucy's car. Her hands were trembling from the interaction inside, but as they walked, Lucy's anger started to outweigh her fear. Ivan was frightening because they didn't know the depth of his powers, but Lucy felt like she was becoming more evenly matched with Kayla.

With a glance around to make sure they weren't being watched, Kayla moved to the far side of Lucy's vehicle and made an exaggerated pout. "Oh no, it looks like you have a flat," she said.

Like Leon taught her, Lucy recognized the quick inhale of Kayla readying to attack. Kayla let out a piercing hawk-like sound, targeting Lucy's back tire.

Lucy reacted quickly, releasing her own tone, successfully blocking the strike.

Kayla's eyes narrowed. "I see you've learned something since last time. Did you fix your phone yet?" she sneered.

Lucy instinctively clutched her bag with her phone inside, as if that would protect it from a repeat of last time. Kayla laughed and sent another shot to her purse, now targeting her phone.

Once again, Lucy was able to block the attack. She was so filled with rage now at the thought of almost having to fix her phone a second time, that she readied herself to send a tremor roll towards Kayla, but Noor leaned in and whispered, "Don't show your hand."

Lucy released her breath without returning fire. Noor was right—better for Kayla to think they only learned how to block. No need to tip the dark side off to the full depths of their new skills.

Noor crossed her arms. "You're outnumbered, Kayla. I think you'd better be on your way."

Kayla huffed and sent a blast towards Lucy's windshield out of sheer displeasure at her second failure. This time Noor blocked the blow, causing Kayla to stamp her foot like a toddler.

In her rage, Kayla sent three rapid thrusts, like a child throwing a tantrum. The first two landed at Lucy and Noor's feet, causing them to jump back to avoid the blast. Unable to block in the seconds it took them to regain their balance, a third shot hit the front headlight, cracking the cover. "Consider this your second warning. There will be no third," Kayla barked and stormed back to the building.

Lucy looked at her broken headlight. "Why is it always my car?" she said, and briefly explained how her tire had previously been slashed by dark magicians.

"Sorry, that sucks. First your phone, now your car. It could have been worse though—she could have cracked the windshield."

"That's true—nice defense," Lucy said with a grin that belied how her heart was pounding.

"You too. Seems all that training at the ranch paid off," replied Noor.

Lucy nodded, then both women stood in silence for a minute, reflecting on what had just happened.

When Lucy's pulse had slowed and her throat began to unclench, she said, "What are we going to do? Something tells me we aren't welcome here."

"Yeah. I don't think singing with the choir is an option anymore."

Lucy sighed in disappointment at her entire choir experience. "Well, we've gotten as much information as we were likely to get from being at rehearsals anyway. And it wasn't like it was fun, knowing what we do."

"I agree. Better to quit rehearsing and let them think we gave in. They can't stop us from attending the concert."

"No, they cannot," said Lucy. "I guess we'd better buy tickets—looks like we'll have to stop them from the audience."

Chapter 37

SOMETHING ABOUT RESEARCH MADE LUCY feel calm. Even if it wouldn't make a shred of difference in the upcoming battle, just having faces to go with the names made her feel more prepared. One thing she had learned from her previous run-in with dark magicians was that learning about their lives made them seem more human.

She imagined Kayla watching Beavis and Butt-Head and eating Sour Patch Kids. She probably didn't do either, but surely she watched some kind of TV show and had a weakness for a certain candy, and in that way, she was just like Lucy.

Lucy started with Ileana Banis. Many of the articles about her were in Greek, but she found a few concert programs with bios in English. The woman went to university in Greece and seemed to perform only in Europe, so how she was recruited to work with Scordatura seemed a mystery. But then Lucy found a human-interest article talking about two sweetheart lovebirds, a singer married to a violinist, Ileana and her husband. And the husband had played in the very ensemble Ivan had formed with Pierre. But which had come first? Did Ileana know song magic before she met her husband or did she fall in love and join him in solidarity?

Next, she looked up Sergio Diaz. He had sung featured guest roles with several small city operas throughout the United States, and he had gotten his graduate degree in Chicago. It was likely that he was recruited in college like Kayla.

Russell Penner was easy, as it turned out that the Voce Nocturna ensemble toured with Ivan's early music ensemble across Europe. It was starting to seem that even if Ivan wasn't part of the corporate management of Scordatura, he was a key figure in the dark song magic world, the connector, excelling in recruiting and seeking out opportunities for himself and his followers.

Finally, she searched for Fiona Lee. Something about the fact that she went to school right here in Northbrook made her heart pinch. She hated to think that any young person she saw on the playgrounds around town could fall into dark magic just by following their passion in music performance, or animal science in college. Or who knows what subjects the other types of magic use to find potential practitioners.

Fiona looked so fresh-faced and innocent, probably about 26, her whole life ahead of her. She had gotten a full scholarship to study performance at Northbrook University. Lucy wondered if the scholarship always went to a student who displayed potential for song magic, or even to students who already used it.

Lucy found Fiona's webpage, and a chill went through her spine when she saw a photo of Fiona and a cat that looked similar to Cloud, save for a white mark like a locket on his chest. Did this dark magician love her cat as much as Lucy loved Cloud? It was all too confusing for Lucy, this idea that someone could partition her life like that, use dark magic to achieve selfish goals, then do volunteer work with the honors society and love a sweet, gray cat.

She was starting to lose herself in rumination, which was never a good thing, as she tended to fall down a rabbit hole of helplessness, wondering what effect she could possibly have on such a world.

Luckily, her phone rang. It was Noor.

"Hi Lucy. I have a weird favor to ask."

"Oookay," Lucy said, dreading what it could be.

"Evan's mom Debbie told me that he has been having nightmares and hasn't been sleeping because he claims there is a spiky monster living in the tree outside their apartment. She's really worried about him."

"Poor Evan. That sounds terrible, but I'm not sure what I can do about a little boy's nightmare."

"Well, I was thinking since you and Maya use animal magic, you could take a look around, make sure there's nothing there. And then, since Maya is a wildlife expert, Evan might feel better to know that a professional investigated."

"I don't mind, and I'm sure Maya won't either. Let me see if she is free. When were you wanting to do this?" asked Lucy.

"As soon as possible, so poor Evan can get a good night's sleep. And Debbie, too."

An hour and a half later, the three women met in the apartment complex parking lot. Debbie came out and walked around the two-story building to show them the tree that was outside of Evan's window. The building was nestled into a stand of juniper woods above a small creek that ran through the property.

"Thanks so much for taking a look. I'm sure if you can tell Evan you didn't find anything, he'll feel better. He has a lot of respect for expertise," said Debbie.

"No problem, we're happy to help," said Maya.

"Why don't you go back inside, and we'll knock on the door when we're done," suggested Noor, knowing the other two would want some privacy to use their animal magic.

They waited for Debbie to turn the corner.

"I think this task is for you, Lucy. Can you sense anything?" asked Maya.

"Let me see," she said and closed her eyes. She listened to the sound of an owl hooting, smelled the woodsy scent of juniper bark, like a piney car air freshener, and began to scan the animals around her. She felt all sorts of birds, squirrels, and mice, and quite a number of insects including beetles, wasps, roaches, and ants. She sensed the pets inside the apartments, cats and dogs, hamsters, and a gerbil that could only be Evan's.

"Wait," she said. "There's an animal here that I've never sensed before."

"Do you know where?" said Noor.

"Up high in this tree."

The streetlamps from the parking lot and the light from the apartment windows were not enough to illuminate the area. Maya took a flashlight out of her coat and shined it up the trunk of the tree. "You know what—I do see a clump up there. Kind of the way squirrels make big, messy nests out of leaves, but this one is even bigger and seems to be made more like a beaver dam."

"That's interesting. But you can't see anything in it?" said Lucy.

"Not from down here."

Lucy nodded. She had to think about how she could get a good view without endangering any other wildlife, since they didn't know what they'd find up there. She needed something with keen eyes that could perch above it and look down. She surveyed the area for nocturnal birds, as she didn't want to disturb any roosting species. Lucy heard a lone mockingbird singing, the sound a mournful one of desperation, a male without a mate. She felt remorse for disturbing his woeful tirade, but she knew it would only be a minute.

She centered herself and found the mockingbird's door. It looked to her like an arched entranceway with white wooden paneling. She asked for permission and the bird allowed her entry into its mind. Lucy navigated the creature into the tree above the mystery nest. When she was carefully perched, she looked down.

Lucy's jaw dropped. "It can't be…" she said.

"What is it?" said Maya and Noor.

"We don't have porcupines around here, do we?" said Lucy.

Maya's face lit up with delight. "Yes! They're rare, but there have been more sightings in the area in the past few years. I can't believe it—I wish I could see it up close."

Lucy took another look to be sure of what she was seeing and then released the mockingbird with heartfelt thanks.

"It all makes sense," said Noor. "What would a porcupine look like to a kid but a spiky monster?"

Maya laughed. "You have a point there."

"Let's go tell Debbie. She is going to be relieved."

Debbie was shocked when she heard the news. "I had no idea that was possible. Is it dangerous? Should I report it?"

"No, they aren't aggressive unless threatened. It's safe enough to let it be, as long as we teach Evan about it. And it won't stay in that tree longer than a few months, most likely."

Debbie called to her son and got her laptop out to show him what his monster creature really was.

Evan's eyes got wide when he saw the photo. "That's him!"

"Yep. He's got a nest in that tree out there," said Maya. "But there is no reason to be scared of him. Porcupines are amazing."

"But they're sharp," said Evan.

"That's true, they have long quills that would hurt if they stuck in you, but it's not true that they throw their quills. When a porcupine gets scared it gets all bristly and if another animal or a human tried to brush against it, the quills will come out. So as long as you keep a safe distance, there's no danger."

Maya showed Evan a video of a porcupine eating an apple and making silly little grunty noises, kind of like Alvin and the Chipmunks. Evan pointed at the screen and laughed.

Debbie's mom put her hand on Evan's shoulder. "What do you think? Porcupines aren't as scary as we thought."

"No, they're different. I like them," said Evan.

Debbie smiled, glad her son would be able to sleep once again, and mouthed, "Thank you," to the three women.

"Animal magic for the win," said Noor as they walked to their cars. "Do you think I could learn it too?"

"No reason why not," Lucy said. "Let's start your training as soon as the concert is behind us."

Noor grinned. "I can't wait!"

Chapter 38

IT WAS MAYA WHO HAD requested another song magic practice session. Lucy groaned, because as much as she wanted to be prepared for the big event, she was tired of the constant focus on song magic. But Noor promised she'd find a way to make training fun this time, and reminded Lucy that it was understandable that Maya felt behind, since she hadn't embraced her own song magic until recently.

In retrospect Lucy found it odd that she and Maya hadn't realized that song magic wasn't only for elite musicians. One of the first things Maya had taught her about animal magic was that anyone could learn it, albeit to different levels of expertise, if they could just learn to be in the same time and space as their animal counterparts and were willing to put in the work. Why wouldn't it be the same for song magic? Once you know it exists, the path opens automatically, Lucy reasoned.

When Lucy and Maya arrived at Northbrook Harmony, they were greeted with the shimmering lights of a disco ball projector and the upbeat sounds of Donna Summer's "Bad Girls." They laughed as they panned the room. Noor had gone all out.

"First station, ladies, the song magic nutcracker." Lucy gave Maya a confused glance and they followed her to a plastic tray lined with walnuts. Lucy chuckled.

"Find the cracks, Lucy first," said Noor. Lucy grinned and scanned the walnuts, and selected one where she could see a crack just beginning to form. She sent her voice to the seam and with a shrill zipping noise, the walnut lay perfectly cracked in two.

"Woo hoo! Nice one. Do you want to try next?" Noor said to Maya.

Maya scrunched up her face. "Um, I'm not sure I know how to do this part, I'm in more of a throw it and hope it hits something stage."

"No problem, I'll talk you through it," Noor said. "I'm going to pick one, then try to become aware of its faults, sense where it wants to open. Then I send the soundwave there, like I'm chopping it with a knife." Noor demonstrated with a sharp screech and the nut fell open.

"Alright, I'll give it a go," said Maya. She focused on a nut, then sent out an uncontrolled whoop. Instead of cracking the nuts, the force of the soundwave blew them off the tray, scattering them across the floor, causing all three women to laugh as they cleaned up the magical mess.

"That's okay, still powerful song magic," said Lucy as she popped a walnut in her mouth. They practiced with the walnuts for a while longer, and Maya showed quick improvement.

"Second station, art. Why only practice the ugly parts of magic, right?" Noor began to sing over a shallow wooden box of sand set on the floor. As the pure tone and haunting melody skimmed the grains, the sands began to shift, creating shapes of flowers with fine petals, reminiscent of Leon's canvas in the dunes.

"That's so pretty," said Lucy. "I don't even want to erase it."

"Nah, it's sand. It's meant to be ephemeral."

Lucy used her song magic to send a smooth wind over the box, creating a blank canvas. Then she began to sing a simple tune, guiding the sands as they moved into spirals, large and small.

"Wow, you two make it look so easy," said Maya. She stood over the box, and started singing, shaky at first, a lively tune. The sands bumped around and leapt into place, forming a blocky geometric pattern of connected squares. It wasn't soft and elegant like Lucy and Noor's patterns, but it was strong and neat.

Noor gasped. "It's actually really hard to do squares, Maya. That's impressive!"

Maya grinned, surprised at herself.

"Time for levitation station," Noor said.

"Levitation?" asked Lucy, shocked. "You figured out how to levitate things with song magic? The best I can do is knock things down."

"I figured it out by accident a few days ago and I've been working on it so I could show you both. You basically cause the object to balance on the sound, like a surfer on an ocean wave. Focus on supporting it from beneath. It's easier to start with something that's already in the air."

Noor had strung up three small paper cranes from the top of the door frame leading to the kitchen. She released a steady swooshing sound and the middle crane rose.

"Whoa—that's neat! Let me try," said Lucy, who attempted to replicate Noor's sound, like the soft roar of a jet engine. The crane on the left jerked forward and swung back and forth.

"Think of lifting it from beneath, gliding the sound just under it, then raising it up," instructed Noor.

Lucy tried again, and this time, the crane floated upwards.

Maya stood up to take her turn and was surprised when the crane on the right levitated, somewhat jerkily.

"Yes! We are three awesome song magicians. Keep practicing this one, I'm sure it will come in handy someday."

"Absolutely," said Lucy.

"For sure," said Maya.

"And now, let's party," said Noor and she tapped her phone and the chill groove of "Rock the Boat" filled the room.

"You're the best at cracking things, so—do your thing," Noor said to Lucy as she pointed to a coconut on the counter in the small kitchen.

Lucy laughed as Noor got out some frozen pineapple from the mini freezer.

"Piña Coladas?" said Maya.

"Yep, we deserve a break, don't you think?"

#   #   #

After another weekend of practicing song battle magic, even as much fun as song magic disco jam was, Lucy was actually relieved to come back to work. It was ridiculous that the office was now the most relaxing place for her to be, but here she didn't worry about getting attacked by anyone. She still had anxiety at work, but now it paled in comparison to the fears that Ivan Novak, Kayla, and Scordatura summoned within her.

Lucy sipped her white pear tea as usual, and today she found the sound of Anuk's Monday morning voice rather soothing, lulling her into a meditative state. The sameness, the stability of the office, had become a welcome part of her life, which surprised Lucy. The kick of Maya's foot on her leg startled her back into the room.

Anuk was looking at her expectantly.

"I'm sorry, can you repeat that?" Lucy said, not wanting to risk guessing at an appropriate response like she had last time. Her face burned with embarrassment as her coworkers chuckled at her inattentiveness.

"Crazy weekend?" Bethany joked.

"Something like that," said Lucy.

"I was saying that we have a superstar in our midst," continued Anuk.

"What?"

"The lead for the disaster recovery program said you are the employee with the fastest processing speed while maintaining the highest accuracy. It's no small accomplishment—you should be proud. He wants to talk with you about other opportunities with his team."

"Wow, Lucy, like, way to go!" said Bethany.

Lucy blushed and looked down at her hands. "Um, thanks. It has been a really cool project."

Seeing how uncomfortable the attention made her, Anuk realized the error he had made and swiftly moved on to the next agenda item. Lucy was thankful that her manager was so empathetic; it was a rare trait.

She was glad Tyler was on the east coast doing the GPS work; she could picture the grand scowl he would have made if he had been here to witness Anuk's praise of her. Bethany would undoubtedly tell him when he returned, as much just to gossip, as to keep him informed in this fictitious battle between Team Lucy and Team Tyler.

If Bethany only had any idea of the real battles, with dangerous consequences, that she was dealing with, her head would, like, totally explode. Last week's incident with Kayla put her petty competition with Tyler into perspective. Not that she still didn't plan to win the bird-off, just that the stakes felt lower than they had several weeks ago.

In the courtyard, now wearing sweaters and flannel to stave off the late fall breeze, Lucy and Maya ate their lunches amidst the wilted flowers and fallen leaves; winter was approaching. The squirrels seemed frantic in their last-ditch effort to hoard nuts before it was too late.

"Sounds like this disaster recovery thing might be a big opportunity for you," said Maya.

Her friend's tone sounded neutral, but Lucy suspected there was a big question behind it. "Perhaps. I need to find out more about it."

"But you think it's something you might want to pursue?"

"I don't know yet. Why—do you not want me to?"

Maya scrunched up her face. "That's not it, of course I want you to follow whatever path is the best for you, whatever makes you happy. I just like getting to do fieldwork with you, that's all."

"Me too. And there's nothing to say I can't do both," said Lucy, even though in her heart she knew that it wouldn't be fair to Tyler to follow both paths, when he was clearly only suited towards the fieldwork and showed little aptitude for the disaster recovery work. But maybe when he returned from the GPS work on the project, that might have changed; maybe that was his new calling.

"I would hate not getting to do bird surveys with you. But Anuk will eventually hire another avian specialist anyway, and then..." said Lucy.

"No more surveys for you," said Maya. "I guess that's true—it would be a shame if you missed out on another career option and still didn't get to do the bird surveys. I'm just being selfish, thinking of having to work with Tyler in the short-term."

"Nothing's been decided. I'm still committed to the bird-off, I just feel the need to explore this other path too."

"I know. I'll support you either way, I promise."

"Thanks, Maya—you're an awesome friend."

"I know," she said with a chuckle.

Chapter 39

INSTEAD OF ATTENDING REHEARSAL ON Wednesday night as she had for several months prior, Lucy arrived with Maya at the music therapy studio to the sounds of Noor playing her Celtic lap harp. They let themselves in and found Evan sitting on the floor, listening attentively to the music.

When the song ended, he declared, "Fuchsia and cerulean."

Maya looked at Lucy in confusion; she'd have to explain Evan's synesthesia to her later. What was impressive to Lucy was that the boy knew such specific color names, many more than you'd find in the typical box of crayons.

She wondered what dark song magic would look like to Evan, but it was hardly appropriate to subject the boy to that kind of influence. Still, there might be some knowledge gained by his perspective.

"Hi Evan," said Lucy. "Do you remember that day that Noor and I sang and made gerbil Evan feel better?"

He nodded. Noor gave Lucy a questioning look but let her continue, trusting her friend's judgement.

"Do you remember what colors you saw then? That helped him feel better?" She knew it was a long shot, since human Evan had been agitated and pacing at the time, so she was shocked when he answered immediately, without hesitation.

"Pearl white, swirled with pistachio, with a glow like fairy lights."

"Interesting, thank you," Lucy said as the tinkle of wind chimes sounded, and Evan's mom Debbie came to collect her son.

"Thanks Noor, have a good night," said Debbie, giving a wave to Lucy and Maya.

"No problem. Bye, Evan," said Noor as the pair exited. She turned back to Lucy. "I see the wheels turning—what are you thinking?"

"Not exactly sure, I was just wondering if Evan can see the difference between light and dark magic, and if light and dark magic each had their own color spectrums. And now I wonder if only song magic has this glow he mentioned."

"That's an interesting idea, but he seems to name a lot of different colors even when I'm not using song magic, so I haven't picked up on any particular color combos."

"Oh well, it was just a thought."

"Speaking of patterns, the reason I asked you here is that I heard back from Ricky about the CD from Scordatura," said Maya.

"Did he find something?" asked Noor.

"Kind of. He was able to isolate a certain part of the sound by importing the single line parts from the other tracks and overlaying them with the suspicious track. It took a long time because he had to manually sift through the soundwaves to extract the parts that didn't belong."

"What was left over?" asked Lucy.

"I don't know, exactly. He sent me an MP3 file with it. Even though he thinks what we are suggesting is absurd, he was still reluctant to listen to it himself. Just in case."

Noor laughed. "I like this guy, covers his bases...or basses, ba-dum-tss."

Lucy and Maya groaned. "I've never heard you make a terrible joke," said Lucy.

"And you probably won't again, it just flowed out of me this one time," said Noor.

"So, it's up to us to listen to the track. How can we possibly test it without risking harm?" asked Lucy.

"I've been thinking about this—remember how I said noise cancelling headphones work by playing the inverse of the soundwave—could it be used to reverse the effects?" said Noor.

"It's a good theory, but how could we possibly test it?" said Maya.

The three women pondered this problem for a few minutes, Lucy tapping her foot on the floor, Maya looking out the front window, and Noor resting her head in her hands.

"I have an idea," said Lucy. "There is no difference between light and dark song magic in terms of how it works, right?"

"Right," said Noor. "I think I see where you're going with this. We could test it with something that's not harmful."

"Like sleep! Noor, you could put Lucy to sleep with your harp, then we could see if the inverse wakes her up," said Maya.

"That's a perfect example, but I'd have to use a computer to create the opposite," Noor explained.

"Do you have a recording device here?" said Lucy.

Noor nodded and without further discussion she set up her microphone and recorder next to her stool and picked up her lap harp. "You'd better wait outside unless you want to take a nap," she said.

When Noor gave the all clear, the two women returned inside. Lucy fired up her laptop and Noor uploaded the file. A quick search of 'soundwave inverse' brought up an audio tool designed to do just that. "Wow, finally something that's easy—you literally just select the wave and click the invert button," said Lucy, demonstrating as she spoke.

The three women watched the progress bar as it calculated. "Alright, you ready?" said Noor.

"As I'll ever be," Lucy replied. Of everything she had experienced, and what she knew was possible, being magicked asleep didn't sound like that bad of a thing. She plugged in her headphones and pressed play on the original track. Her eyes blinked wearily as the soothing timbres of the harp floated through her and soon her lids were too heavy to keep open and she felt herself falling backwards into the cushions.

The next thing she knew, Noor and Maya were standing over her while the inverted track played. Lucy sat upright, perfectly alert, as if she hadn't been asleep at all.

"It works!" said Noor.

"This is a huge breakthrough," said Lucy. "This means even if we fail to stop them, we could potentially reverse the impacts of the enchantment before they use the trigger."

"In theory, yes, but in practicality that's nearly impossible. We'd have to be able to record it, invert it, and play it back loud enough for everyone to hear, and not like the dark magicians are just going to stand still while we do that," said Maya.

"One step at a time," said Lucy.

"Back to the original question—what's on the rehearsal CD?" asked Noor.

"Not it!" shouted Lucy.

"I'll listen to it," said Maya. "Get the inverse ready because I have no idea what's going to happen. I could go all zombie and try to eat your brains."

"I hope not," said Lucy with a laugh.

"Please don't," said Noor.

Maya put in the headphones and Lucy and Noor watched her with concern, looking for any sign of discomfort, Lucy's hand on the mouse, ready to switch to the inverse track at a moment's notice.

Nothing seemed to be happening. Maya shrugged. "I don't feel any different," she said after a few minutes.

"Maybe it's making changes in your brain, maybe it's part of Project Puppet," said Lucy.

"I don't know why, but I don't think so. For some reason all I can think about is how I really want those hard candy caramels my lita loves so much."

Lucy looked puzzled.

"Do you like them?" said Noor.

"The hard candy caramels?" asked Maya.

"Yes, did you eat them whenever your grandmother had them around?" pressed Noor.

Maya shook her head. Noor began to laugh.

"What's so funny?" said Lucy.

"Let's play the inverse," said Noor. Lucy clicked the other track.

Maya's eyes widened. "That's so weird. Now I don't want them at all."

Now Lucy laughed too. "All this fuss over song magic that is just trying to sell caramels to grannies?"

Maya took out the headphones and the three of them roared with laughter until they had tears running down their faces.

When they finally regained their composure, Lucy said, "The thing I'm wondering is if recorded song magic works just as well, why bother recruiting highly accomplished musicians to cast magic during live performances?" said Lucy.

"I wondered the same thing," said Noor, "so I researched the topic online. There were a few journals with studies on how live and recorded music affect the brain differently. One study found that the brain waves of an audience listening to live music synchronized more than with pre-recorded. That could be important for the collective soldier mentality Scordatura is trying to achieve."

"Hmm, so maybe recording for minor stuff, like selling products, but in-person for the big things, like controlling people," said Maya.

"I think there's a good chance that is the case," said Noor.

Chapter 40

LUCY DROVE BACK FROM THE studio feeling optimistic. They were finally starting to understand song magic and uncover tools to thwart Scordatura's endeavors. She couldn't wait to get home, indulge in some chocolate, and watch a movie.

Nothing looked amiss at her house as she pulled into the driveway, but when she got out of the car and walked around to the porch, she shrieked. The sunburst glass inset in her front door was cracked like a spiderweb. She knew it was tempered glass and purposely shatter resistant, and that could only mean one thing. This wasn't random vandalism, this was a warning, just like her phone and headlight.

"Cloud!" she yelled. If they hurt her sweet boy there would be hell to pay. She scrambled to undo the lock and burst into the entranceway. When he wasn't by the door to greet her, she started to panic.

"Cloud, where are you?"

In here, Lucy.

She rushed into the bedroom and crouched down to see her poor little furball hunched under the bed.

"Are you okay?"

Yes, now that you're home.

"Come on out, buddy. It's safe now—I'll never let anybody hurt you."

Cloud slinked out from beneath the bed and Lucy scooped him up and held him close.

"That was smart to hide under the bed. If you ever hear anyone else in the house or outside the door, that's what you should do."

Lucy sat cross-legged on the bedroom floor and pet Cloud until she felt his fears recede. She had never been so angry in her life. It was one thing to target her, but to come to her house and upset her innocent feline friend was unconscionable. A dark flame of rage burned within her.

Kayla would pay for this.

Cloud stopped purring and lifted his head.

"What is it, sweetheart?"

You feel different. Don't let them change you.

Lucy nodded. Had Cloud felt the vengeance that had just coursed through her? She kissed the top of his furry head. He was right, of course, the last thing she wanted was to become like Kayla, to seek power only to use it for her own gain. She would have to be careful.

"Let's go watch a movie. I'm not going to be able to sleep for a while."

Cloud followed her to the kitchen, where she made some tea and put a few chocolate sandwich cookies on a plate. She also gave Cloud a couple of treats, which he gobbled up as usual. Always a good way to test if he was okay; she knew if he ever stopped eating, there was a real problem.

With her cat shadowing her every move, to the point of being underfoot, Lucy navigated carefully to the couch with her tea and cookies. The pair settled in to watch the heartfelt *The Bells of St. Mary's*, starring the graceful Ingrid Bergman as a nun trying to save her run-down inner-city school from closing. Lucy hoped that the spirit of generosity and community in the film would help realign her values and shift away from the dark thoughts of revenge floating through her head.

#   #   #

Lucy's eyes welled with tears when she recounted the evening's event to Maya in the courtyard the following day.

"I just worry they might hurt Cloud. I mean, we know Kayla knows animal magicians, too."

Maya patted her arm. "That must have been awful, but there's no reason to think they even know you have a cat. The window was just a sign, like you said. Like a horsehead in the bed sort of thing."

"Ugh—seriously?" Lucy screeched. "That's the analogy you choose?"

Maya scrunched up her face. "Sorry. That was tactless. I was just thinking the dark magic syndicate has a real mafia vibe."

"That's not making me feel better."

"Look, the point is, so far we don't know of anyone who has actually been killed by the dark magicians, right? There's no real reason to think they are coming after you or that they would target Cloud; they're just trying to scare you off."

"Well, it's working. And remember, they did put Darlene in the hospital. I really don't think I'm cut out for this," said Lucy, collapsing back in the chair. She felt physically and emotionally exhausted and just wanted to go back home and sleep.

"Who is? Only a very sick person would do all of this for fun. You said it yourself—how can we turn our backs on one thousand people?"

"I know, I know," said Lucy, "but that doesn't mean I can do this— I'm not strong enough. I can't risk getting Cloud, or you or Noor hurt just because we know about magic."

"Noor and I are responsible for our own decisions, not you. And I don't know anyone stronger."

Lucy slumped further into the chair and closed her eyes, knowing Maya was right but just wanting a moment to imagine she could walk away, never join another choir, never do fieldwork, just make maps in her cubicle and watch movies with Cloud. It wouldn't be such a terrible life. She felt like she understood Leon a little more each day, why he would purposely choose the quiet life of a hermit.

"Let's do something fun, take your mind off all of this. Why don't we go to the Holiday Market? I need to look for presents for a zillion relatives."

Lucy was unsure. She felt like every time she left the house there were just more reminders of dark magic being used all around her. Was it so unreasonable that she just wanted to hide in her house until she absolutely had to leave it on December 14th?

"I don't know—I don't really feel like it," said Lucy.

"Come on, they have all sorts of food and drinks. I'll buy you a hot chocolate."

"You're sneaky," Lucy said with a grin. "You know I can't turn down chocolate."

Maya laughed.

The Holiday Market was buzzing with activity when they arrived. Lucy tensed when she heard carolers wandering through the market but relaxed again when she failed to detect any song magic. Sometimes singers were just singing, to spread joy and holiday spirit, she reminded herself.

They hit the hot chocolate stand first, Lucy selecting a double chocolate with whipped cream, while Maya chose peppermint.

"Ooh—they have buñuelos, too. You have to try one." Maya bought two of the crispy fried dough discs covered in cinnamon sugar and handed one to Lucy.

She took a bite, the sweetness and fat melting on her tongue. "This is delicious," she said. "Kind of like a funnel cake."

"A bit. There are lot of versions of fried dough out there. And I'm happy to eat them all, no matter what they're called," said Maya with a grin.

"I second that," said Lucy as she alternated between the buñuelo and the hot chocolate. She was glad she had decided to come.

The two women walked up and down the stalls adorned with white twinkling lights. It rarely snowed in Northbrook, so the best the city could do was fake plastic snowmen, reindeer statues, and snowflake decorations to create that special winter feeling from the movies.

Maya found a vendor selling handmade tree ornaments. "These will be perfect for a few of my cousins. And lita's tree can never be busy enough. I bet she'd love this tiny carousel one."

"That's so pretty and intricate," said Lucy, admiring the craftsmanship.

Something at the stall caught Maya's eye, then she quickly turned to Lucy.

"Hey, I'm kind of chilly and I left my scarf in your car," said Maya.

"No problem. I'll get it while you pick out your ornaments."

When Lucy returned, Maya had a smug smile on her face, and a bag full of presents.

"Geez—how long was I gone? Did you buy out the whole market?"

"Ha! Maybe so. I've crossed off the most important people in my life."

It occurred to Lucy that she hadn't known Maya last year, and she needed to start thinking about a good gift for her new friend. In truth, she hadn't had many people to exchange presents with in recent years, save for Bethany's annoying attempts at an office Secret Santa or White Elephant gift exchange.

"Want me to take your picture with Santa?" joked Maya as they walked past a North Pole scene, complete with fake snow lining the ground, and a jolly, costumed man with a white beard sitting on a red velvet chair.

"Ewww! I'm not sitting in some strange man's lap," said Lucy.

"Fair enough," Maya said, laughing. "Plus, who knows how many kids have peed on that costume. Or worse."

"That's a disgusting thought."

"You're welcome," said Maya with a smirk.

Chapter 41

IT HAD BEEN MAYA'S IDEA for the three of them to hang out the night before the big concert. They all knew they wouldn't be able to sleep a wink, so why not have some fun? Lucy protested when Maya said she had planned a surprise; Lucy had been thinking of something more like a movie night. But Maya had promised it would be to her liking, and despite her distaste for surprises, she trusted her friend.

Maya and Noor met at Lucy's house and carpooled to the secret destination, Maya refusing to give any hints along the way. When Maya pulled the car to a stop, Lucy looked out and read the medieval lettering on the sign, "Saffron and Sage: An Apothecary."

"Please don't tell me I'm here to learn herbal magic," said Lucy. "Believe me, I'm curious about the other branches of magic, but I'm up to my neck in the two I already know."

Her friends just laughed. "Please, give me a little credit," said Maya.

Lucy pursed her lips together, still doubtful, but no one knew her better, so she followed her friend inside.

"Welcome!" said a bald man with a British accent. "I'm Archie Chatham." He gave each of them a firm handshake as they introduced themselves. "Do come in, we're set up in here."

The women followed him to a side room with an oak cabinet housing dozens of square drawers, each lovingly labeled by hand in cursive. There was a large table in the middle, the entire top a cutting board, set with ocean blue ceramic bowls, a mortar and pestle, a scale, and several single serve cast iron pots.

Lucy looked puzzled. "What is all this?" she asked.

"Ah," said Archie, "So this is *your* surprise. Well, Lucy, tonight we are going to make your perfect blend of tea, one that is created with just you in mind."

Maya and Noor waited for her reaction. Lucy's jaw dropped and her eyes widened. "Tea? The perfect Lucy tea?" She turned to her friends, "This is the best present anyone has ever given me."

Archie smiled broadly, with a twinkle in his eye. This man clearly loved his job; how rare to be able to make a living at one's calling. "Then let's get started, shall we?"

Lucy grinned and took her place at the table. She was in paradise as Archie talked through the most common leaves, seeds, petals, and roots used in herbal teas, allowing the women to smell each one, then sample it brewed.

He talked about their properties like a wine connoisseur, each with their own notes and colors, depth and body, and of the effects each could have on the mind and body. Lavender is not simply floral but light and sweet, with hints of earthiness akin to rosemary, and as Lucy already knew, is touted for its calming properties. Definitely in the Lucy pile.

Their teacher encouraged them to find one or two ingredients to use as a base, a scent or flavor, something that would momentarily take them somewhere else, a brief escape from this world. Lucy chose chamomile as her base, Noor selected elderflower, and Maya, chicory root.

Next, they experimented with adding additional flavors, slowly building a blend unique to each woman. Lucy added a tiny dash of lavender and vanilla to hers, and declared it was the most soothing thing she ever tasted, delighting their host. Even Maya said her blend gave coffee a run for its money, although she wouldn't likely be converting anytime soon.

"Come back anytime, ladies," said Archie as he walked them towards the exit. "You can create blends for different purposes. Many people use tea to destress, but truly, there are teas to find courage, summon strength, build patience, or anything you want more of in your lives."

Lucy clutched the large sachet with her own personal blend and the recipe to recreate it. "Thanks so much, Archie, this was really fantastic."

When they were outside, she hugged both of her friends, "And thanks to you wonderful ladies—you're awesome!"

Back at Lucy's, they went over the plan for the next day one more time, and called Jeremy to make sure he was prepared as well. Knowing there was nothing to do but wait for time to pass, Lucy made gourmet popcorn drizzled in chocolate and sea salt and they gathered in the living room to watch a movie.

"Any suggestions?" asked Lucy. "Maya knows I mostly watch old movies, preferably in black and white, so I'm not that well-versed in anything more modern."

"Except for *Alias*," corrected Maya.

Noor looked surprised. "The TV series? That's an odd exception to your rule."

"Well Jennifer Garner seems super nice and she kicks ass as Sydney Bristow," said Lucy. "Although lately my life is too much like *Alias* for my comfort."

Noor laughed. "Since you like that show, have you ever seen *Point of No Return?*"

"Never heard of it," said Lucy.

"I've never seen it either," said Maya. "What's it about?"

"It stars Bridget Fonda as a violent drug addict who is reformed by the government to become a skilled assassin. She kicks ass too, but there's also a lot of heart in it," said Noor.

"I'm in," said Lucy and searched the streaming services for the film. Within minutes, Cloud was curled up in her lap, and the three women were engrossed in the movie, mindlessly crunching popcorn, tomorrow's trial far from their minds.

While the credits rolled, Noor stood up and stretched her back. "Well, what did you think?"

"I liked it," said Maya, "but not sure about the scene that was like a remake of the fancy dog dinner from Lady and the Tramp with ravioli instead of spaghetti."

Lucy and Noor hooted with laughter. "That was a weird scene, for sure," said Lucy. "I loved the movie though. It made me wonder if even someone like Kayla could be rehabilitated, if she could find a way out of the dark magic syndicate."

Maya raised her eyebrow. "That's what you took away from the movie?"

Lucy shrugged and Noor just shook her head in amusement as she put on her jacket.

After the two women were gone and Lucy was alone again with only Cloud for company, she once again felt an ominous dread, one she could no longer push to the recesses of her mind: tomorrow she would once again be facing dark magicians. She thought back to the day before the Sienna Falls Forest battle. It was different then because she and Maya had been on the outs, and she didn't know if Maya would ever forgive her. In contrast, tonight was a celebration of friendship, and she knew whatever happened tomorrow, they would have her back.

Chapter 42

LUCY STOOD OUTSIDE THE ENTRANCE to the concert hall, feeling like a giant was sitting on her chest, crushing her lungs. The weight of the task at hand was overwhelming, but it was too late to back down now. They had a plan, and she just needed to follow it. She took a deep breath in to remind herself she could and released it as she handed her ticket to the usher.

If she had been there for any other reason, she would have been charmed by the festive tree in the lobby, dressed only in silver and gold balls and white lights, the garlands of holly and ivy, the wreaths of spruce with pinecones, and the oversized velvet red bows adorning the end of each aisle.

When she reached her seat, she glanced around covertly, trying to find the others. The four of them had arrived separately at the concert hall, trying not to draw attention from Kayla or any of the dark magicians who would be more likely to recognize Lucy and Noor together.

Dispersed throughout the audience for maximum coverage, Lucy was seated in the front middle; she was the first line of protection. Noor was seated off center, further back to the left, and Maya to the back right. Jeremy was all the way in the rear, in the shadows, trying to hide that he had snuck a caged merlin into the performance.

Lucy slipped in her Bluetooth headphones and started streaming white noise from an app on her phone. This way she would be free to focus on deflecting the song magic without worry of falling prey to any enchantment were they to fail at their task. She put her phone into night mode with the lowest brightness and set it face up at the bottom of her purse.

Luckily, the 'Sing it Yourself *Messiah*' was less a formal classical concert and more of a family affair, with squirmy children being hushed by their parents and older ladies in fancy hats trying to quietly unwrap the crinkliest cough drops, to no avail. Normally that would annoy Lucy, but she was glad she would be able to check her phone, shielded in her purse, at intervals throughout the evening, without raising too much ire from her neighbors.

Lucy surveyed the concert hall. The stage was set with risers for the choir, and the conductor's platform housed a music stand where the score lay open. Musicians in the orchestra began tuning their instruments and warming up, creating a quiet cacophony of sound as the lights flashed and latecomers scrambled to find their seats. Just before the house lights dimmed, Lucy suppressed a gasp; she had just spotted the woman with the curly black hair in the audience, to the lower left of her. Did Scordatura have people in the audience too? Wasn't Kayla, Ivan, and the four soloists enough?

The choir filed out onto the risers and Lucy cringed when she saw Kayla standing tall and confident in the alto section. It burned again that Lucy was forced to sit out here instead of performing with the choir.

The four soloists took the stage to enthusiastic applause, the two men in suits and the two women in stylish gowns, one a mint green, and the other a deep crimson. And then Ivan Novak walked out on stage.

Before he reached the platform, he stopped by a microphone and addressed the audience. "Good evening," Ivan said, flashing his signature crocodile smile. "Before we begin, I have a very special announcement. Due to the generous sponsorship of Scordatura Solutions, the orchestra is playing on period instruments, much like the ones that would have been used during Handel's time. As you know, we welcome you to sing along with the choir this evening. Without further ado, please enjoy tonight's performance."

Ivan took the podium and soon the stately "Sinfony" overture began, the baroque ornamentation, trills, and passing of parts between the stringed instruments setting the tone for the story to come. To Lucy's ears, the *Messiah* had none of the drama of the *Requiem* she had sung at the last concert; this music was crisper and even in a minor key had a lighter quality than the Mozart.

She sat on the edge of her seat during the first solo of the piece, the clear tenor voice ringing through the hall. Unlike the *Requiem*, these solos were lengthy, several minutes long, compared with the thirty seconds Kayla had alone during her solo at the previous concert.

Sure enough, as Ivan's handpicked tenor Sergio sang, Lucy felt that familiar tingle of song magic fall upon her, like a light rain that's more akin to a fog, moistening, but not pelting. She hummed as quietly as possible, not trying to sing along with the solo, but along with the changing chords, blending her voice with the orchestra, but willing the sound to spread out like a three-dimensional fan, blanketing the audience in front of her.

She strained to reach further, but it was clear her protections wouldn't be able to cover far enough to reach everyone in her area; even if Maya, Noor, and Jeremy could cover as much as she, there would still be gaps. This was bad.

The solo ended and Lucy relaxed as the choir took over, and the audience joined in. Surely she could rest during these sections, with so many soundwaves bouncing around, it would be pointless for the dark magicians to try and overpower the choir. She allowed herself to be lost in the energy, the glory and triumph of the music. This was the natural magic of a choir singing as one, what she longed to find again if she could ever return to the choir.

Before she knew it, another soloist began, and she once again had to concentrate on blocking the dark magic emanating from him. She scanned the audience and saw Noor, her face fixed in concentration. Lucy could swear it was as Evan had described, that she could see the barely perceptible glow of the song magic, and where the dark and light magic met, the glow turned to pinpoint sparks, each one a miniature battle.

She glanced back and saw the same scene with Maya, but her glow covered a smaller area. That was okay; they knew that Lucy and Noor were stronger than Maya and Jeremy at song magic and they could only hope that the people further back were at less risk of the dark magic reaching them.

Another choral section began, and Lucy relaxed again. She was beginning to doubt that she would have the energy to fight for the entire length of the concert, but she could only do her best. When the famous "Hallelujah" chorus began, the fraction of the audience that joined in the singing doubled, and she could feel the joy of the voices around her, hundreds of people singing in harmony, nothing short of transcendent. The powerful sections of unison singing, followed by the rich, full chords of call and response was exhilarating.

Lucy knew that she only had to last twenty-five more minutes, but she felt her energy draining with each solo. She could see her protective barrier faltering with each passing minute, the area slowly shrinking like a drought-ridden lake. And then the worst happened. She watched as a glassy-eyed stare overtook one member of the audience in the area just outside her protective shield. Then the affliction spread to another, and another.

They were being enchanted and there was nothing she could do to stop it.

Chapter 43

TEARS STARTED TO STING HER eyes; they had failed, and yet she still had to continue to limit the damage for the rest of the concert, save as many as she could. During the next choral section, Lucy glanced back and caught Noor's eye, but she just shook her head sadly; her protection was failing, too. Lucy didn't need to look back at Maya or Jeremy to know it would be the same story for them, since their song magic was even weaker. She just had to hope the dark magic didn't reach as strongly all the way to the back of the hall.

As the chorus sang, Lucy noticed the audience singing along was suddenly more together, unified in rhythm and intonation. They were becoming more synchronized because of the enchantment. A collective. A chill went through her bones at the realization.

When the trumpet triumphantly serenaded during "The trumpet shall sound," Lucy turned her gaze to the orchestra. She recognized the other instruments, violins, viola, cello, timpani, oboe, bassoon, and harpsichord. The period instruments did have a slightly different timbre than the modern ones she was more familiar with.

Lucy froze. The instruments that Scordatura had sponsored. Why hadn't she thought of this earlier? They had been so worried about the four soloists that they hadn't considered the orchestra. If Scordatura supplied special instruments that could only mean one thing. Lucy scrambled in her purse to send a group text.

Lucy: orchestra=trigger?

Noor: Maybe

Maya: which instrument?

Lucy: IDK

Jeremy: keep watch

Trying not to let her focus lapse during the remaining solos, as she sensed more and more people around her falling under the enchantment despite her best efforts, she scanned the orchestra members one by one. During the next choral section, she took out the opera glasses that Carmela had lent them. She didn't see a glow emanating from any of the musicians in the orchestra. Maybe she was wrong.

The final chorale, the "Amen," with the glorious harmonies and explosive energy, flew by as Lucy tried to solve the puzzle. When the final note ceased, the audience erupted with applause, with standing ovations for each of the dark magician soloists. Lucy was still straining to see the orchestra through the standing crowds.

The house lights rose and people, unaware that they had been magicked, collected their belongings, and made their way to the exit, clogging the main aisle immediately. The soloists exited toward the green room and the choir followed in single file. The musicians began to loosen their bows and pack up their music.

And then she saw it. Next to the oboist sat a second instrument on a metal stand, a light wood color, nondescript in anyway, yet somehow menacing. The man set down the oboe he had played during the performance and picked up the alternate, bringing it to his mouth.

The trigger.

Lucy stood with one foot on either arm rest and waved at Jeremy in the back of the hall, mouthing "The trigger!" and pointing to the oboist. Jeremy didn't hesitate but bent down out of sight to retrieve Silver. Lucy watched in terror as she saw the swirling glow from the oboe, the trigger magic, nearing the audience as they waited for the line to move. The sound would hit them in seconds. Soon Noor was by her side, and together they let out a series of tones to interrupt the wave, but it wouldn't work for long.

There was a shrill scream, then a second and third as Silver swooped above the audience, heading towards the stage. The oboist shrieked when he saw her approaching and raised his instrument to fend her off. Silver grabbed the oboe with her talons and raced back to Jeremy.

She was halfway there when a sudden blast of sound hit the bird and Silver was thrown off course from the blow; the oboe clattered to the floor among the seats. Lucy screamed as a pain seared through her heart as if she had been struck and not Silver; she was devastated by the chance that her avian friend had been seriously hurt.

Jeremy barreled over the rows and raced towards the injured bird but motioned for Lucy and the others to carry on. Lucy knew his highest priority would be to attend to Silver; the rest of them had to find the trigger.

Lucy could hear the oboe slowly rolling down the slanted aisles row by row, heading towards the stage. She jumped from arm rest to arm rest, running on top of the rows trying to reach it, while Maya pushed her way through the crowds to the right and Noor to the left. But they weren't the only ones.

The oboist was clambering down the side steps from the stage and two of the soloists burst from the green room door. Lucy saw Noor approaching from the left, just a few aisles from the bottom, but the oboist was down the steps and nearing the front row. She wasn't going to make it in time.

"Lucy, duck!" shouted Noor. Lucy dropped between the first and second rows as Noor sent a sound slap at the oboist, knocking his eyeglasses to the floor. As he scrambled to find them, Lucy reached beneath the seats, grabbed the oboe, and made a break towards the side exit.

A voice bellowed, "They have the trigger—west door!"

Lucy pushed past the ushers and ran outside, Noor and Maya close behind. Night had fallen and the half-moon was the only illumination on this side of the building, which held a grassy area for day picnics, closed after dark. The parking garage was to the east of the building, but Lucy reasoned that even if they made it there, they'd be stuck in the lines of cars in the multi-level lot. Best to make their way to the front entrance, which would still be crowded with patrons milling about. Lucy turned to run left toward the lighted area, but halted when a man turned the corner of the building.

It was Ivan.

"This way," Lucy said, and the women instead ran to the right, toward the playground. Lucy let out a low growl and the lock on the gate broke open. Inside, it was dark and shadowed by tall oak trees, swing sets creaking as they swung in the breeze. Lucy hid behind a thick trunk while her eyes adjusted to the darkness, and Noor and Maya did the same. She listened for the sounds of crunching feet and wondered if everyone could hear her heart pounding and her heavy breaths.

"We don't want to hurt you," came Ivan's voice, dripping with honey as he moved through the gate. "Just give us the oboe."

Lucy stayed still and quiet, listening. She peeked around the trunk to see Kayla had joined him, followed by Sergio and Ileana. She caught a slight motion from the corner of her eye. The curly haired woman was with them, too, sneaking around the side.

Five against three. Lucy had dealt with worse odds. She didn't need to defeat them, she just needed to get away with the trigger.

"I'm getting impatient, ladies," Ivan rasped. "Last chance. 5...4...3...2..." On the last count, Ivan inhaled and let out a booming roar that made Lucy's bones ache and her head pound. She braced herself against the tree to remain upright as the sonic wave passed by her.

Lucy scanned the park behind her and guessed that there would be a second exit in the back corner, across the foot bridge over the creek. She caught Noor's gaze and nodded her head in that direction. Noor motioned for Lucy to run, that she and Maya would cover her.

As much as she didn't want to abandon her friends, the trigger was dangerous and had to be destroyed.

Lucy took off in a sprint.

"Over there!" shouted Kayla and readied to strike.

Noor let out an operatic tone and a tree limb came crashing down in front of the dark magicians, catching Ileana in the leg. A spreading stain of blood soaked the fabric of her dress where a branch impaled her.

"You bitch! Do you know how expensive this was?" Ileana screeched and targeted Noor with a pained squawking sound before her leg gave out and she crumpled to the grass. Noor easily evaded the distracted attack.

"Oh, it's on now," Kayla snarled. She sent a sound slap, catching Maya's ankle as she ran through the sand pit by the slide. Maya yelped in pain, but recovered quickly and used the tremor roll to throw sand back at Kayla, who shrieked as she tried to protect her eyes.

Lucy turned back and took a moment to sense the area, taking inventory of any animals who could help her, unwilling to leave her friends to fend for themselves after all. She reached out to a great horned owl, and he swept down from his perch and landed on Ivan Novak's head.

Ivan screamed in agony as the talons pierced his skull. His hands flailed over his head, trying to remove the owl, but the bird's sharp hooked beak took a chunk out of his finger, and he resorted to thrashing his head side to side screaming, "Get off me!" in an attempt to dislodge the creature.

"That's it. No more games. Get them!" Ivan screamed at Kayla and Sergio, blood dripping down his forehead, his hair matted with crimson. The owl released him, and Ivan cowered low, fearing a second attack from the skies.

Kayla cackled, glad to finally be unleashed, and slammed Noor in the back with a mighty thrust of sound, throwing her to the ground. Noor groaned but quickly turned over and returned fire. Kayla blocked easily and laughed.

Sergio sent a sweeping scale of notes across his path, targeting all three women. Lucy and Noor blocked the attack, but Maya fell again, her ankle weakened by the previous blow.

Noor looked at Maya and back at Lucy. "You need to go on ahead. I'll fight them and protect Maya. Run as fast as you can."

Lucy nodded and started to race toward the back corner. She heard a hissing sound and a crippling pain hit her shoulder. She cried out and held her arm in support but never loosened her grasp on the oboe. She glanced back to see Kayla with a satisfied grin on her face.

While Kayla reveled in her small triumph, she failed to see Noor standing behind the concrete water fountain. Noor let out a guttural sound from her core, rising in pitch as she guided the water higher and higher until it formed an immense wall, then, in a mighty holler released it in a massive tidal wave, knocking Kayla and Sergio to the ground. They moaned and slithered around in the mud but neither got back to their feet. Seeing no other imminent attacks, Noor ran over to help Maya.

Lucy crossed the wooden footbridge, trying to ignore the searing pain radiating down her arm. She was nearing the back where the second gate should be, and then she'd be free.

She looked around desperately, but there was no gate, just a six-foot-high shrub lining the back. Lucy pushed aside the branches, hoping to force her way through, but she hit a chain link fence. She heard the crunch of leaves and slowly turned around to find the curly-haired woman standing before her.

Lucy was trapped.

Chapter 44

"STAND BACK," SAID LUCY. "I'M warning you."

The woman put her hands up in surrender. "I'm not who you think I am," she said.

"Yeah, sure. So then, you're not after this?" Lucy said, holding up the oboe, tightly grasped with both hands.

"I am. But not for the reasons you think."

Lucy pursed her lips. "Enlighten me, then."

"I'm on your side. I want to stop them from using the trigger."

"Bullshit!" snapped Lucy. "I saw you at the health expo. And at the last concert."

The woman nodded. "That's true, I was. But only because I was monitoring Kayla. We thought she could be turned into a double agent."

Lucy's eyes narrowed. "Hah! Now I know you're lying. Kayla is evil to the core."

"You'd be surprised," said the woman. "We've seen people like her before, approval seeking, recruited in college. Sometimes they jump at a chance for a way out."

The woman's assessment of Kayla was so similar to the one that Lucy herself had given not long ago that it gave Lucy pause. But how could she trust this total stranger with something so important?

"I understand your suspicion, Lucy, I do. But let me ask you this? What do you plan to do with the oboe?"

Lucy looked down at the wooden instrument, the realization of the responsibility she held in her hands. How many triggers were there? Was this the only one? Were there dozens more? She had no way of knowing. "Destroy it, of course, as soon as I can."

The woman didn't flinch. "And that would be sensible, with the limited resources you and your friends have access to. But if you turn it over to me, we can reverse engineer it. Come up with an antidote for the people who were already affected."

Lucy paused to consider that—an antidote would be ideal. But she still wasn't sure. "If you knew all about what they were doing, why didn't you step in to stop it?"

"Because there is a bigger game at stake. I was only sent to monitor, not to interfere. But now that you already have, there is an opportunity."

"You expect me to believe that?" said Lucy.

"I do, because it's the truth," the woman said with a sigh. "Look, Lucy, since I started watching Kayla, I've seen you in action. If *we* know about you, then *they* know about you, too. It's only a matter of time before things get ugly if you continue to meddle in their affairs."

Lucy narrowed her eyes. "That sounded like a threat."

"Not from me, not from my side. But you won't go unnoticed after tonight, and if you give me the trigger, we can help keep you safe."

"Who is *we*?"

"That's a discussion for another time. I'm going to leave you a card. If you want to know more, text the number. You're not alone in this."

Lucy felt so tired, the pressure of the past months had drained all of her energy, and now her body ached and her shoulder throbbed. If there was any chance it wasn't her, Maya, Noor, and Jeremy against the world, she wanted that to be true more than anything. "There are other people trying to stop Scordatura?" she said.

The woman smiled. "Surely you didn't think only dark magicians are organized?"

Lucy considered this, being a rather organized person herself, and felt the words rang true. "If I hand this over, you'll use it for good?"

"I swear my life on it," the woman said, crossing her heart.

"Okay." Lucy walked to the woman and held out the oboe. In exchange, the woman handed Lucy a white card, but it missed her fingers and fell in the grass. She picked it up and slipped it into her coat pocket.

"Hey, what was the trigger going to do tonight?" Lucy asked as she straightened, but when she looked up, the woman was gone.

Lucy walked back to check on her friends. There was no sign of Ivan, Kayla, or the two soloists as she tread cautiously through the trees. When she reached the gate, she saw Noor waving across the lawn.

"Come quick!"

Lucy sprinted across the grass. Maya and Jeremy were standing around Silver's cage. Lucy's stomach lurched as she neared. Please let Silver be okay.

Jeremy looked up, his eyes brimming with tears, his face ashen. "She's hurt real bad."

Silver lay at the bottom of her cage, motionless, her small chest barely rising and falling.

Noor pulled Lucy to the side. "I don't know if she'll make it to an emergency vet."

"Can we heal her?" whispered Lucy.

"I don't know, but we need to try."

Lucy nodded. She knew she needed to connect with Silver, but she dreaded feeling the poor bird's pain, guilty for involving her in this dangerous scheme. What had they been thinking, involving an innocent animal, and yet, if it weren't for Silver, the trigger would have worked. Silver was a hero; the least Lucy could do was share her pain. Lucy closed her eyes and found the door to the merlin's mind. What had once been a steadfast, heavy wooden door was now splintered and frail. Lucy entered without resistance.

She fell back onto the grass, overwhelmed by the pain. Noor put her hand on Lucy's shoulder, and said, "Can you tell what's wrong?"

Lucy shook her head. She needed to stay with the pain, uncover the source. She refocused inside Silver, her breathing short, trying to lessen the pain of each inhale. As she surveyed the merlin's body, she didn't detect broken bones or damaged organs. It seemed the effect was more of a curse than injury. As upsetting as that was, that meant it might be possible to use song magic to counter the damage.

"You start," Lucy directed, and Noor sang in her most soothing, clearest tone, washing over Silver's still body. Lucy could feel Silver sigh in relief. But it wasn't enough.

Noor grabbed her hand and squeezed it. "Add the harmony."

Lucy tried to match Noor's timbre as she added another note. She could feel something shift in Silver, the bird fighting for her life, trying to find the light and stay on this side.

"We need more—Maya," said Lucy.

"You know I can't sing," Maya protested.

"Of course, you can. Doesn't have to be pretty," said Noor. "Sing on this pitch."

Maya let out an unsteady note, then Noor came back in, and Lucy completed the chord. With the other two women there to ground her, Maya put all her focus into matching their tone, and it soon evened out. Jeremy stood back, both devastated and hopeful, while Maya grasped Lucy and Noor's hands and the three women formed a circle around Silver's cage. Suddenly something clicked into place and a fourth overtone rung out over their heads. A soft glowing pearl white, swirled with pistachio green enveloped the bird.

Silver slowly opened one of her eyes. Lucy reached inside the bird again and the door was repairing itself. Inside, she still felt Silver's pain, but it was receding.

"It's working—keep it going," said Lucy.

The three women held the chord again, this time triumphantly, as Jeremy's tears changed to ones of joy and relief. By the end of the fourth round of singing, Silver was standing in her cage and even stretched her wings out to the side, testing them.

"She's going to be okay," said Lucy, and they broke the circle to allow Jeremy to join in a group hug around Silver's cage.

I'm glad you're safe, Lucy said telepathically to Silver.

The merlin tilted her head in a slight bow, even in near-death, retaining her regal fashion.

Noor was the first to break the circle, her eyes wide. "Lucy—where's the oboe?"

"It's a long story, but everything's okay. I'll tell you all about it later."

Chapter 45

THE FOLLOWING EVENING, THE FOUR women once again sat in Carmela's living room. Maya had reasoned that since lita would want to know everything that happened, Lucy might as well explain the fate of the oboe to them all at once.

Maya began by catching lita up on the concert, their failure to protect portions of the audience from enchantment and the identification of the trigger instrument. Carmela gasped and covered her eyes as Maya acted out the scene from the park and then demanded to know if any of them were injured.

Maya tucked her ankle, wrapped in an ace bandage, beneath the coffee table, Lucy's hand reflexively went to her bruised shoulder, and Noor stretched her sore back, but the three women assuaged Carmela's fears and assured her they were fine, in a 'you should see the other guys' sort of way.

Carmela's eyes moistened when Maya told of Silver's injury and treatment and how it took all three of them doing song magic to save her.

"See, what did I tell you?" said Carmela. "Three is a powerful number—I knew you would do great things together."

Lucy, Maya, and Noor looked at each other in turn, each wondering if some unknowable force attracted them to one another.

"I'm just glad we were all there to save Silver," said Lucy.

Carmela nodded. "I'm glad you were too, for Silver's sake, and for Jeremy's."

"So that brings us to Lucy—I'm dying to know what happened with the oboe," said Noor.

Lucy recited her conversation with the curly haired woman in as much detail as possible.

"But how did you know she was telling the truth?" asked Maya, looking dubious. "What if after all that, you just handed the trigger back to Scordatura?"

Lucy shook her head. "I just knew. It's hard to explain, but now that I've been around song and animal magic for a while, I can feel it. Dark magic leaves a residue on a person."

"Like an aura?" asked Noor.

"Something like that, but not so much a visible sign as a feeling, a heaviness, like the emotional equivalent of burnt, blackened wood."

"Hmm, I think I understand that. Well, I believe you. If you trust her, so do I," said Noor.

"Okay, I'm convinced as well," said Maya. "Who would have thought that there would be a light magic syndicate? That's not the right word, though—syndicate sounds so mob-ish. Light magic *consortium*?" said Maya.

"I've been telling you girls," said Carmela, "there is an underlying force that keeps our world in balance. It comes in many forms, but it seems you three are helping to balance light and dark magic."

"Wow, no pressure!" laughed Maya.

"Right?" said Lucy. "Now I feel like some kind of superhero."

"What was it Leon called song magic? We could be 'The Three Sound Shifters,'" said Noor.

Maya grimaced. "Umm, maybe not that, exactly."

"I'm just spit balling here," said Noor.

"Let's put a pin in brainstorming our superhero trio name," said Lucy. "I'm still not committed to fighting dark magicians full time. I just wanted to sing in a choir and do some fieldwork, that's all."

Carmela patted Lucy's hand. "My poor child. You can't unsee the truth, and to try and look the other way will only bring pain."

"Yeah, I don't think we can pretend we don't know what we do," said Maya.

"I'm not saying we ignore it. There is a huge difference between rising to an occasion and seeking out trouble," said Lucy.

"I agree with Lucy," said Noor. "I have every intention of going back to my normal life with my music therapy and my Kayla-free choir. But if my skills are needed in the future, I won't say no."

"I would love a Kayla-free choir," said Lucy.

Noor cracked a wide grin. "You haven't seen it yet? They sent out an e-mail update this morning—Darlene is out of the hospital and recovering well. She'll resume conducting the choir in January."

"Yes! That's the best news I've heard in a long time. I'm so glad she's okay. What are we singing next season?"

"The e-mail said that after Darlene's ordeal, she wanted to do something uplifting. So instead of one large choral work, we're doing a lighter concert of pieces that celebrate spring, in early April."

"Oh, that sounds perfect—I can't wait!" Lucy could practically hear the uplifted voices around her, heralding renewal and the change of seasons, honoring mother earth. Maybe this would finally be the choir experience she had always longed for.

"That's wonderful, girls. At least you have that part of your lives worked out," said Carmela.

"That *is* great, but what are you going to do about the mystery woman, Lucy? Are you going to text the number on the card?" asked Maya.

Lucy's head was spinning. So much had happened in such a short time, she didn't have time to think. "I don't know. I just need some quiet time to recharge, with nothing crazy happening. Maybe in the New Year. I feel like my life is a hare running far out ahead of me, lost in the woods, and I'm trying to catch up."

Carmela nodded in sympathy. "Remember, your path is yours alone. No one can tell you how to live, and you don't have to accept every opportunity."

"Thanks, Carmela. I need to remember that."

Maya pulled something from the glass bowl on the end table. "Catch, Lucy!"

She caught the object and opened her palm to reveal a caramel hard candy, causing the three younger women to roar with laughter.

"What's so funny?" said Carmela, but they were too hysterical to explain, tears of amusement running down their faces.

Chapter 46

LUCY DRANK TWO CUPS OF tea that morning, trying to calm her nerves. The day of the bird-off had finally arrived. In some ways, this was nearly as terrifying as the concert had been. Funny thing how the brain classifies threats—the fear of losing, embarrassing herself in front of her colleagues was as anxiety-producing as battling Ivan and Kayla.

"You ready?" Maya said as she popped into Lucy's cubicle. "Oh dear, you look a bit green."

"Gee, thanks. Just the pep talk I needed."

"Sorry. I mean you totally got this! You have been studying like crazy and you did so great in the field during the last survey."

"That's better," said Lucy. She inhaled and released her breath in a huff. "I do know my stuff, but my anxiety gets in the way when I get nervous. What if my mind goes blank?"

"Then take a sip of tea, center yourself. Keep it in perspective."

Lucy rolled her eyes. "Mindfulness, stay in the moment. That doesn't work when the moment is awful."

"You're impossible. Now stop stalling, you're going to do great."

Lucy reluctantly trudged her heavy feet out of the cubicle down to the conference room. She almost passed out when she saw the set up.

Bethany had gone all out, with a giant poster that said, "1st Annual

TerraPlaya Bird-off," with streamers hanging from the ceiling, and party whistles for the audience. There were two contestant chairs set up with a low partition between them, and Anuk was wearing a bow tie and held a highlighter pen up as a microphone. "And now, entering the room, with fourteen years at TerraPlaya—Lucy!"

The office applauded and hooted and hollered. "And with six years at TerraPlaya—Tyler!" More applause filled the room.

Lucy's mouth felt sticky, but she reminded herself this was just a fun distraction for the office, and she took her seat at the front next to Tyler.

"May the best *man* win," he whispered to Lucy. She scowled in return. Don't let him psych you out, she thought.

Anuk spoke into his pen, "There will be three rounds. First round is photo identification. I am going to put twenty birds up on the screen. Common names are accepted but must be specific enough to differentiate among species. You will each write your answers on the paper provided. Audience, you're welcome to play along, but keep silent."

One by one, each bird was projected onto the screen for thirty seconds. Lucy's hand was shaking as she wrote, and she struggled to keep her writing legible. The first few she felt pretty good about as they were common or distinctive birds. She smiled when she saw a merlin falcon, she would never forget the regal markings of Silver's feathers and her gorgeous yellow-ringed eyes.

As they neared the end of the round, the birds were more challenging, and she had to make a few guesses between two species with similar features.

"And time is up! Please hand me your papers. Thank you. You might as well all learn something, so here's the same presentation with the bird names labeled." Anuk pressed play and checked Lucy's and Tyler's answers as the photos appeared.

Lucy cringed a few times, angry at herself for guessing wrong. How could she have confused a house finch with a Cassin's finch? So stupid, she chided herself. She was letting her nerves get the better of her—she needed to concentrate.

"And we're back," said Anuk. "The first round goes to…Lucy! She had seventeen correct answers, compared to Tyler's fifteen. This is going to be a tight race, folks!"

Maya grinned at Lucy and gave her a thumbs up. "You got this, Lucy!"

Bethany scowled at Maya and said, "This next one's all yours Tyler—you rock at the bird calls."

"All right," said Anuk. "This time, we're going to hear twenty bird calls, each repeated three times, and you'll once again write down the name of the bird. Here we go."

Lucy smiled as she thought of that first time she had played the birding CD and Cloud had gone into attack mode. Concentrate, Lucy! She barely had time to hear the first bird song and had to guess at the species. This round was much harder. Each bird could have multiple calls and regional variations. She struggled to focus as her anxiety started building, making it difficult to think clearly. Focus on your breathing, she told herself. Better to miss one and breathe, than blank out on the whole second half.

The fog in her mind began to clear as she slowed her breath, and she felt good about the last few.

"Time! Papers, please," said Anuk. He played the calls again, this time announcing the species out loud. "This round goes to…Tyler! He correctly identified twelve of the calls, while Lucy got ten. Don't judge them, folks, calls are no easy feat."

Lucy had a sinking feeling she was going to lose. She hated thinking of Tyler out there at Brighton Island with Maya. Not only did she want to survey birds with her friend, but she wanted to check in on Leon and let him know what happened. Maya wouldn't be able to do that with Tyler tagging along.

"Third round is a little different. I have five cards here, with specific habitats listed. I'll have Bethany here randomly choose two cards. Then Lucy and Tyler, you're going to list the birds most likely found in that habitat. In order to get credit, you need to specify if the bird is a common year-round inhabitant or only during migration or breeding. To discourage guessing, a half a point will be deducted for each bird on the list that would not be found there. Bethany, please do the honors."

Anuk first shuffled, then fanned out the five index cards. Bethany chose the first one. "Coastal Prairie," she announced, then pulled a second card, "and Pineywoods."

"Thank you, Bethany. There you have it folks. You have ten minutes to write down as many as you can."

Lucy was thankful that Maya had taught her to make lists of common birds by habitat. If she could at least get the year-round ones, she had a chance. She had to think strategically. Better to only list the ones she was sure about than risk deductions.

She got to work, listing all the ones she was sure of first. She knew songbirds were common in the Coastal Prairie, so she listed all the species of wrens, thrushes, warblers, and sparrows she could think of, plus the common birds that lived practically anywhere, like blue jays and cardinals. Her time was half up.

The Pineywoods was trickier. It included hardwood forests, pine forests, and swamps, among others, much more diverse. That meant more birds to list, but more room for error. She started with woodpeckers and nuthatches, then various vireos, wrens, hawks, and owls. Her hand was beginning to cramp but she kept writing, determined to prove herself, not just to Anuk, Tyler, Bethany, or anyone else in the office, but to herself, that she could be whatever she wanted.

"End of round three!" announced Anuk. "This will take longer to score, so good thing the pizza is here. Grab some food and talk amongst yourselves." Anuk took the papers from Lucy and Tyler and went back to his office to check it against the regional lists.

Lucy was too nervous to eat, and she hated that Tyler was already downing his second slice, without any sign of stress. Maya sat down with a slice of her own. Lucy appreciated that Maya didn't ask her why she wasn't eating; Maya already knew.

"Whatever happens, I'm proud of you," she whispered.

"Aww, thanks," said Lucy. The truth was she learned a lot about birding and even if she lost, none of that time would have been a waste. Knowledge never was, not to Lucy. She sipped a Sprite to settle her stomach and thought about her future. There were so many unknowns, but for the first time in her life she had options, and that was awesome. If she won the bird-off then the choice would be hers to make, and that was an invaluable prize.

Anuk returned, waving a piece of cardstock. "Without further ado, the winner of the First Annual TerraPlaya Bird-off is…Lucy!" He handed her a certificate with a gold border and her name printed in the middle. She was definitely going to hang this in her cubicle.

Maya gave her a hug, "Great job!"

Tyler walked over and extended his hand, "You're a tough competitor, Lucy, but you won fair and square. Congratulations."

Lucy shook his hand, surprised by the classy gesture on Tyler's part. "Thanks—I had to study a ton if that helps at all."

"Yeah, probably my idea of studying a lot versus yours is much different."

"Probably," she said, and they both chuckled.

Chapter 47

IT WAS THE LAST DAY of work before a week-long holiday break. Even though there was a chilly wind, Lucy and Maya decided to have one final lunch in the courtyard before the new year.

"I have something for you," Maya said, pulling a small, wrapped box from her coat pocket.

"Aww, you didn't need to get me anything. Your friendship is more than enough," said Lucy.

"It's nothing big, don't get too excited about it."

Lucy untied the bow and carefully removed the red foil. Inside, was a handmade ornament from the Holiday Market. "Ooooh, it looks just like my little Cloud!" Lucy exclaimed.

"I know, right—the resemblance is uncanny. I knew it belonged on your miniature tree."

"Aha—that's why you sent me back to the car that day—sneaky. Thank you, I love it. I can just imagine Cloud's face when he sees it."

"He'll probably say something like 'that's not what I look like.'"

"Or 'Is that supposed to be me?'" They both laughed at the thought. "I have something for you, too," said Lucy, handing Maya a small bag tied with a silver ribbon. "It's actually not just from me. It's from Buck Henshaw, too."

"The park ranger who patrols Sienna Falls Forest?" Maya pulled on the ribbon and pulled out a small, framed photograph. "Is that…"

"Yep. It's a Silver-winged Warbler. Turns out the dark magicians hadn't destroyed all the nests. We saved the forest just in time. Buck snapped this photo in late fall, before the birds headed south for winter. When we go back to do nesting surveys next year, there's a good chance they'll be there again."

Maya's eyes were glossy. "This is the best present ever, to know that the birds we fought so hard to protect have a chance now. I'm putting this on my desk so I can see it every day. Thank you."

A fierce gust of wind blew through the courtyard and Lucy hugged her jacket tight. She looked off into the distance.

"What are you thinking about—you suddenly look a million miles away," asked Maya.

"I was thinking about Leon. It's not like he'll freeze on the coast, but the winter isn't exactly mild, either. That's no way for an old man to live."

"Yeah, I think about that too. And every time we go back for a survey, I'll worry that we'll find him dead."

Lucy frowned. "But what can we do? He doesn't want to return to society, so it's not like he's going to live in a shelter."

"I agree. If only there was some place where he could be autonomous and have access to the outdoors, which he seems to love, but still be close to heating and plumbing."

"And someone to notice if he needs medical care."

"Somewhere he could find purpose."

"Purpose, yes. He seems to like nature—he knew all about sea beans."

Maya's eyes lit up. "That's it!"

"What is?"

"Red Bluff Ranch—it has everything we listed. Leon could live in the little ranch hand hut, which has been empty for ages. And he could help Jeremy with the raptors."

"Do you think Jeremy would go for it? Leon is a complete stranger."

"I think they'd get along great—Jeremy can only handle people in small doses, too, so it's perfect. They could live as two hermits on one ranch."

"Oh goodness, that sounds like an idea for a TV show," Lucy said with a chuckle.

"Hah! I can imagine the theme song, 'Two hermits, One ra-a-anch….'" Maya sang in an out of tune voice.

Lucy cracked up, snorting with laughter. Then she turned serious. "You know, when I first started visiting Mrs. Kleinbaum at the retirement home, I saw myself in her—no children to look after her, alone in the world. But then I watched her, at 83, make a new best friend in Mrs. Perez. Such good friends that they moved to Florida together, and Mrs. Kleinbaum is having the time of her life."

"As long as I'm alive, you'll never be alone, Lucy."

"Thanks Maya. Likewise. Although you have three hundred other friends and infinite family to keep you company."

"Nah, none of those friendships are like ours. We have something in common that none of them do—magic."

Lucy grinned. "Two kinds of magic," she said. "So, you think if I ever left TerraPlaya we'd still stay friends? If we didn't see each other every day for work?"

"Of course. It would take more effort, but yes, absolutely. Wait—does this mean you're thinking of talking to the mystery woman?"

"I am thinking about it. I need more information. I don't even know what she wants to talk to me about—it could be nothing, just asking what else we learned about Kayla or Scordatura."

"I think we can guess what she wants, though, and it's more than that."

"No, I don't want to make any assumptions," said Lucy. "I need to know all the parameters of all my options before I can make any decisions."

"It seems like you *have* made a decision though," Maya said softly.

When Lucy got home that evening, she pet Cloud's chin and kissed his furry head. Then she went to the closet and reached into the pocket of the coat she had worn on the night of the concert and took out the business card the mystery woman had given her. She flipped it over.

It was blank.

What the heck? Had Lucy been duped? Was there never a secret light magic organization at all, and she really had handed the trigger back over to Scordatura? Was it a mistake to trust her instincts?

She flipped the card over twice more, sure that she was missing something. She even held it up to the light, in case it used secret ink.

It didn't.

Then she held it close to the light bulb and took it into the dark closet to see if it glowed.

It didn't.

She was distraught. This can't be the end to everything they had been through, since that first evening when Kayla joined the choir, to the wild night that almost killed her merlin friend. There had to be more. Think, Lucy! She was starting to become hysterical, worrying she had made a terrible error in judgement.

She tried something that had never occurred to her before and began to sing, attempting to cast calming song magic on herself. In theory it should work as well as it would on anyone else. As the melody floated all around her, she saw Cloud stretch and yawn and curl up into a ball. Lucy was starting to feel centered and calm as she walked around the room like Cinderella singing to the birds.

When the song was over, she sat back on the couch and looked down at the card on the coffee table. She blinked twice in confusion, then grabbed the card and held it up to her face. It was no longer blank—a phone number had appeared in a glowing golden font, triggered by her song magic.

It wasn't a ruse. Part of her was relieved, elated at the thought of a light magic counterpart to Scordatura. The other part of her was so anxious about the possibilities that her stomach threatened to return her supper.

Her hand trembled as she considered her options. She wasn't sure if she was ready to see what fate had in store for her, to find out if her journey was now irrevocably dominated by her aptitude for magic, if she was destined to battle dark magicians again and again. But the wise Carmela had assured her that the path was hers to choose.

Lucy took a deep breath in and entered the number into her phone. She closed her eyes for another moment to reflect, and when she opened them, she hit the send button.

Now she just had to wait for her next adventure to begin.

CASTLE BRIDGE MEDIA RECOMMENDS...

If you liked this book, you might also enjoy reading the following titles from Castle Bridge Media available on Amazon or by order at your favorite book store:

ANIMAL CHARMER
Animal Charmer
By Rain Nox
Magic & Melody
By Rain Nox

Austinites
By In Churl Yo

Bloodsucker City
By Jim Towns

The Burning Gem
By Don Sawyer

THE CASTLE OF HORROR ANTHOLOGY SERIES
Volume 1
Volume 2: Holiday Horrors
Volume 3: Scary Summer Stories
Volume 4: Women Running From Houses
Volume 5: Thinly Veiled: The 70s
Volume 6: Femme Fatales*
Volume 7: Love Gone Wrong
Volume 8: Thinly Veiled: The 80s
Volume 9: Young Adult
Volume 10: Thinly Veiled: Saturday Mournings
Volume 11: Revenge
Edited By Jason Henderson and In Churl Yo
*Edited By P.J. Hoover

Castle of Horror Podcast Book of Great Horror
Edited By Jason Henderson

Cherry Dark
By R.L. Wilburn

Dream State
By Martin Ott

Dominic
By Lee Guzman

FRENCH DECEPTION
A Forgery in Paris
By Janice Nagourney
A Forgery in Lyon
By Janice Nagourney
A Forgery in Marseille
By Janice Nagourney

FuturePast Sci-Fi Anthology
Edited by In Churl Yo

GLAZIER'S GAP
Ghosts of the Forbidden
By Leanna Renee Hieber

Hellfall
By Jay Gould

Isonation
By In Churl Yo

JAYU CITY CHRONICLES
The Hermes Protocol
By Chris M. Arnone
Necropolis Alpha
By Chris M. Arnone

Junk Film: Why Bad Movies Matter
By Katharine Coldiron

MID-LIFE CRISIS THRILLERS
18 Miles From Town
By Jason Henderson
Lost Angel
By Sam Knight
Ties That Kill
By Deven Greene

Nightwalkers: Gothic Horror Movies
By Bruce Lanier Wright

THE PATH
The Blue-Spangled Blue
By David Bowles
The Deepest Green
By David Bowles

St. Damned
By Ty Drago

SURF MYSTIC
Night of the Book Man
By Peyton Douglas
Dark of the Curl
By Peyton Douglas

The 23rd Hero
By Rebecca Anne Nguyen

The Thing That Happened When We Were Little
By Caroline Kelly Franklin

Vinyl Wonderland
By Mark Rigney

Yesterday's Tomorrows: The Golden Age of Science Fiction Movies
By Bruce Lanier Wright

Please remember to leave us your reviews on Amazon and Goodreads!
w**THANK YOU FOR SUPPORTING INDEPENDENT PUBLISHERS AND AUTHORS!**
castlebridgemedia.com

www.ingramcontent.com/pod-product-compliance
Lightning Source LLC
Chambersburg PA
CBHW032034310726
48972CB00002B/669